ANNALS

OF A

QUIET NEIGHBOURHOOD.

BY

GEORGE MAC DONALD M.A.,

AUTHOR OF "ALEC FORBES OF HOWGLEN," ETC.

COPYRIGHT EDITION.

IN TWO VOLUMES.

VOL. I.

LEIPZIG

BERNHARD TAUCHNITZ

1867.

CONTENTS

OF VOLUME I.

ANNALS

OF A

QUIET NEIGHBOURHOOD.

CHAPTER I.

Despondency and Consolation.

Before I begin to tell you some of the things I have seen and heard, in both of which I have had to take a share, now from the compulsion of my office, now from the leading of my own heart, and now from that destiny which, including both, so often throws the man who supposed himself a mere on-looker, into the very vortex of events — that destiny which took form to the old pagans as a gray mist high beyond the heads of their gods, but to us is known as an infinite love, revealed in the mystery of man — I say before I begin, it is fitting that, in the absence of a common friend to do that office for me, I should introduce myself to your acquaintance, and I hope coming friendship. Nor can there be any impropriety in my telling you about myself, seeing I remain concealed behind my own words. You can never look me in the eyes, though you may look me in the soul. You may find me out, find my faults, my vanities, my sins, but you will not *see* me, at least in this world. To you I am but a voice of revealing, not a form of vision; therefore I am bold behind the mask, to speak to you heart to heart; bold, I say, just so much the more that I do not speak to you face to face. And when we meet in heaven — well, there I know there is no hiding; there, there is no reason for hiding anything; there, the whole desire will be alternate revelation and vision.

I am now getting old — faster and faster. I cannot help my gray hairs, nor the wrinkles that gather so slowly yet ruthlessly; no, nor the quaver that will come in my voice, nor the sense of being feeble in the knees, even when I walk only across the floor of my study. But I have not got used to age yet. I do not *feel* one atom older than I did at three-and-twenty. Nay, to tell all the truth, I feel a good deal younger. — For then I only felt that a man had to take up his cross; whereas now I feel that a man has to follow Him; and that makes an unspeakable difference. — When my voice quavers, I feel that it is mine and not mine; that it just belongs to me like my watch, which does not go well now, though it went well thirty years ago — not more than a minute out in a month. And when I feel my knees shake, I think of them with a kind of pity, as I used to think of an old mare of my father's of which I was very fond when I was a lad, and which bore me across many a field and over many a fence, but which at last came to have the same weakness in her knees that I have in mine; and she knew it too, and took care of them, and so of herself, in a wise equine fashion. These things are not me — or *I*, if the grammarians like it better, (I always feel a strife between doing as the scholar does and doing as other people do;) they are not me, I say; I *have* them — and, please God, shall soon have better. For it is not a pleasant thing for a young man, or a young woman either, I venture to say, to have an old voice, and a wrinkled face, and weak knees, and gray hair, or no hair at all. And if any moral Philistine, as our queer German brothers over the Northern fish-pond would call him, say that this is all rubbish, for that we *are* old, I would answer: "Of all children how can the children of God be old?"

So little do I give in to calling this outside of me, *me*, that I should not mind presenting a minute description of my own person such as would at once clear me from any suspicion of vanity in so introducing myself. Not that my honesty would result in the least from indifference to the external — but from comparative indifference to the transitional; not to the transitional in itself, which is of eternal significance and result, but to the particular form of imperfection which it may have reached at any individual moment of its infinite progression towards the complete. For no sooner have I spoken the word *now*, than that *now* is dead and another is dying; nay, in such a regard, there is no *now* — only a past of which we know a little, and a future of which we know far less and far more. But I will not speak at all of this body of my earthly tabernacle, for it is on the whole more pleasant to forget all about it. And besides, I do not want to set any of my readers to whom I would have the pleasure of speaking far more openly and cordially than if they were seated on the other side of my writing-table — I do not want to set them wondering whether the vicar be this vicar or that vicar; or indeed to run the risk of giving the offence I might give, if I were anything else than "a wandering voice."

I did not feel as I feel now when first I came to this parish. For, as I have said, I am now getting old very fast. True, I was thirty when I was made a vicar, an age at which a man might be expected to be beginning to grow wise; but even then I had much yet to learn.

I well remember the first evening on which I wandered out from the vicarage to take a look about me — to find out, in short, where I was, and what aspect the sky and earth here presented. Strangely enough, I had never been here before; for the presentation had been made me while I was abroad. — I was depressed. It was depressing weather. Grave doubts as to whether I was in my place in the Church, would keep rising and floating about, like rain-clouds within me. Not that I doubted about the Church; I only doubted about myself. "Were my motives pure?" "What were my motives?" And, to tell the truth, I did not know what my motives were, and therefore I could not answer about the purity of them. Perhaps seeing we are in this world in order to become pure, it would be expecting too

much of any young man that he should be absolutely certain that he was pure in anything. But
the question followed very naturally: "Had I then
any right to be in the Church — to be eating her
bread and drinking her wine without knowing whether
I was fit to do her work?" To which the only answer I could find was, "The Church is part of God's
world. He makes men to work; and work of some
sort must be done by every honest man. Somehow
or other I hardly know how, I find myself in the
Church. I do not know that I am fitter for any
other work. I see no other work to do. There is
work here which I can do after some fashion. With
God's help I will try to do it well."

This resolution brought me some relief, but still
I was depressed. It was depressing weather. — I
may as well say that I was not married then, and
that I firmly believed I never should be married —
not from any ambition taking the form of self-denial;
nor yet from any notion that God takes pleasure in
being a hard master; but there was a lady — Well,
I *will* be honest, as I would be. — I had been refused a few months before, which I think was the
best thing ever happened to me except one. That
one, of course, was when I was accepted. But this
is not much to the purpose now. Only it was depressing weather.

For is it not depressing when the rain is falling,
and the steam of it is rising? when the river is
crawling along muddily, and the horses stand stock-
still in the meadows with their spines in a straight
line from the ears to where they fail utterly in the

tails? I should only put on goloshes now, and think
of the days when I despised damp. Ah! it was
mental waterproof that I needed then; for let me
despise damp as much as I would, I could neither
keep it out of my mind, nor help suffering the spiritual rheumatism which it occasioned. Now, the damp
never gets farther than my goloshes and my Macin-
tosh. And for that worst kind of rheumatism — I
never feel it now.

But I had begun to tell you about that first
evening. — I had arrived at the vicarage the night
before, and it had rained all day, and was still
raining, though not so much. I took my umbrella
and went out.

For as I wanted to do my work well (everything taking far more the shape of work to me,
then, and duty, than it does now — though, even
now, I must confess things have occasionally to be
done by the clergyman because there is no one else
to do them, and hardly from other motive than a
sense of duty, — a man not being able to shirk
work because it may happen to be dirty) — I say,
as I wanted to do my work well, or rather, perhaps,
because I dreaded drudgery as much as any poor
fellow who comes to the treadmill in consequence —
I wanted to interest myself in it; and therefore I
would go and fall in love, first of all, if I could,
with the country round about. And my first step
beyond my own gate was up to the ankles in mud.

Therewith, curiously enough, arose the distract-
ing thought how I could possibly preach *two* good
sermons a Sunday to the same people, when one of

the sermons was in the afternoon instead of the
evening, to which latter I had been accustomed in
the large town in which I had formerly officiated as
curate in a proprietary chapel. I, who had de-
claimed indignantly against excitement from without, who had been inclined to exalt the intellect at
the expense even of the heart, began to fear that
there must be something in the darkness, and the
gas-lights, and the crowd of faces, to account for a
man's being able to preach a better sermon, and for
servant-girls preferring to go out in the evening.
Alas! I had now to preach, as I might judge with
all probability beforehand, to a company of rustics,
of thought yet slower than of speech, unaccustomed
in fact to *think* at all, and that in the sleepiest,
deadest part of the day, when I could hardly think
myself, and when, if the weather should be at all
warm, I could not expect many of them to be awake.
And what good might I look for as the result of
my labour? How could I hope in these men and
women to kindle that fire which in the old days of
the outpouring of the Spirit made men live with the
sense of the kingdom of heaven about them, and the
expectation of something glorious at hand just outside that invisible door which lay between the
worlds?

I have learned since that perhaps I overrated the
spirituality of those times, and underrated, not being
myself spiritual enough to see all about me, the
spirituality of these times. I think I have learned
since, that the parson of a parish must be content to
keep the upper windows of his mind open to the

holy winds and the pure lights of heaven; and the
side windows of tone; of speech, of behaviour open
to the earth, to let forth upon his fellow-men the
tenderness and truth which those upper influences
bring forth in any region exposed to their operation.
Believing in his Master, such a servant shall not
make haste; shall feel no feverous desire to behold
the work of his hands; shall be content to be as his
Master, who waiteth long for the fruits of his earth.

But surely I am getting older than I thought;
for I keep wandering away from my subject, which
is this my first walk in my new cure. My excuse
is, that I want my reader to understand something
of the state of my mind, and the depression under
which I was labouring. He will perceive that I
desired to do some work worth calling by the name
of work, and that I did not see how to get hold of
a beginning.

I had not gone far from my own gate before the
rain ceased, though it was still gloomy enough for
any amount to follow. I drew down my umbrella,
and began to look about me. The stream on my
left was so swollen that I could see its brown in
patches through the green of the meadows along its
banks. A little in front of me, the road, rising
quickly, took a sharp turn to pass along an old
stone bridge that spanned the water with a single
fine arch, somewhat pointed; and through the arch
I could see the river stretching away up through
the meadows, its banks bordered with pollards. Now
pollards always made me miserable. In the first
place, they look ill-used; in the next place, they

look tame; in the third place, they look very ugly. I had not learned then to honour them on the ground that they yield not a jot to the adversity of their circumstances; that, if they must be pollards, they still will be trees; and what they may not do with grace, they will yet do with bounty; that, in short, their life bursts forth, despite of all that is done to repress and destroy their individuality. When you have once learned to honour anything, love is not very far off; at least that has always been my experience. But, as I have said, I had not yet learned to honour pollards, and therefore they made me more miserable than I was already.

When, having followed the road, I stood at last on the bridge, and, looking up and down the river through the misty air, saw two long rows of these pollards diminishing till they vanished in both directions, the sight of them took from me all power of enjoying the water beneath me, the green fields around me, or even the old-world beauty of the little bridge upon which I stood, although all sorts of bridges have been from very infancy a delight to me. For I am one of those who never get rid of their infantile predilections, and to have once enjoyed making a mud bridge, was to enjoy all bridges for ever.

I saw a man in a white smock-frock coming along the road beyond, but I turned my back to the road, leaned my arms on the parapet of the bridge, and stood gazing where I saw no visions, namely, at those very poplars. I heard the man's footsteps coming up the crown of the arch, but I would not

turn to greet him. I was in a selfish humour if
ever I was; for surely if ever one man ought to
greet another, it was upon such a comfortless afternoon. The footsteps stopped behind me, and I
heard a voice: —

"I beg yer pardon, sir; but be you the new
vicar?"

I turned instantly and answered, "I am. Do
you want me?"

"I wanted to see yer face, sir, that was all, if
ye'll not take it amiss."

Before me stood a tall old man with his hat in
his hand, clothed as I have said, in a white smock-
frock. He smoothed his short gray hair with his
curved palm down over his forehead as he stood.
His face was of a red brown, from much exposure
to the weather. There was a certain look of roughness, without hardness, in it, which spoke of en-
durance rather than resistance, although he could
evidently set his face as a flint. His features were
large and a little coarse, but the smile that parted
his lips when he spoke, shone in his gray eyes as
well, and lighted up a countenance in which a man
might trust.

"I wanted to see yer face, sir, if you'll not take
it amiss."

"Certainly not," I answered, pleased with the
man's address, as he stood square before me, looking
as modest as fearless. "The sight of a man's face
is what everybody has a right to; but, for all that,
I should like to know why you want to see my
face."

"Why, sir, you be the new vicar. You kindly told me so when I axed you."

"Well, then, you'll see my face on Sunday in church — that is, if you happen to be there."

For, although some might think it the more dignified way, I could not take it as a matter of course that he would be at church. A man might have better reasons for staying away from church than I had for going, even though I was the parson, and it was my business. Some clergymen separate between themselves and their office to a degree which I cannot understand. To assert the dignities of my office seems to me very like exalting myself; and when I have had a twinge of conscience about it, as has happened more than once, I have then found comfort in these two texts: "The Son of man came not to be ministered unto but to minister;" and "It is enough that the servant should be as his master." Neither have I ever been able to see the very great difference between right and wrong in a clergyman, and right and wrong in another man. All that I can pretend to have yet discovered comes to this: that what is right in another man is right in a clergyman; and what is wrong in another man is much worse in a clergyman. Here, however, is one more proof of approaching age. I do not mean the opinion, but the digression.

"Well, then," I said, "you'll see my face in church on Sunday, if you happen to be there."

"Yes, sir; but you see, sir, on the bridge here, the parson is the parson like, and I'm old Rogers; and I looks in his face, and he looks in mine, and

I says to myself, 'This is my parson.' But o' Sundays he's nobody's parson: he's got his work to do, and it mun be done, and there's an end on't."

That there was a real idea in the old man's mind was considerably clearer than the logic by which he tried to bring it out.

"Did you know parson that's gone, sir?" he went on.

"No," I answered.

"Oh, sir! he wur a good parson. Many's the time he come and sit at my son's bedside — him that's dead and gone, sir — for a long hour, on a Saturday night, too. And then when I see him up in the desk the next mornin', I'd say to myself, 'Old Rogers, that's the same man as sat by your son's bedside last night. Think o' that, old Rogers!' But, somehow, I never did feel right sure o' that same. He didn't seem to have the same cut, somehow; and he didn't talk a bit the same. And when he spoke to me after sermon, in the churchyard, I was always of a mind to go into the church again and look up to the pulpit to see if he war really out ov it; for this warn't the same man, you see. But you'll know all about it, better than I can tell you, sir. Only I always likes parson better out o' the pulpit, and that's how I come to want to make you look at me, sir, instead o' the water down there, afore I see you in the church to-morrow mornin'."

The old man laughed a kindly laugh; but he had set me thinking, and I 'did not know what to say to him all at once. So after a short pause, he resumed:

"You'll be thinking me a queer kind of a man, sir, to speak to my betters before my betters speaks to me. But mayhap you don't know what a parson is to us poor folk that has ne'er a friend more larned than theirselves but the parson. And, besides, sir, I'm an old salt, — an old man-o'-war's man, — and I've been all round the world, sir; and I ha' been in all sorts o' company, pirates and all, sir; and I aint a bit frightened of a parson. No; I love a parson, sir. And I'll tell you for why, sir. He's got a good telescope, and he gits to the masthead, and he looks out. And he sings out, 'Land ahead!' or 'Breakers ahead!' and gives directions accordin'. Only I can't always make out what he says. But when he shuts up his spyglass, and comes down the riggin', and talks to us like one man to another, then I don't know what I should do without the parson. Good evenin' to you, sir, and welcome to Marshmallows."

The pollards did not look half so dreary. The river began to glimmer a little; and the old bridge had become an interesting old bridge. The country altogether was rather nice than otherwise. I had found a friend already! — that is, a man to whom I might possibly be of some use; and that was the most precious friend I could think of in my present situation and mood. I had learned something from him too; and I resolved to try all I could to be the same man in the pulpit that I was out of it. Some may be inclined to say that I had better have formed the resolution to be the same man out of the pulpit that I•was in it. But the one will go quite right

with the other. Out of the pulpit I would be the
same man I was in it — seeing and feeling the
realities of the unseen; and in the pulpit I would be
the same man I was out of it — taking facts as
they are, and dealing with things as they show themselves in the world.

One other occurrence before I went home that
evening, and I shall close the chapter. I hope I
shall not write another so dull as this. I dare not
promise, though; for this is a new kind of work
to me.

Before I left the bridge, — while, in fact, I was
contemplating the pollards with an eye, if not of
favour, yet of diminished dismay, — the sun, which,
for anything I knew of his whereabouts, either from
knowledge of the country, aspect of the evening, or
state of my own feelings, might have been down for
an hour or two, burst his cloudy bands, and blazed
out as if he had just risen from the dead, instead of
being just about to sink into the grave. Do not
tell me that my figure is untrue, for that the sun
never sinks into the grave, else I will retort that it
is just as true of the sun as of a man; for that no
man sinks into the grave. He only disappears.
Life is a constant sunrise, which death cannot interrupt, any more than the night can swallow up the
sun. "God is not the God of the dead, but of the
living; for all live unto him."

Well, the sun shone out gloriously. The whole
sweep of the gloomy river answered him in gladness; the wet leaves of the pollards quivered and
glanced; the meadows offered up their perfect green,

fresh and clear out of the trouble of the rain; and away in the distance, upon a rising ground covered with trees, glittered a weathercock. What if I found afterwards that it was only on the roof of a stable? It shone, and that was enough. And when the sun had gone below the horizon, and the fields and the river were dusky once more, there it glittered still over the darkening earth, a symbol of that faith which is "the evidence of things not seen." It made my heart swell as at a chant from the prophet Isaiah. What matter then whether it hung over a stable-roof or a church-tower?

I stood up and wandered a little farther — off the bridge, and along the road. I had not gone far before I passed a house, out of which came a young woman leading a little boy. They came after me, the boy gazing at the red and gold and green of the sunset sky. As they passed me, the child said, —·

"Auntie, I think I should like to be a painter."

"Why?" returned his companion.

"Because, then," answered the child, "I could help God to paint the sky."

What his aunt replied I do not know; for they were presently beyond my hearing. But I went on answering him myself all the way home. Did God care to paint the sky of an evening, that a few of His children might see it, and get just a hope, just an aspiration, out of its passing green, and gold, and purple, and red? and should I think my day's labour lost, if it wrought no visible salvation in the earth?

But was the child's aspiration in vain? Could I tell him God did not want his help to paint the sky? True he could mount no scaffold against the infinite of the glowing west. But might he not with his little palette and brush, when the time came, show his brothers and sisters what he had seen there, and make them see it too? Might he not thus come, after long trying, to help God to paint this glory of vapour and light inside the minds of His children? Ah! if any man's work is not *with* God, its results shall be burned, ruthlessly burned, because poor and bad.

"So, for my part," I said to myself, as I walked home, "if I can put one touch of a rosy sunset into the life of any man or woman of my cure, I shall feel that I have worked with God. He is in no haste; and if I do what I may in earnest, I need not mourn if I work no great work in the earth. Let God make His sunsets: I will mottle my little fading cloud. To help the growth of a thought that struggles towards the light; to brush with gentle hand the earth-stain from the white of one snow-drop — such be my ambition! So shall I scale the rocks in front, not leave my name carved upon those behind me."

People talk about special providences. I believe in the providences, but not in the specialty. I do not believe that God lets the thread of my affairs go for six days, and on the seventh evening takes it up for a moment. The so-called special providences are no exception to the rule — they are common to all men at all moments. But it is a fact that God's care is more evident in some instances of it than in others to the dim and often bewildered vision of humanity. Upon such instances men seize and call them providences. It is well that they can; but it would be gloriously better if they could believe that the whole matter is one grand providence.

I was one of such men at the time, and could not fail to see what I called a special providence in this, that on my first attempt to find where I stood in the scheme of Providence, and while I was discouraged with regard to the work before me, I should fall in with these two — an old man whom I could help, and a child who could help me; the one opening an outlet for my labour and my love, and the other reminding me of the highest source of the most humbling comfort, — that in all my work I might be a fellow-worker with God.

CHAPTER II.

My first Sunday at Marshmallows.

THESE events fell on the Saturday night. On
the Sunday morning, I read prayers and preached.
Never before had I enjoyed so much the petitions of
the Church, which Hooker calls "the sending of
angels upward," or the reading of the lessons, which
he calls "the receiving of angels descended from
above." And whether from the newness of the parson, or the love of the service, certainly a congregation more intent, or more responsive, a clergyman
will hardly find. But, as I had feared, it was different in the afternoon. The people had dined, and
the usual somnolence had followed; nor could I find
in my heart to blame men and women who worked
hard all the week, for being drowsy on the day of
rest. So I curtailed my sermon as much as I could,
omitting page after page of my manuscript; and
when I came to a close, was rewarded by perceiving
an agreeable surprise upon many of the faces round
me. I resolved that, in the afternoons at least,
my sermons should be as short as heart could
wish.

But that afternoon there was at least one man
of the congregation who was neither drowsy nor in-
attentive. Repeatedly my eyes left the page off

which I was reading and glanced towards him. Not
once did I find his eyes turned away from me.
There was a small loft in the west end of the
church, in which stood a little organ, whose voice,
weakened by years of praising and possibly of ne-
glect, had yet among a good many tones that were
rough, wooden, and reedy, a few remaining that
were as mellow as ever praiseful heart could wish to
praise withal. And these came in amongst the rest
like trusting thoughts amidst "eating cares;" like
the faces of children borne in the arms of a crowd
of anxious mothers; like hopes that are young pro-
phecies amidst the downward sweep of events. For,
though I do not understand music, I have a keen
ear for the perfection of the single tone, or the com-
pleteness of the harmony. But of this organ more
by and by.

Now this little gallery was something larger than
was just necessary for the organ and its ministrants,
and a few of the parishioners had chosen to sit in
its fore-front. Upon this occasion there was no one
there but the man to whom I have referred.

The space below this gallery was not included
in the part of the church used for the service. It
was claimed by the gardener of the place, that is
the sexton, to hold his gardening tools. There were
a few ancient carvings in wood lying in it, very
brown in the dusky light that came through a small
lancet window, opening not to the outside, but into
the tower, itself dusky with an enduring twilight.
And there were some broken old headstones, and the
kindly spade and pickaxe — but I have really no-

thing to do with these now, for I am, as it were, in
the pulpit, whence one ought to look beyond such
things as these.

Rising against the screen which separated this
mouldy portion of the church from the rest, stood an
old monument of carved wood, once brilliantly
painted in the portions that bore the arms of the family over whose vault it stood, but now all bare and
worn; itself gently flowing away into the dust it
commemorated. It lifted its gablet, carved to look
like a canopy, till its apex was on a level with the
book-board on the front of the organ-loft; and over
— in fact upon this apex appeared the face of the
man whom I have mentioned. It was a very remarkable countenance — pale, and very thin, without any hair, except that of thick eyebrows that far
overhung keen, questioning eyes. Short bushy hair,
gray, not white, covered a well-formed head with a
high narrow forehead. As I have said, those keen
eyes kept looking at me from under their gray eyebrows all the time of the sermon — intelligently
without doubt, but whether sympathetically or otherwise I could not determine. And indeed I hardly
know yet.

My vestry door opened upon a little group of
graves, simple and green, without headstone or slab;
poor graves, the memory of whose occupants no one
had cared to preserve. Good men must have pre-
ceded me here, else the poor would not have lain so
near the chancel and the vestry-door. All about
and beyond were stones, with here and there a
monument; for mine was a large parish, and there

were old and rich families in it, more of which buried their dead here than assembled their living. But close by the vestry-door, there was this little billowy lake of grass. And at the end of the narrow path leading from the door, was the churchyard wall, with a few steps on each side of it, that the parson might pass at once from the churchyard into his own shrubbery, here tangled, almost matted, from luxuriance of growth. But I would not creep out the back way from among my people. That way might do very well to come in by; but to go out, I would use the door of the people. So I went along the church, a fine old place, such as I had never hoped to be presented to, and went out by the door in the north side into the middle of the churchyard. The door on the other side was chiefly used by the few gentry of the neighbourhood; and the Lychgate, with its covered way, (for the main road had once passed on that side,) was shared between the coffins and the carriages, the dead who had no rank but one, that of the dead, and the living who had more money than their neighbours. For let the old gentry disclaim it as they may, mere wealth, derived from whatever source, will sooner reach their level, than poor antiquity, or the rarest refinement of personal worth; although, to be sure, the oldest of them will sooner give to the rich their sons or their daughters to wed, to love if they can, to have children by, than they will yield a jot of their ancestral pre-eminence, or acknowledge any equality in their sons or daughters-in-law. The carpenter's son is to them an old myth, not an

everlasting fact. To Mammon alone will they yield
a little of their rank — none of it to Christ. Let
me glorify God that Jesus took not on Him the
nature of nobles, but the seed of Adam; for what
could I do without my poor brothers and sisters?

I passed along the church to the northern door,
and went out. The churchyard lay in bright sun-
shine. All the rain and gloom were gone. "If one
could only bring this glory of sun and grass into
one's hope for the future!" thought I; and looking
down I saw the little boy who aspired to paint the
sky, looking up in my face with mingled confidence
and awe.

"Do you trust me, my little man?" thought I.
"You shall trust me then. But I won't be a priest
to you. I'll be a big brother."

For the priesthood passes away, the brotherhood
endures. The priesthood passes away, swallowed
up in the brotherhood. It is because men cannot
learn simple things, cannot believe in the brotherhood, that they need a priesthood. But as Dr. Arnold
said of the Sunday, "They *do* need it." And I,
for one, am sure that the priesthood needs the
people much more than the people needs the priesthood.

So I stooped and lifted the child and held him
in my arms. And the little fellow looked at me
one moment longer, and then put his arms gently
round my neck. And so we were friends. When
I had set him down, which I did presently, for I
shuddered at the idea of the people thinking that I
was showing off the *clergyman*, I looked at the boy.

In his face was great sweetness mingled with great
rusticity, and I could not tell whether he was the
child of gentlefolk or of peasants. He did not say
a word, but walked away to join his aunt, who was
waiting for him at the gate of the churchyard. He
kept his head turned towards me, however, as he
went, so that, not seeing where he was going, he
stumbled over the grave of a child, and fell in the
hollow on the other side. I ran to pick him up.
His aunt reached him at the same moment.

"Oh, thank you, sir!" she said, as I gave him
to her, with an earnestness which seemed to me dis-
proportionate to the deed, and carried him away
with a deep blush over all her countenance.

At the churchyard-gate, the old man-of-war's
man was waiting to have another look at me. His
hat was in his hand, and he gave a pull to the
short hair over his forehead, as if he would gladly
take that off too, to show his respect for the new
parson. I held out my hand gratefully. It could
not close around the hard unyielding mass of fingers
which met it. He did not know how to shake
hands, and left it all to me. But pleasure sparkled
in his eyes.

"My old woman would like to shake hands
with you, sir," he said.

Beside him stood his old woman in a portentous
bonnet, beneath whose gay yellow ribbons appeared
a dusky old face wrinkled like a ship's timbers, out
of which looked a pair of keen black eyes, where
the best beauty, that of loving-kindness, had not
merely lingered, but triumphed.

"I shall be in to see you soon," I said, as I shook hands with her. "I shall find out where you live."

"Down by the mill," she said; "close by it, sir. There's one bed in our garden that always thrives, in the hottest summer, by the plash from the mill, sir."

"Ask for Old Rogers, sir," said the man. "Everybody knows Old Rogers. But if your reverence minds what my wife says, you won't go wrong. When you find the river, it takes you to the mill; and when you find the mill, you find the wheel; and when you find the wheel, you haven't far to look for the cottage, sir. It's a poor place, but you'll be welcome, sir."

CHAPTER III.

My first Monday at Marshmallows.

THE next day I might expect some visitors. It is a fortunate thing that English society now regards the parson as a gentleman, else he would have little chance of being useful to the *upper classes*. But I wanted to get a good start of them, and see some of my poor before my rich came to see me. So after breakfast, on as lovely a Monday in the beginning of autumn as ever came to comfort a clergyman in the reaction of his efforts to feed his flock on the Sunday, I walked out, and took my way to the village. I strove to dismiss from my mind every feeling of *doing duty*, of *performing my part*, and all that. I had a horror of becoming a moral policeman as much as of "doing church." I would simply enjoy the privilege, more open to me in virtue of my office, of ministering. But as no servant has a right to force his service, so I would be the *neighbour* only, until such time as the opportunity of being the servant should show itself.

The village was as irregular as a village should be, partly consisting of those white houses with intersecting parallelograms of black which still abound in some regions of our island. Just in the centre, however, grouping about an old house of red brick, which had once been a manorial residence, but was now subdivided in all modes that analytic ingenuity could devise, rose a portion of it which, from one point of view, might seem part of an old town. But you had only to pass round any one of three visible corners to see stacks of wheat and a farm-yard; while in another direction the houses went straggling away into a wood that looked very like the beginning of a forest, of which some of the village orchards appeared to form part. From the street the slow-winding, poplar-bordered stream was here and there just visible.

I did not quite like to have it between me and my village. I could not help preferring that homely relation in which the houses are built up like swallow-nests on to the very walls of the cathedrals themselves, to the arrangement here, where the river flowed, with what flow there was in it, between the church and the people.

A little way beyond the farther end of the village, appeared an iron gate, of considerable size, dividing a lofty stone wall. And upon the top of that one of the stone pillars supporting the gate which I could see, stood a creature of stone, whether *natant*, *volant*, *passant*, *couchant*, or *rampant*, I could not tell, only it looked like something terrible enough for a quite antediluvian heraldry.

As I passed along the street, wondering with myself what relations between me and these houses were hidden in the future, my eye was caught by the window of a little shop, in which strings of beads and elephants of gingerbread formed the chief samples of the goods within. It was a window much broader than it was high, divided into lozenge-shaped panes. Wondering what kind of old woman presided over the treasures in this cave of Aladdin, I thought to make a first of my visits by going in and buying something. But I hesitated, because I could not think of anything I was in want of — at least that the old woman was likely to have. To be sure I wanted a copy of Bengel's "Gnomon;" but she was not likely to have that. I wanted the fourth plate in the third volume of Law's "Behmen;" she was not likely to have that either. I did not care for gingerbread, and I had no little girl to take home beads to.

But why should I not go in without an ostensible errand? For this reason: there are dissenters everywhere, and I could not tell but I might be going into the shop of a dissenter. Now, though, I confess, nothing would have pleased me better than that all the dissenters should return to their old home in the Church, I could not endure the suspicion of laying myself out to entice them back by canvassing or using any personal influence. Whether they returned or not, however, (and I did not expect many would,) I hoped still, some day, to stand towards every one of them in the relation of the parson of the parish, that is, one of whom each might feel certain that he was ready to serve him or her at any hour when he might be wanted to render a service. In the meantime, I could not help hesitating.

I had almost made up my mind to ask if she had a small pocket compass, for I had seen such things in little country shops — I am afraid only

in France, though — when the door opened, and
out came the little boy whom I had already seen
twice, and who was therefore one of my oldest friends
in the place. He came across the road to me, took
me by the hand, and said —

"Come and see mother."

"Where, my dear?" I asked.

"In the shop there," he answered.

"Is it your mother's shop?"

"Yes."

I said no more, but accompanied him. Of course
my expectation of seeing an old woman behind the
counter had vanished, but I was not in the least prepared for the kind of woman I did see.

The place was half a shop and half a kitchen.
A yard or so of counter stretched inwards from the
door, just as a hint to those who might be intru-
sively inclined. Beyond this, by the chimney-corner,
sat the mother, who rose as we entered. She was
certainly one — I do not say of the most beautiful,
but, until I have time to explain further — of the
most remarkable women I had ever seen. Her face
was absolutely white — no, pale cream-colour —
except her lips and a spot upon each cheek, which
glowed with a deep carmine. You would have said
she had been painting, and painting very inartisti-
cally, so little was the red shaded into the surround-
ing white. Now this was certainly not beautiful.
Indeed, it occasioned a strange feeling, almost of
terror, at first, for she reminded one of the spectre
woman in the "Rime of the Ancient Mariner." But
when I got used to her complexion, I saw that the

form of her features was quite beautiful. She might indeed have been *lovely* but for a certain hardness which showed through the beauty. This might have been the result of ill health, ill-endured; but I doubted it. For there was a certain modelling of the cheeks and lips which showed that the teeth within were firmly closed; and, taken with the look of the eyes and forehead, seemed the expression of a constant and bitter self-command. But there were indubitable marks of ill health upon her, notwithstanding; for not to mention her complexion, her large dark eye was burning as if the lamp of life had broken and the oil was blazing; and there was a slight expansion of the nostrils, which indicated physical unrest. But her manner was perfectly, almost dreadfully, quiet; her voice soft, low, and chiefly expressive of indifference. She spoke without looking me in the face, but did not seem either shy or ashamed. Her figure was remarkably graceful, though too worn to be beautiful. — Here was a strange parishioner for me! — in a country toy-shop, too!

As soon as the little fellow had brought me in, he shrunk away through a half-open door that revealed a stair behind.

"What can I do for you, sir?" said the mother, coldly, and with a kind of book-propriety of speech, as she stood on the other side of the little counter, prepared to open box or drawer at command.

"To tell the truth, I hardly know," I said. "I am the new vicar; but I do not think that I should have come in to see you just to-day, if it had not

3*

been that your little boy there — where is he gone
to? He asked me to come in and see his mother."

"He is too ready to make advances to strangers,
sir."

She said this in an incisive tone.

"Oh, but," I answered, "I am not a stranger
to him. I have met him twice before. He is a
little darling. I assure you he has quite gained my
heart."

No reply for a moment. Then just "Indeed!"
and nothing more.

I could not understand it.

But a jar on a shelf, marked *Tobacco*, rescued me
from the most pressing portion of the perplexity,
namely, what to say next.

"Will you give me a quarter of a pound of tobacco?" I said.

The woman turned, took down the jar, arranged
the scales, weighed out the quantity, wrapped it up,
took the money, — and all without one other word
than, "Thank you, sir;" which was all I could return, with the addition of, "Good morning."

For nothing was left me but to walk away with
my parcel in my pocket.

The little boy did not show himself again. I
had hoped to find him outside.

Pondering, speculating, I now set out for the
mill, which, I had already learned, was on the village side of the river. Coming to a lane leading
down to the river, I followed it, and then walked
up a path outside the row of pollards, through a
lovely meadow, where brown and white cows were

eating and shining all over the thick deep grass.
Beyond the meadow, a wood on the side of a rising
ground went parallel with the river a long way. The
river flowed on my right. That is, I knew that it
was flowing, but I could not have told how I knew,
it was so slow. Still swollen, it was of a clear
brown, in which you could see the browner trouts
darting to and fro with such a slippery gliding that
the motion seemed the result of will, without any
such intermediate and complicate arrangement as
brain and nerves and muscles. The water-beetles
went spinning about over the surface; and one glorious dragon-fly made a mist about him with his
long wings. And over all the sun hung in the sky,
pouring down life; shining on the roots of the wil-
lows at the bottom of the stream; lighting up the
black head of the water-rat as he hurried across to
the opposite bank; glorifying the rich green lake of
the grass; and giving to the whole an utterance of
love and hope and joy which was, to him who could
read it, a more certain and full revelation of God
than any display of power in thunder, in avalanche,
in stormy sea. Those with whom the feeling of religion is only occasional, have it most when the awful
or grand breaks out of the common; the meek who
inherit the earth, find the God of the whole earth
more evidently present — I do not say more present, for there is no measuring of His presence —
more evidently present in the commonest things.
That which is best He gives most plentifully, as is
reason with Him. Hence the quiet fulness of ordinary nature; hence the Spirit to them that ask it.

I soon came within sound of the mill; and presently, crossing the stream that flowed back to the river after having done its work on the corn, I came in front of the building, and looked over the halfdoor into the mill. The floor was clean and dusty. A few full sacks, tied tight at the mouth — they always look to me as if Joseph's silver cup were just inside — stood about. In the farther corner, the flour was trickling down out of two wooden spouts into a wooden receptacle below. The whole place was full of its own faint but pleasant odour. No man was visible. The spouts went on pouring the slow torrent of flour, as if everything could go on with perfect propriety of itself. I could not even see how a man could get at the stones that I heard grinding away above, except he went up the rope that hung from the ceiling. So I walked round the corner of the place, and found myself in the company of the water-wheel, mossy and green with ancient waterdrops, looking so furred and overgrown and lumpy, that one might have thought the wood of it had taken to growing again in its old days, and so the wheel was losing by slow degrees the shape of a wheel, to become some new awful monster of a pollard. As yet, however, it was going round; slowly, indeed, and with the gravity of age, but doing its work, and casting its loose drops in the alms-giving of a gentle rain upon a little plot of Master Rogers's garden, which was therefore full of moisture-loving flowers. This plot was divided from the mill-wheel by a small stream which carried away the surplus water, and was now full and running rapidly.

Beyond the stream, beside the flower bed, stood
a dusty young man, talking to a young woman with
a rosy face and clear honest eyes. The moment
they saw me they parted. The young man came
across the stream at a step, and the young woman
went up the garden towards the cottage.

"That must be Old Rogers's cottage?" I said
to the miller.

",Yes, sir," he answered, looking a little sheepish.

"Was that his daughter — that nice-looking
young woman you were talking to?"

"Yes, sir, it was."

And he stole a shy pleased look at me out of
the corners of his eyes.

"It's a good thing," I said, "to have an honest
experienced old mill like yours, that can manage to
go on of itself for a little while now and then."

This gave a great help to his budding confidence.
He laughed.

"Well, sir, it's not very often it's left to itself.
Jane isn't at her father's above once or twice a
week at most."

"She doesn't live with them, then?"

"No, sir. You see they're both hearty, and they
ain't over well to do, and Jane lives up at the Hall,
sir. She's upper housemaid, and waits on one of
the young ladies. — Old Rogers has seen a great
deal of the world, sir."

"So I imagine. I am just going to see him.
Good morning."

I jumped across the stream, and went up a little
gravel-walk, which led me in a few yards to the

cottage-door. It was a sweet place to live in, with honeysuckle growing over the house, and the sounds of the softly-labouring mill-wheel ever in its little porch and about its windows.

The door was open, and Dame Rogers came from within to meet me. She welcomed me, and led the way into her little kitchen. As I entered, Jane went out at the back-door. But it was only to call her father, who presently came in.

"I'm glad to see ye, sir. This pleasure comes of having no work to-day. After harvest there come slack times for the likes of me. People don't care about a bag of old bones when they can get hold of young men. Well, well, never mind, old woman. The Lord 'll take us through somehow. When the wind blows, the ship goes; when the wind drops, the ship stops; but the sea is His all the same, for He made it; and the wind is His all the same too."

He spoke in the most matter-of-fact tone, unaware of anything poetic in what he said. To him it was just common sense, and common sense only.

"I am sorry you are out of work," I said. "But my garden is sadly out of order, and I must have something done to it. You don't dislike gardening, do you?"

"Well, I beant a right good hand at garden-work," answered the old man, with some embarrassment, scratching his gray head with a troubled scratch.

There was more in this than met the ear; but

what, I could not conjecture. I would press the
point a little. So I took him at his own word.

"I won't ask you to do any of the more ornamental part," I said, — "only plain digging and
hoeing."

"I would rather be excused, sir."

"I am afraid I made you think" —

"I thought nothing, sir. I thank you kindly,
sir."

"I assure you I want the work done, and I
must employ some one else if you don't under-
take it."

"Well, sir, my back's bad now — no, sir, I
won't tell a story about it. I would just rather not,
sir."

"Now," his wife broke in, "now, Old Rogers,
why won't 'ee tell the parson the truth, like a man,
downright? If ye won't, I'll do it for 'ee. The
fact is, sir," she went on, turning to me, with a
plate in her hand, which she was wiping, "the fact
is, that the old parson's man for that kind o' work
was Simmons, t'other end of the village; and my
man is so afeard o' hurtin' e'er another, that he'll
turn the bread away from his own mouth and let it
fall in the dirt."

"Now, now, old 'oman, don't 'ee belie me. I'm
not so bad as that. You see, sir, I never was good
at knowin' right from wrong like. I never was
good, that is, at tellin' exactly what I ought to do.
So when anything comes up, I just says to myself,
'Now, Old Rogers, what do you think the Lord
would best like you to do?' And as soon as I ax

myself that, I know directly what I've got to do;
and then my old woman can't turn me no more
than a bull. And she don't like my obstinate fits.
But, you see, I daren't, sir, once I axed myself
that."

"Stick to that, Rogers," I said.

"Besides, sir," he went on, "Simmons wants it
more than I do. He's got a sick wife; and my old
woman, thank God, is hale and hearty. And there
is another thing besides, sir: he might take it hard
of you, sir, and think it was turning away an old
servant like; and then, sir, he wouldn't be ready to
hear what you had to tell him, and might, mayhap,
lose a deal o' comfort. And that I would take worst
of all, sir."

"Well, well, Rogers, Simmons shall have the
job."

"Thank ye, sir," said the old man.

His wife, who could not see the thing quite
from her husband's point of view, was too honest to
say anything; but she was none the less cordial to
me. The daughter stood looking from one to the
other with attentive face, which took everything,
but revealed nothing.

I rose to go. As I reached the door, I re-
membered the tobacco in my pocket. I had not
bought it for myself. I never could smoke. Nor
do I conceive that smoking is essential to a clergyman in the country; though I have occasionally
envied one of my brethren in London, who will sit
down by the fire, and, lighting his pipe, at the same
time please his host and subdue the bad smells of

the place. And I never could hit his way of talking to his parishioners either. He could put them at their ease in a moment. I think he must have got the trick out of his pipe. But in reality, I seldom think about how I ought to talk to anybody I am with.

That I didn't smoke myself was no reason why I should not help Old Rogers to smoke. So I pulled out the tobacco.

"You smoke, don't you, Rogers?" I said.

"Well, sir, I can't deny it. It's not much I spend on baccay, anyhow. Is it, dame?"

"No, that it bean't," answered his wife.

"You don't think there's any harm in smoking a pipe, sir?"

"Not the least," I answered, with emphasis.

"You see, sir," he went on, not giving me time to prove how far I was from thinking there was any harm in it, "You see, sir, sailors learns many ways they might be better without. I used to take my pan o' grog with the rest of them; but I give that up quite, 'cause as how I don't want it now."

"'Cause as how," interrupted his wife, "you spend the money on tea for me, instead. You wicked old man to tell stories!"

"Well, I takes my share of the tea, old woman, and I'm sure it's a deal better for me. But, to tell the truth, sir, I was a little troubled in my mind about the baccay, not knowing whether I ought to have it or not. For you see, the parson that's gone didn't more than half like it, as I could tell by the turn of his hawse-holes when he come in at the door

and me a-smokin'. Not as he said anything; for,
ye see, I was an old man, and I daresay that kep
him quiet. But I did hear him blow up a young
chap i' the village he come upon promiscus with a
pipe in his mouth. He did give him a thunderin'
broadside! to be sure! So I was in two minds
whether I ought to go on with my pipe or not."

"And how did you settle the question, Rogers?"

"Why I followed my own old chart, sir."

"Quite right. One mustn't mind too much what
other people think."

"That's not exactly what I mean, sir."

"What do you mean then? I should like to
know."

"Well, sir, I mean that I said to myself, 'Now,
Old Rogers, what do you think the Lord would say
about this here baccay business?'"

"And what did you think He would say?"

"Why, sir, I thought He would say, 'Old Rogers,
have yer baccay; only mind ye don't grumble when
you 'aint got none.'"

Something in this — I could not at the time
have told what — touched me more than I can express. No doubt it was the simple reality of the
relation in which the old man stood to his Father in
heaven that made me feel as if the tears would come
in spite of me.

"And this is the man," I said to myself,
"whom I thought I should be able to teach! Well,
the wisest learn most, and I may be useful to him
after all."

As I said nothing, the old man resumed —

"For you see, sir, it is not always a body feels he has a right to spend his ha'pence on baccay; and sometimes, too, he 'aint got none to spend."

"In the meantime," I said, "here is some that I bought for you as I came along. I hope you will find it good. I am no judge."

The old sailor's eyes glistened with gratitude. "Well, who'd ha' thought it. You didn't think I was beggin' for it, sir, surely?"

"You see I had it for you in my pocket."

"Well that *is* good o' you, sir!"

"Why, Rogers, that'll last you a month!" exclaimed his wife, looking nearly as pleased as himself.

"Six weeks at least, wife," he answered. "And ye don't smoke yourself, sir, and yet ye bring baccay to me! Well, it's just like yer Master, sir."

I went away resolved that Old Rogers should have no chance of "grumbling" for want of tobacco, if I could help it.

CHAPTER IV.

The Coffin.

ON the way back, my thoughts were still oc-
cupied with the woman I had seen in the little shop.
The old man-of-war's man was probably the nobler
being of the two; and if I had had to choose
between them, I should no doubt have chosen him.
But I had not to choose between them; I had only
to think about them; and I thought a great deal
more about the one I could not understand than the
one I could understand.   For Old Rogers wanted
little help from me; whereas the other was evidently
a soul in pain, and therefore belonged to me in peculiar right of my office; while the readiest way in
which I could justify to myself the possession of
that office was to make it a shepherding of the sheep.
So I resolved to find out what I could about her, as
one having a right to know, that I might see 'whether
I could not help her.   From herself it was evident
that her secret, if she had one, was not to be easily
gained; but even the common reports of the village
would be some enlightenment to the darkness I was
in about her.

As I went again through the village, I observed
a narrow lane striking off to the left, and resolved
to explore in that direction.   It led up to one side
of the large house of which I have already spoken.

As I came near, I smelt what has been to me always a delightful smell — that of fresh deals under the hands of the carpenter. In the scent of those boards of pine is enclosed all the idea the tree could gather of the world of forest where it was reared. It speaks of many wild and bright but chiefly clean and rather cold things. If I were idling, it would draw me to it across many fields. — Turning a corner, I heard the sound of a saw. And this sound drew me yet more. For a carpenter's shop was the delight of my boyhood; and after I began to read the history of our Lord with something of that sense of reality with which we read other histories, and which, I am sorry to think, so much of the well-meant instruction we receive in our youth tends to destroy, my feeling about such a workshop grew stronger and stronger, till at last I never could go near enough to see the shavings lying on the floor of one, without a spiritual sensation such as I have in entering an old church; which sensation, ever since having been admitted on the usual conditions to a Mohammedan mosque, urges me to pull off, not only my hat, but my shoes likewise. And the feeling has grown upon me, till now it seems at times as if the only cure in the world for social pride would be to go for five silent minutes into a carpenter's shop. How one can think of himself as above his neighbours, within sight, sound, or smell of one, I fear I am getting almost unable to imagine; and one ought not to get out of sympathy with the wrong. Only as I am growing old now, it does not matter so much, for I daresay my time will not be very long.

So I drew near to the shop, feeling as if the Lord might be at work there at one of the benches. And when I reached the door, there was my pale-faced hearer of the Sunday afternoon, sawing a board for a coffin-lid.

As my shadow fell across and darkened his work, he lifted his head and saw me.

I could not altogether understand the expression of his countenance as he stood upright from his labour and touched his old hat with rather a proud than a courteous gesture. And I could not believe that he was glad to see me, although he laid down his saw and advanced to the door. It was the gentleman in him, not the man, that sought to make me welcome, hardly caring whether I saw through the ceremony or not. True, there was a smile on his lips, but the smile of a man who cherishes a secret grudge; of one who does not altogether dislike you, but who has a claim upon you — say, for an apology, of which claim he doubts whether you know the existence. So the smile seemed tightened, and stopped just when it got half-way to its width, and was about to become hearty and begin to shine.

"May I come in?" I said.

"Come in, sir," he answered.

"I am glad I have happened to come upon you by accident," I said.

He smiled as if he did not quite believe in the accident, and considered it a part of the play between us that I should pretend it. I hastened to add —

"I was wandering about the place, making some acquaintance with it, and with my friends in it, when I came upon you quite unexpectedly. You know I saw you in church on Sunday afternoon."

"I know you saw me, sir," he answered, with a motion as if to return to his work; "but, to tell the truth, I don't go to church very often."

I did not quite know whether to take this as proceeding from an honest fear of being misunderstood, or from a sense of being in general superior to all that sort of thing. But I felt that it would be of no good to pursue the inquiry directly. I looked therefore for something to say.

"Ah! your work is not always a pleasant one," I said, associating the feelings of which I have already spoken with the facts before me, and looking at the coffin, the lower part of which stood nearly finished upon trestles on the floor.

"Well, there are unpleasant things in all trades," he answered. "But it does not matter," he added, with an increase of bitterness in his smile.

"I didn't mean," I said, "that the work was unpleasant — only sad. It must always be painful to make a coffin."

"A joiner gets used to it, sir, as you do to the funeral 'service. But, for my part, I don't see why it should be considered so unhappy for a man to be buried. This isn't such a good job, after all, this world, sir, you must allow."

"Neither is that coffin," said I, as if by a sudden inspiration.

The man seemed taken aback, as Old Rogers

might have said. He looked at the coffin and then
looked at me.

"Well, sir," he said, after a short pause, which
no doubt seemed longer both to him and to me than
it would have seemed to any third person, "I don't
see anything amiss with the coffin. I don't say it'll
last till doomsday, as the gravedigger says to Hamlet,
because I don't know so much about doomsday as
some people pretend to; but you see, sir, it's not
finished yet."

"Thank you," I said; "that's just what I meant.
You thought I was hasty in my judgment of your
coffin; whereas I only said of it knowingly what
you said of the world thoughtlessly. How do you
know that the world is finished any more than your
coffin? And how dare you then say that it is a bad
job?"

The same respectfully scornful smile passed over
his face, as much as to say, "Ah! it's your trade
to talk that way, so I must not be too hard upon
you."

"At any rate, sir," he said, "whoever made it
has taken long enough about it, a person would
think, to finish anything he ever meant to finish."

"One day is with the Lord as a thousand years,
and a thousand years as one day," I said. '

"That's supposing," he answered, "that the Lord
did make the world. For my part, I am half of a
mind that the Lord didn't make it at all."

"I am very glad to hear you say so," I answered.

Hereupon I found that we had changed places a

little. He looked up at me. The smile of superiority was no longer there, and a puzzled questioning, which might indicate either "Who would have expected that from you?" or, "What can he mean?" or both at once, had taken its place. I, for my part, knew that on the scale of the man's judgment I had risen nearer to his own level. As he said nothing, however, and I was in danger of being misunderstood, I proceeded at once.

"Of course it seems to me better that you should not believe God had done a thing, than that you should believe He had not done it well?"

"Ah! I see, sir. Then you will allow there is some room for doubting whether He made the world at all?"

"Yes; for I do not think an honest man, as you seem to me to be, would be able to doubt without any room whatever. That would be only for a fool. But it is just possible, as we are not perfectly good ourselves — you'll allow that, won't you?"

"That I will, sir; God knows."

"Well, I say — as we're not quite good ourselves, it's just possible that things may be too good for us to do them the justice of believing in them.".

"But there are things, you must allow, so plainly wrong!"

"So much so, both in the world and in myself, that it would be to me torturing despair to believe that God did not make the world; for then, how would it ever be put right? Therefore I prefer the theory that He has not done making it yet."

"But wouldn't you say, sir, that God might have
4*

managed it without so many slips in the making as
your way would suppose? I should think myself a
bad workman if I worked after that fashion."

"I do not believe that there are any slips. You
know you are making a coffin; but are you sure
you know what God is making of the world?"

"That I can't tell, of course, nor anybody else."

"Then you can't say that what looks like a slip
is really a slip, either in design or in the workman-
ship. You do not know what end He has in view;
and you may find some day that those slips were
just the straight road to that very end."

"Ah! maybe. But you can't be sure of it, you
see."

"Perhaps not, in the way you mean; but sure
enough, for all that, to try it upon life — to order
my way by it, and so find that it works well. And
I find that it explains everything that comes near it.
You know that no engineer would be satisfied with
his engine on paper, nor with any proof whatever
except seeing how it will go."

He made no reply.

It is a principle of mine never to push anything
over the edge. When I am successful in any argument, my one dread is of humiliating my opponent.
Indeed I cannot bear it. It humiliates me. And if
you want him to think about anything, you must
leave him room, and not give him such associations
with the question that the very idea of it will be
painful and irritating to him. Let him have a hand
in the convincing of himself. I have been surprised
sometimes to see my own arguments come up fresh

and green, when I thought the fowls of the air had devoured them up. When a man reasons for victory and not for the truth in the other soul, he is sure of just one ally, the same that Faust had in fighting Gretchen's brother — that is, the Devil. But God and good men are against him. So I never follow up a victory of that kind, for, as I said, the defeat of the intellect is not the object in fighting with the sword of the Spirit, but the acceptance of the heart. In this case, therefore, I drew back.

"May I ask for whom you are making that coffin?"

"For a sister of my own, sir."

"I'm sorry to hear that."

"There's no occasion. I can't say I'm sorry, though she was one of the best women I ever knew."

"Why are you not sorry, then? Life's a good thing in the main, you will allow."

"Yes, when it's endurable at all. But to have a brute of a husband coming home at any hour of the night or morning, drunk upon the money she had earned by hard work, was enough to take more of the shine out of things than church-going on Sundays could put in again, regular as she was, poor woman! I'm as glad as her brute of a husband, that she's out of his way at last."

"How do you know he's glad of it?"

"He's been drunk every night since she died."

"Then he's the worse for losing her?"

"He may well be. Crying like a hypocrite, too, over his own work!"

"A fool he must be. A hypocrite, perhaps not. A hypocrite is a terrible name to give. Perhaps her death will do him good."

"He doesn't deserve to be done any good to. I would have made this coffin for him with a world of pleasure."

"I never found that I deserved anything, not even a coffin. The only claim that I could ever lay to anything was that I was very much in want of it."

The old smile returned — as much as to say, "That's your little game in the church." But I resolved to try nothing more with him at present; and indeed was sorry that I had started the new question at all, partly because thus I had again given him occasion to feel that he knew better than I did, which was not good either for him or for me in our relation to each other.

"This has been a fine old room once," I said, looking round the workshop.

"You can see it wasn't a workshop always, sir. Many a grand dinner-party has sat down in this room when it was in its glory. Look at the chimney-piece there."

"I have been looking at it," I said, going nearer.

"It represents the four quarters of the world, you see."

I saw strange figures of men and women, one on a kneeling camel, one on a crawling crocodile, and others differently mounted; with various besides of Nature's bizarre productions creeping and flying in stone-carving over the huge fire-place, in which,

in place of a fire, stood several new and therefore
brilliantly red cart-wheels. The sun shone through
the upper part of a high window, of which many of
the panes were broken, right in upon the cart-wheels,
which, glowing thus in the chimney under the sombre
chimney-piece, added to the grotesque look of the
whole assemblage of contrasts. The coffin and the
carpenter stood in the twilight occasioned by the
sharp division of light made by a lofty wing of the
house that rose flanking the other window. The
room was still wainscotted in panels, which, I presume for the sake of the more light required for
handicraft, had been washed all over with white. At
the level of labour they were broken in many places.
Somehow or other, the whole reminded me of Albert
Dürer's "Melencholia."

Seeing I was interested in looking about his
shop, my new friend — for I could not help feeling
that we should be friends before all was over, and so
began to count him one already — resumed the conversation. He had never taken up the dropped thread
of it before.

"Yes, sir," he said; "the owners of the place
little thought it would come to this — the deals
growing into a coffin there on the spot where the
grand dinner was laid for them and their guests!
But there is another thing about it that is odder still:
my son is the last male" —

Here he stopped suddenly, and his face grew very
red. As suddenly he resumed —

"I'm not a gentleman, sir; but I will tell the
truth. Curse it! — I beg your pardon, sir," — and

here the old smile — "I don't think I got that from
their side of the house. — My son's *not* the last male
descendant."

Here followed another pause.

As to the imprecation, I knew better than to
take any notice of a mere expression of excitement
under a sense of some injury with which I was not
yet acquainted. If I could get his feelings right in
regard to other and more important things, a reform
in that matter would soon follow; whereas to make
a mountain of a mole-hill would be to put that very
mountain between him and me. Nor would I ask
him any questions, lest I should just happen to ask
him the wrong one; for this parishioner of mine evidently wanted careful handling, if I would do him
any good. And it will not do any man good to
fling even the Bible in his face. Nay, a roll of
bank-notes, which would be more evidently a good
to most men, would carry insult with it if presented
in that manner. You cannot expect people to accept
before they have had a chance of seeing what the
offered gift really is.

After a pause, therefore, the carpenter had once
more to recommence, or let the conversation lie. I
stood in a waiting attitude. And while I looked at
him, I was reminded of some one else whom I knew
— with whom, too, I had pleasant associations —
though I could not in the least determine who that
one might be.

"It's very foolish of me to talk so to a stranger,"
he resumed.

"It is very kind and friendly of you," I said,

still careful to make no advances. "And you yourself belong to the old family that once lived in this old house?"

"It would be no boast to tell the truth, sir, even if it were a credit to me, which it is not. That family has been nothing but a curse to ours."

I noted that he spoke of that family as different from his, and yet implied that he belonged to it. The explanation would come in time. But the man was again silent, planing away at half the lid of his sister's coffin. And I could not help thinking that the closed mouth meant to utter nothing more on this occasion.

"I am sure there must be many a story to tell about this old place, if only there were any one to tell them," I said at last, looking round the room once more. — "I think I see the remains of paintings on the ceiling."

"You are sharp-eyed, sir. My father says they were plain enough in his young days."

"Is your father alive, then?"

"That he is, sir, and hearty too, though he seldom goes out of doors now. Will you go up stairs and see him? He's past ninety, sir. He has plenty of stories to tell about the old place — before it began to fall to pieces, like." .

"I won't go to-day," I said, partly because I wanted to be at home to receive any one who might call, and partly to secure an excuse for calling again upon the carpenter sooner than I should otherwise have liked to do. "I expect visitors myself, and it is time I were at home. Good morning."

"Good morning, sir."

And away home I went with a new wonder in
my brain. The man did not seem unknown to me.
I mean the state of his mind woke no feeling of
perplexity in me. I was certain of understanding it
thoroughly when I had learned something of his
history; for that such a man must have a history of
his own was rendered only the more probable from
the fact that he knew something of the history of
his forefathers, though indeed there are some men
who seem to have no other. It was strange, however, to think of that man working away at a trade
in the very house in which such ancestors had eaten
and drunk, and married and given in marriage. The
house and family had declined together — in outward appearance at least; for it was quite possible
both might have risen in the moral and spiritual
scale in proportion as they sank in the social one.
And if any of my readers are at first inclined to
think that this could hardly be, seeing that the man
was little if anything better than an infidel, I would
just like to hold one minute's conversation with them
on that subject. A man may be on the way to the
truth just in virtue of his doubting. I will tell you
what Lord Bacon says, and of all writers of English
I delight in him: "So it is in contemplation: if a
man will begin with certainties, he shall end in
doubts; but if he will be content to begin with doubts,
he shall end in certainties." Now I could not tell
the kind or character of this man's doubt; but it was
evidently real and not affected doubt; and that was
much in his favour. And I could see that he was a

thinking man; just one of the sort I thought I should get on with in time, because he was honest — notwithstanding that unpleasant smile of his, which did irritate me a little, and partly piqued me into the determination to get the better of the man, if I possibly could, by making friends with him. At all events, here was another strange parishioner. And who could it be that he was like?

CHAPTER V.

Visitors from the Hall.

WHEN I came near my own gate, I saw that it was open; and when I came in sight of my own door, I found a carriage standing before it, and a footman ringing the bell. It was an old-fashioned carriage, with two white horses in it, yet whiter by age than by nature. They looked as if no coachman could get more than three miles an hour out of them, they were so fat and knuckle-kneed. But my attention could not rest long on the horses, and I reached the door just as my housekeeper was pronouncing me absent. There were two ladies in the carriage, one old and one young.

"Ah, here is Mr. Walton!" said the old lady, in a serene voice, with a clear hardness in its tone; and I held out my hand to aid her descent. She had pulled off her glove to get a card out of her card-case, and so put the tips of two old fingers, worn very smooth, as if polished with feeling what things were like, upon the palm of my hand. I then offered my hand to her companion, a girl apparently about fourteen, who took a hearty hold of it, and jumped down beside her with a smile. As I followed them into the house, I took their card from the housekeeper's hand, and read *Mrs. Oldcastle and Miss Gladwyn.*

I confess here to my reader, that these are not really the names I read on the card. I made these up this minute. But the names of the persons of humble position in my story, are their real names. And my reason for making the difference will be plain enough. You can never find out my friend Old Rogers: you *might* find out the people who called on me in their carriage with the ancient white horses.

When they were seated in the drawing-room, I said to the old lady —

"I remember seeing you in church on Sunday morning. It is very kind of you to call so soon."

"You will always see me in church," she returned with a stiff bow, and an expansion of deadness on her face, which I interpreted into an assertion of dignity, resulting from the implied possibility that I might have passed her over in my congregation, or might have forgotten her after not passing her over.

"Except when you have a headache, grannie," said Miss Gladwyn, with an arch look first at her grandmother and then at me. "Grannie has bad headaches sometimes."

The deadness melted a little from Mrs. Oldcastle's face, as she turned with half a smile to her grandchild, and said —

"Yes, Pet. But you know that cannot be an interesting fact to Mr. Walton."

"I beg your pardon, Mrs. Oldcastle," I said. "A clergyman ought to know something, and the more the better, of the troubles of his flock. Sympathy is one of the first demands he ought to be able to meet. — I know what a headache is."

The former expression, or rather non-expression, returned; this time unaccompanied by a bow.

"I trust, Mr. Walton, I *trust* I am above any morbid necessity for sympathy. But, as you say, amongst the poor of your flock, — it *is* very desirable that a clergyman should be able to sympathize."

"It's quite true what grannie says, Mr. Walton, though you mightn't think it. When she has a headache, she shuts herself up in her own room, and doesn't even let me come near her — nobody but Sarah; and how she can prefer her to me, I'm sure I don't know."

And here the girl pretended to pout, but with a sparkle in her bright gray eye.

"The subject is not interesting to me, Pet. Pray, Mr. Walton, is it a point of conscience with you to wear the surplice when you preach?"

"Not in the least," I answered. "I think I like it rather better on the whole. But that's not why I wear it."

"Never mind grannie, Mr. Walton. *I* think the surplice is lovely. I'm sure it's much liker the way we shall be dressed in heaven, though I don't think I shall ever get there, if I must read the good books grannie reads."

"I don't know that it is necessary to read any good books but *the* good book," I said.

"There, grannie!" exclaimed Miss Gladwyn,

triumphantly. "I'm so glad I've got Mr. Walton on my side!"

"Mr. Walton is not so old as I am, my dear, and has much to learn yet."

I could not help feeling a little annoyed, (which was very foolish, I know,) and saying to myself, "If it's to make me like you, I had rather not learn any more;" but I said nothing aloud, of course.

"Have you got a headache to-day, grannie?"

"No, Pet. Be quiet. I wish to ask Mr. Walton *why* he wears the surplice."

"Simply," I replied, "because I was told the people had been accustomed to it under my predecessor."

"But that can be no good reason for doing what is not right — that people have been accustomed to it."

"But I don't allow that it's not right. I think it is a matter of no consequence whatever. If I find that the people don't like it, I will give it up with pleasure."

"You ought to have principles of your own, Mr. Walton."

"I hope I have. And one of them is, not to make mountains of molehills; for a molehill is not a mountain. A man ought to have too much to do in obeying his conscience and keeping his soul's garments clean, to mind whether he wears black or white when telling his flock that God loves them, and that they will never be happy till they believe it."

"They may believe that too soon."

"I don't think any one can believe the truth too soon."

A pause followed, during which it became evident to me that Miss Gladwyn saw fun in the whole affair, and was enjoying it thoroughly. Mrs. Old-castle's face, on the contrary, was illegible. She resumed in a measured still voice, which she meant to be meek, I daresay, but which was really authoritative —

"I am sorry, Mr. Walton, that your principles are so loose and unsettled. You will see my honesty in saying so when you find that, objecting to the surplice, as I do, on Protestant grounds, I yet warn you against making any change because you may discover that your parishioners are against it. You have no idea, Mr. Walton, what inroads Radicalism, as they call it, has been making in this neighbour-hood. It is quite dreadful. Everybody, down to the poorest, claiming a right to think for himself, and set his betters right! There's one worse than any of the rest — but he's no better than an atheist — a carpenter of the name of Weir, always talking to his neighbours against the proprietors and the magistrates, and the clergy too, Mr. Walton, and the game-laws, and what not? And if you once show them that you are afraid of them by going a step out of your way for *their* opinion about anything, there will be no end to it; for the beginning of strife is-like the letting out of water, as you know. *I* should know nothing about it, but that my daughter's maid — I came to hear of it through her — a de-cent girl of the name of Rogers, and born of decent parents, but unfortunately attached to the son of one of your churchwardens, who has put him into that mill on the river you can almost see from here."

"Who put him in the mill?"

"His own father, to whom it belongs."

"Well, it seems to me a very good match for her."

"Yes, indeed, and for him too. But his foolish father thinks the match below him, as if there was any difference between the positions of people in that rank of life! Every one seems striving to tread on the heels of every one else, instead of being content with the station to which God has called them. I am content with mine. I had nothing to do with putting myself there. Why should they not be content with theirs? They need to be taught Christian humility and respect for their superiors. That's the virtue most wanted at present. The poor have to look up to the rich" —

"That's right, grannie! And the rich have to look down on the poor."

"No, my dear. I did not say that. The rich have to be *kind* to the poor."

"But, grannie, why did you marry Mr. Old castle?"

"What does the child mean?"

"Uncle Stoddart says you refused ever so many offers when you were a girl."

"Uncle Stoddart has no business to be talking about such things to a chit like you," returned the grandmother, smiling, however, at the charge, which so far certainly contained no reproach.

"And grandpapa was the ugliest and the richest of them all — wasn't he, grannie? and Colonel Markham the handsomest and the poorest?"

A flush of anger crimsoned the old lady's pale face. It looked dead no longer.

"Hold your tongue," she said. "You are rude."

And Miss Gladwyn did hold her tongue, but nothing else, for she was laughing all over.

The relation between these two was evidently a very odd one. It was clear that Miss Gladwyn was a spoiled child, though I could not help thinking her very nicely spoiled, as far as I saw; and that the old lady persisted in regarding her as a cub, although her claws had grown quite long enough to be dangerous. Certainly, if things went on thus, it was pretty clear which of them would soon have the upper hand, for grannie was vulnerable, and Pet was not.

It really began to look as if there were none but characters in my parish. I began to think it must be the strangest parish in England, and to wonder that I had never heard of it before. "Surely it must be in some story-book at least!" I said to myself.

But her grand-daughter's tiger-cat-play drove the old lady nearer to me. She rose and held out her hand, saying, with some kindness:

"Take my advice, my dear Mr. Walton, and don't make too much of your poor, or they'll soon

be too much for you to manage. — Come, Pet: it's
time to go home to lunch. — And for the surplice,
take your own way and wear it. *I* shan't say anything more about it."

"I will do what I can see to be right in the
matter," I answered as gently as I could; for I did
not want to quarrel with her, although I thought
her both presumptuous and rude.

"I'm on your side, Mr. Walton," said the girl,
with a sweet comical smile, as she squeezed my hand
once more.

I led them to the carriage, and it was with a
feeling of relief that I saw it drive off.

The old lady certainly was not pleasant. She
had a white smooth face over which the skin was
drawn tight, gray hair, and rather lurid hazel eyes.
I felt a repugnance to her that was hardly to be accounted for by her arrogance to me, or by her super-
ciliousness to the poor; although either would have
accounted for much of it. For I confess that I have
not yet learned to bear presumption and rudeness
with all the patience and forgiveness with which I
ought by this time to be able to meet them. And
as to the poor, I am afraid I was always in some
danger of being a partizan of theirs against the
rich; and that a clergyman ought never to be. And
indeed the poor rich have more need of the care of
the clergyman than the others, seeing it is hardly
that the rich shall enter into the kingdom of heaven,
and the poor have all the advantage over them in
that respect.

5*

"Still," I said to myself, "there must be some good in the woman — she cannot be altogether so hard as she looks, else how should that child dare to take the liberties of a kitten with her? She doesn't look to *me* like one to make game of! However, I shall know a little more about her when I return her call, and I will do my best to keep on good terms with her."

I took down a volume of Plato to comfort me after the irritation which my nerves had undergone, and sat down in an easy-chair beside the open window of my study. And with Plato in my hand, and all that outside my window, I began to feel as if after all a man might be happy, even if a lady had refused him. And there I sat, without opening my favourite vellum-bound volume, gazing out on the happy world, whence a gentle wind came in as if to bid me welcome with a kiss to all it had to give me. And then I thought of the wind that bloweth where it listeth, which is everywhere, and I quite forgot to open my Plato, and thanked God for the Life of life whose story and whose words are in that best of books, and who explains everything to us, and makes us love Socrates and David and all good men ten times more; and who follows no law but the law of love, and no fashion but the will of God; for where did ever one read words less like moralizing and more like simple earnestness of truth than all those of Jesus? And I prayed my God that He would make me able to speak good common heavenly sense to my people, and forgive me for feeling so cross and proud towards the unhappy old

lady — for I was sure she was not happy — and
make me into a rock which swallowed up the waves
of wrong in its great caverns, and never threw them
back to swell the commotion of the angry sea whence
they came. Ah, what it would be actually to an-
nihilate wrong in this way! — to be able to say, it
shall not be wrong against me, so utterly do I forgive it! How much sooner, then, would the wrong-
doer repent, and get rid of the wrong from his side
also! But the painful fact will show itself, not less
curious than painful, that it is more difficult to forgive small wrongs than great ones. Perhaps, however, the forgiveness of the great wrongs is not so
true as it seems. For do we not think it is a fine
thing to forgive such wrongs, and so do it rather
for our own sakes than for the sake of the wrong-
doer? It is dreadful not to be good, and to have
bad ways inside one.

Such thoughts passed through my mind. And
once more the great light went up on me with regard
to my office, namely, that just because I was parson
to the parish, I must not be *the person* to myself.
And I prayed God to keep me from feeling *stung*
and proud, however any one might behave to me;
for all my value lay in being a sacrifice to Him and
the people.

So when Mrs. Pearson knocked at the door, and
told me that a lady and gentleman had called, I
shut my book which I had just opened, and kept
down as well as I could the rising grumble of the
inhospitable Englishman, who is apt to be forgetful

to entertain strangers, at least in the parlour of his
heart. And I cannot count it perfect hospitality to
be friendly and plentiful towards those whom you
have invited to your house — what thank has a
man in that? — while you are cold and forbidding
to those who have not that claim on your attention.
That is not to be perfect as our Father in heaven is
perfect. By all means tell people, when you are
busy about something that must be done, that you
cannot spare the time for them except they want
you upon something of yet more pressing necessity;
but *tell* them, and do not get rid of them by the
use of the instrument commonly called *the cold
shoulder*. It is a wicked instrument that, and ought
to have fallen out of use by this time.

I went and received Mr. and Miss Boulderstone,
and was at least thus far rewarded — that the *eerie*
feeling, as the Scotch would call it, which I had
about my parish, as containing none but *characters*,
and therefore not being *cannie*, was entirely removed.
At least there was a wholesome leaven in it of
honest stupidity. Please, kind reader, do not fancy
I am sneering. I declare to you I think a sneer the
worst thing God has not made. A curse is nothing
in wickedness to it, it seems to me. I do mean that
honest stupidity I respect heartily, and do assert my
conviction that I do not know how England at least
would get on without it. But I do not mean the
stupidity that sets up for teaching itself to its neighbour, thinking itself wisdom all the time. That I
do not respect.

Mr. and Miss Boulderstone left me a little

fatigued, but in no way sore or grumbling. They
only sent me back with additional zest to my Plato,
of which I enjoyed a hearty page or two before any
one else arrived. The only other visitors I had that
day were an old surgeon in the navy who since his
retirement had practised for many years in the
neighbourhood, and was still at the call of any one
who did not think him too old-fashioned — for even
here the fashions, though decidedly elderly young
ladies by the time they arrived, held their sway
none the less imperiously — and Mr. Brownrigg,
the churchwarden. More of Dr. Duncan by and by.

Except Mr. and Miss Boulderstone, I had not
yet seen any common people. They were all decidedly uncommon, and, as regarded most of them,
I could not think I should have any difficulty in
preaching to them. For, whatever place a man may
give to preaching in the ritual of the church — indeed it does not properly belong to the ritual at all
— it is yet the part of the so-called *service* with
which his personality has most to do. To the influences of the other parts he has to submit himself,
ever turning the openings of his soul towards them,
that he may not be a mere praying-machine; but
with the sermon it is otherwise. That he produces.
For that he is responsible. And therefore, I say, it
was a great comfort to me to find myself amongst a
people from which my spirit neither shrunk in the
act of preaching, nor with regard to which it was
likely to feel that it was beating itself against a
stone wall. There was some good in preaching to
a man like Weir or Old Rogers. Whether there

was any good in preaching to a woman like Mrs. Oldcastle I did not know.

The evening I thought I might give to my books, and thus end my first Monday in my parish; but, as I said, Mr. Brownrigg, the churchwarden, called and stayed a whole weary hour, talking about matters quite uninteresting to any who may hereafter peruse what I am now writing. Really he was not an interesting man: short, broad, stout, red-faced, with an immense amount of mental inertia, discharging itself in constant lingual activity about little nothings. Indeed, when there was no new nothing to be had, the old nothing would do over again to make a fresh fuss about. But if you attempted to convey a thought into his mind which involved the moving round half a degree from where he stood, and looking at the matter from a point even so far new, you found him utterly, totally impenetrable, as pachydermatous as any rhinoceros or behemoth. One other corporeal fact I could not help observing, was, that his cheeks rose at once from the collar of his green coat, his neck being invisible, from the hollow between it and the jaw being filled up to a level. The conformation was just what he himself delighted to contemplate in his pigs, to which his resemblance was greatly increased by unwearied endeavours to keep himself close shaved. — I could not help feeling anxious about his son and Jane Rogers. — He gave a quantity of gossip about various people, evidently anxious that I should regard them as he regarded them; but in all he said concerning them I could scarcely detect

one point of significance as to character or history.
I was very glad indeed when the waddling of hands
— for it was the perfect imbecility of hand-shaking
— was over, and he was safely out of the gate.
He had kept me standing on the steps for full
five minutes, and I did not feel safe from him
till I was once more in my study with the door
shut.

I am not going to try my reader's patience with
anything of a more detailed account of my intro-
duction to my various parishioners. I shall mention
them only as they come up in the course of my
story. Before many days had passed I had found
out my poor, who I thought must be somewhere,
seeing the Lord had said we should have them with
us always. There was a workhouse in the village,
but there were not a great many in it; for the poor
were kindly enough handled who belonged to the
place, and were not too severely compelled to go
into the house; though I believe in this house they
would have been more comfortable than they were
in their own houses.

I cannot imagine a much greater misfortune for
a man, not to say a clergyman, than not to know,
or knowing, no to minister to any of the poor. And
I did not feel that I knew in the least where I was
until I had found out and conversed with almost the
whole of mine.

After I had done so, I began to think it better
to return Mrs. Oldcastle's visit, though I felt greatly

disinclined to encounter that tight-skinned nose again, and that mouth whose smile had no light in it, except when it responded to some nonsense of her grand-daughter's.

————

CHAPTER VI.

Oldcastle Hall.

ABOUT noon, on a lovely autumn day, I set out for Oldcastle Hall. The keenness of the air had melted away with the heat of the sun, yet still the air was fresh and invigorating. Can any one tell me why it is that when the earth is renewing her youth in the spring, man should feel feeble and low-spirited, and gaze with bowed head, though pleased heart, on the crocuses; whereas on the contrary in the autumn, when nature is dying for the winter, he feels strong and hopeful, holds his head erect, and walks with a vigorous step, though the flaunting dahlias discourage him greatly? I do not ask for the physical causes: those I might be able to find out for myself; but I ask, Where is the rightness and fitness in the thing? Should not man and na-ture go together in this world which was made for man — not for science, but for man? Perhaps I have some glimmerings of where the answer lies. Perhaps "I see a cherub that sees it." And in many of our questions we have to be content with such an approximation to an answer as this. And for my part I am content with this. With less, I am not content.

Whatever that answer may be, I walked over the old Gothic bridge with a heart strong enough to

meet Mrs. Oldcastle without flinching. I might have
to quarrel with her — I could not tell: she certainly
was neither safe nor wholesome. But this I was sure
of, that I would not quarrel with her without being
quite certain that I ought. I wish it were *never*
one's duty to quarrel with anybody: I do so hate it.
But not to do it sometimes is to smile in the devil's
face, and that no one ought to do. However, I had
not to quarrel this time.

The woods on the other side of the river
from my house, towards which I was now walking, were of the most sombre rich colour —
sombre and rich, like a life that has laid up trea-
sure in heaven, locked in a casket of sorrow. I
came nearer and nearer to them through the village, and approached the great iron gate with the
antediluvian monsters on the top of its stone pillars.
And awful monsters they were — are still! I see
the tail of one of them at this very moment. But
they let me through very quietly, notwithstanding
their evil looks: I thought they were saying to each
other across the top of the gate, "Never mind; he'll
catch it soon enough." But, as I said, I did not
catch it that day; and I could not have caught it
that day; it was too lovely a day to catch any hurt
even from that most hurtful of all beings under the
sun, an unwomanly woman.

I wandered up the long winding road, through
the woods which I had remarked flanking the meadow on my first walk up the river. These woods
smelt so sweetly — their dead and dying leaves
departing in sweet odours — that they quite made

up for the absence of the flowers. And the wind —
no, there was no wind — there was only a memory
of wind that woke now and then in the bosom of
the wood, shook down a few leaves, like the thoughts
that flutter away in sighs, and then was still
again.

I am getting old, as I told you, my friends.
(See there, you seem my friends already. Do not
despise an old man because he cannot help loving
people he never saw or even heard of.) I say I am
getting old — (is it *but* or *therefore?* I do not know
which) — but, therefore, I shall never forget that
one autumn day in those grandly fading woods.

Up the slope of the hillside they rose like one
great rainbow-billow of foliage — bright yellow,
red-rusty and bright fading green, all kinds and
shades of brown and purple. Multitudes of leaves
lay on the sides of the path, so many that I betook
myself to my old childish amusement of walking in
them without lifting my feet, driving whole armies
of them with ocean-like rustling before me. I did
not do so as I came back. I walked in the middle
of the way then, and I remember stepping over
many single leaves, in a kind of mechanico-merciful
way, as if they had been living creatures — as indeed who can tell but they are, only they must be
pretty nearly dead when they are on the ground.

At length the road brought me up to the house.
It did not look such a large house as I have since
found it to be. And it certainly was not an interesting house from the outside, though its surroundings of green grass and trees would make any whole

beautiful. Indeed the house itself tried hard to look ugly not quite succeeding only because of the kind foiling of its efforts by the Virginia creepers and ivy, which, as if ashamed of its staring countenance, did all they could to spread their hands over it and hide it. But there was one charming group of old chimneys, belonging to some portion behind, which indicated a very different, namely, a very much older, face upon the house once — a face that had passed away to give place to this. Once inside, I found there were more remains of the olden time than I had expected. I was led up one of those grand square oak staircases, which look like a portion of the house to be dwelt in, and not like a ladder for getting from one part of the habitable regions to another. On the top was a fine expanse of landing, another hall, in fact, from which I was led towards the back of the house by a narrow passage, and shown into a small dark drawing-room with a deep stone-mullioned window, wainscoted in oak simply carved and panelled. Several doors around indicated communication with other parts of the house. Here I found Mrs. Oldcastle, reading what I judged to be one of the cheap and gaudy religious books of the present day. She rose and *received* me, and having motioned me to a seat, began to talk about the parish. You would have perceived at once from her tone that she recognized no other bond of connexion between us but the parish.

"I hear you have been most kind in visiting the poor, Mr. Walton. You must take care that they don't take advantage of your kindness, though. I

assure you, you will find some of them very grasping
indeed. And you need not expect that they will give
you the least credit for good intentions."

"I have seen nothing yet to make me uneasy on
that score. But certainly my testimony is of no
weight yet."

"Mine is. I have proved them. The poor of this
neighbourhood are very deficient in gratitude."

"Yes, grannie, — —"

I started. But there was no interruption, such
as I have made to indicate my surprise; although,
when I looked half-round in the direction whence
the voice came, the words that followed were all
rippled with a sweet laugh of amusement.

"Yes, grannie, you are right. You remember
how old dame Hope wouldn't take the money you
offered her, and dropped such a disdainful courtesy.
It was *so* greedy of her, wasn't it?"

"I am sorry to hear of any disdainful reception
of kindness," I said.

"Yes, and she had the coolness, within a fortnight, to send up to me and ask if I would be
kind enough to lend her half-a-crown for a few
weeks."

"And then it was your turn, grannie! You sent
her five shillings, didn't you? — Oh no; I'm wrong.
That was the other woman."

"Indeed, I did not send her anything but a
rebuke. I told her that it would be a very wrong
thing in me to contribute to the support of such an
evil spirit of unthankfulness as she indulged in.

When she came to see her conduct in its true light,
and confessed that she had behaved very abominably,
I would see what I could do for her."

"And meantime she was served out, wasn't she?
With her sick boy at home, and nothing to give
him?" said Miss Gladwyn.

"She made her own bed, and had to lie on it."

"Don't you think a little kindness might have
had more effect in bringing her to see that she was
wrong?"

"Grannie doesn't believe in kindness, except to
me — dear old grannie! She spoils me. I'm sure
I shall be ungrateful some day; and then she'll
begin to read mé long lectures, and prick me with
all manner of headless pins. But I won't stand it,
I can tell you, grannie! I'm *too* much spoiled for
that."

Mrs. Oldcastle was silent — why, I could not
tell, except it was that she knew she had no chance
of quieting the girl in any other way.

I may mention here, lest I should have no opportunity afterwards, that I inquired of dame Hope
as to her version of the story, and found that there
had been a great misunderstanding, as I had suspected. She was really in no want at the time, and
did not feel that it would be quite honourable to
take the money when she did not need it — (some
poor people *are* capable of such reasoning,) and so
had refused it, not without a feeling at the same
time that it was more pleasant to refuse than to accept from such a giver; some stray sparkle of which
feeling, discovered by the keen eye of Miss Glad-

wyn, may have given that appearance of disdain to
her courtesy to which the girl alluded. When, however, her boy in service was brought home ill, she
had sent to ask for what she now required, on the
very ground that it had been offered to her before.
The misunderstanding had arisen from the total in-
capacity of Mrs. Oldcastle to enter sympathetically
into the feelings of one as superior to herself in
character as she was inferior in worldly condition.

But to return to Oldcastle Hall.

I wished to change the subject, knowing that
blind defence is of no use. One must have definite
points for defence, if one has not a thorough understanding of the character in question; and I had
neither.

"This is a beautiful old house," I said. "There
must be strange places about it."

Mrs. Oldcastle had not time to reply, or at least
did not reply, before Miss Gladwyn said,

"Oh, Mr. Walton, have you looked out of the
window yet? You don't know what a lovely place
this is, if you haven't."

And as she spoke she emerged from a recess in
the room, a kind of dark alcove, where she had
been amusing herself with what I took to be some
sort of puzzle, but which I found afterwards to be
the bit and curb-chain of her pony's bridle which
she was polishing up to her own bright mind, because the stable-boy had not pleased her in the
matter, and she wanted both to get them brilliant
and to shame the lad for the future. I followed her

to the window, where I was indeed as much surprised
and pleased as she could have wished.

"There!" she said, holding back one of the
dingy heavy curtains with her small childish hand.

And there indeed I saw an astonishment. It did
not lie in the lovely sweeps of hill and hollow
stretching away to the horizon, richly wooded, and
— though I saw none of them — sprinkled, certainly,
with sweet villages full of human thoughts, loves,
and hopes; the astonishment did not lie in this —
though all this was really much more beautiful to the
higher imagination — but in the fact that, at the
first glance, I had a vision properly belonging to a
rugged or mountainous country. For I had approached the house by a gentle slope, which certainly was long and winding, but had occasioned no
feeling in my mind that I had reached any considerable height. And I had come up that one
beautiful staircase; no more; and yet now, when I
looked from this window, I found myself on the
edge of a precipice — not a very deep one, certainly,
yet with all the effect of many a deeper. For below
the house on this side lay a great hollow, with steep
sides, up which, as far as they could reach, the trees
were climbing. The sides were not all so steep as
the one on which the house stood, but they were all
rocky and steep, with here and there slopes of green
grass. And down in the bottom, in the centre of the
hollow, lay a pool of water. I knew it only by its
slaty shimmer through the fading green of the tree-
tops between me and it.

"There!" again exclaimed Miss Gladwyn; "isn't

that beautiful? But you haven't seen the most beautiful thing yet. Grannie, where's — ah! there she is! There's auntie! Don't you see her down there, by the side of the pond? That pond is a hundred feet deep. If auntie were to fall in she would be drowned before you could jump down to get her out. Can you swim?"

Before I had time to answer, she was off again.

"Don't you see auntie down there?"

"No, I don't see her. I have been trying very hard, but I can't."

"Well, I daresay you can't. Nobody, I think, has got eyes but myself. Do you see a big stone by the edge of the pond, with another stone on the top of it, like a big potato with a little one grown out of it?"

"No."

"Well, auntie is under the trees on the opposite side from that stone. Do you see her yet?"

"No."

"Then you must come down with me, and I will introduce you to her. She's much the prettiest thing here. Much prettier than grannie."

Here she looked over her shoulder at grannie, who, instead of being angry, as, from what I had seen on our former interview, I feared she would be, only said, without even looking up from the little blue-boarded book she was again reading —

"You are a saucy child."

Whereupon Miss Gladwyn laughed merrily.

"Come along," she said, and, seizing me by the hand, led me out of the room, down a back-staircase,

across a piece of grass, and then down a stair in the
face of the rock, towards the pond below. The stair
went in zigzags, and, although rough, was protected
by an iron balustrade, without which, indeed, it
would have been very dangerous.

"Isn't your grandmamma afraid to let you run
up and down here, Miss Gladwyn?" I said.

"Me!" she exclaimed, apparently in the utmost
surprise. "That *would* be fun! For, you know, if
she tried to hinder me — but she knows it's no use;
I taught her that long ago — let me see how long:
oh! I don't know — I should think it must be ten
years at least. I ran away, and they thought I had
drowned myself in the pond. And I saw them, all
the time, poking with a long stick in the pond,
which, if I had been drowned there, never could
have brought me up, for it is a hundred feet deep,
I am sure. How I hurt my sides trying to keep
from screaming with laughter! I fancied I heard one
say to the other, 'We must wait till she swells and
floats!'"

"Dear me! what a peculiar child!" I said to
myself.

And yet somehow, whatever she said — even
when she was most rude to her grandmother — she
was never offensive. No one could have helped
feeling all the time that she was a little lady. — I
thought I would venture a question with her. I stood
still at a turn of the zigzag, and looked down into the
hollow, still a good way below us, where I could
now distinguish the form, on the opposite side of the

pond, of a woman seated at the foot of a tree and stooping forward over a book.

"May I ask you a question, Miss Gladwyn?"

"Yes, twenty if you like; but I won't answer one of them till you give up calling me Miss Gladwyn. We can't be friends, you know, so long as you do that."

"What am I to call you, then? I never heard you called by any other name than Pet, and that would hardly do, would it?"

"Oh, just fancy if you called me Pet before grannie! That's grannie's name for me, and nobody dares to use it but grannie — not even auntie; for, between you and me, auntie is afraid of grannie; I can't think why. I never was afraid of anybody — except, yes, a little afraid of old Sarah. She used to be my nurse, you know; and grandmamma and everybody is afraid of her, and that's just why I never do one thing she wants me to do. It would never do to give in to being afraid of her, you know. — There's auntie, you see, down there, just where I told you before."

"Oh yes! I see her now. — What does your aunt call you, then?"

"Why, what you must call me — my own name, of course."

"What is that?"

"Judy."

She said it in a tone which seemed to indicate surprise that I should not know her name — perhaps read it off her face, as one. ought to know a flower's name by looking at it. But she added instantly, glancing up in my face most comically,

"I wish yours was Punch."

"Why, Judy?"

"It would be such fun, you know."

"Well, it would be odd, I must confess. What is your aunt's name?"

"Oh, such a funny name! — much funnier than Judy: Ethelwyn. It sounds as if it ought to mean something, doesn't it?"

"Yes. It is an Anglo-Saxon word, without doubt."

"What does it mean?"

"I'm not sure about that. I will try to find out when I go home — if you would like to know."

"Yes, that I should. I should like to know everything about auntie. Ethelwyn. Isn't it pretty?"

"So pretty that I should like to know something more about Aunt Ethelwyn. What is her other name?"

"Why, Ethelwyn Oldcastle, to be sure. What else could it be?"

"Why, you know, for anything I knew, Judy, it might have been Gladwyn. She might have been your father's sister."

"Might she? I never thought of that. Oh, I suppose that is because I never think about my father. And now I do think of it, I wonder why nobody ever mentions him to me, or my mother either. But I often think auntie must be thinking about my mother. Something in her eyes, when they are sadder than usual, seems to remind me of my mother."

"You remember your mother, then?"

"No, I don't think I ever saw her. But I've answered plenty of questions, haven't I? I assure you, if you want to get me on to the Catechism, I don't know a word of it. Come along."

I laughed.

"What!" she said, pulling me by the hand, "you a clergyman, and laugh at the Catechism! I didn't know that."

"I'm not laughing at the Catechism, Judy. I'm only laughing at the idea of putting Catechism questions to you."

"You *know* I didn't mean it," she said, with some indignation.

"I know now," I answered. "But you haven't let me put the only question I wanted to put."

"What is it?"

"How old are you?"

"Twelve. Come along."

And away we went down the rest of the stair.

When we reached the bottom, a winding path led us through the trees to the side of the pond, along which we passed to get to the other side.

And then all at once the thought struck me — why was it that I had never seen this auntie, with the lovely name, at church? Was she going to turn out another strange parishioner?

There she sat, intent on her book. As we drew near she looked up and rose, but did not come forward.

"Aunt Winnie, here's Mr. Walton," said Judy.

I lifted my hat and held out my hand. Before our hands met, however, a tremendous splash reached my ears from the pond. I started round. Judy had vanished. I had my coat half off, and was rushing to the pool, when Miss Oldcastle stopped me, her face unmoved, except by a smile, saying, "It's only one of that frolicsome child's tricks, Mr. Walton. It is well for you that I was here, though. Nothing would have delighted her more than to have you in the water too."

"But," I said, bewildered, and not half comprehending, "where is she?"

"There," returned Miss Oldcastle, pointing to the pool, in the middle of which arose a heaving and bubbling, presently yielding passage to the laughing face of Judy.

"Why don't you help me out, Mr. Walton? You said you could swim."

"No, I did not," I answered coolly. "You talked so fast, you did not give me time to say so."

"It's very cold," she returned.

"Come out, Judy dear," said her aunt. "Run home and change your clothes. There's a dear."

Judy swam to the opposite side, scrambled out, and was off like a spaniel through the trees and up the stairs, dripping and raining as she went.

"You must be very much astonished at the little creature, Mr. Walton."

"I find her very interesting. Quite a study."

"There never was a child so spoiled, and never

a child on whom it took less effect to hurt her. I
suppose such things do happen ‚sometimes. She is
really a good girl; though mamma, who has done
all the spoiling, will not allow me to say she is
good."

Here followed a pause, for, Judy disposed of,
what should I say next? And the moment her mind
turned from Judy, I saw a certain stillness — not
a cloud, but the shadow of a cloud — come over
Miss Oldcastle's face, as if she, too, found herself
uncomfortable, and did not know what to say next.
I tried to get a glance at the book in her hand, for
I should know something about her at once if I
could only see what she was reading. She never
came to church, and I wanted to arrive at some
notion of the source of her spiritual life; for that
she had such, a single glance at her face was enough
to convince me. This, I mean, made me even
anxious to see what the book was. But I could
only discover that it was an old book in very shabby
binding, not in the least like the books that young
ladies generally have in their hands.

And now my readers will possibly be thinking
it odd that I have never yet said a word about what
either Judy or Miss Oldcastle was like. If there is
one thing I feel more inadequate to than another, in
taking upon me to relate — it is to describe a lady.
But I will try the girl first.

Judy was rosy, gray-eyed, auburn-haired, sweet-
mouthed. She had confidence in her chin, assertion
in her nose, defiance in her eyebrows, honesty and
friendliness over all her face. No one, evidently,

could have a warmer friend; and to an enemy she
would be dangerous no longer than a fit of passion
might last. There was nothing acrid in her; and
the reason, I presume, was, that she had never yet
hurt her conscience. That is a very different thing
from saying she had never done wrong, you know.
She was not tall, even for her age, and just a little
too plump for the immediate suggestion of grace.
Yet every motion of the child would have been
graceful, except for the fact that impulse was always
predominant, giving a certain jerkiness, like the
hopping of a bird, instead of the gliding of one
motion into another, such as you might see in the
same bird on the wing.

There is one of the ladies.

But the other — how shall I attempt to describe
her?

The first thing I felt was, that she was a lady-
woman. And to feel that is almost to fall in love
at first sight. And out of this whole, the first thing
you distinguished would be the grace over all. She
was rather slender, rather tall, rather dark-haired,
and quite blue-eyed. But I assure you it was not
upon that occasion that I found out the colour of
her eyes. I was so taken with her whole that I
knew nothing about her parts. Yet she was blue-
eyed, indicating northern extraction — some cen-
turies back perhaps. That blue was the blue of the
sea that had sunk through the eyes of some sea-
rover's wife and settled in those of her child, to be
born when the voyage was over. It had been dyed
so deep *ingrayne*, as Spenser would say, that it had

never been worn from the souls of the race since,
and so was every now and then shining like heaven
out at some of its eyes. Her features were what is
called regular. They were delicate and brave. —
After the grace, the dignity was the next thing you
came to discover. And the only thing you would
not have liked, you would have discovered last. For
when the shine of the courtesy with which she received me had faded away, a certain look of negative
haughtiness, of withdrawal, if not of repulsion, took
its place, a look of consciousness of her own high
breeding — a pride, not of life, but of circumstance
of life, which disappointed me in the midst of so
much that was very lovely. Her voice was sweet,
and I could have fancied a tinge of sadness in it, to
which impression her slowness of speech, without
any drawl in it, contributed. But I am not doing
well as an artist in describing her so fully before
my reader has become in the least degree interested
in her. I was seeing her, and no words can make
him see her.

Fearing lest some such fancy as had possessed
Judy should be moving in her mind, namely, that
I was, if not exactly going to put her through her
Catechism, yet going in some way or other to act
the clergyman, I hastened to speak.

"This is a most romantic spot, Miss Oldcastle,"
I said; and as surprising as it is romantic. I could
hardly believe my eyes when I looked out of the
window and saw it first."

"Your surprise was the more natural that the

place itself is not properly natural, as you must have
discovered."

This was rather a remarkable speech for a young
lady to make. I answered:

"I only know that such a chasm is the last thing
I should have expected to find in this gently un-
dulating country. That it is artificial I was no
more prepared to hear than I was to see the place
itself."

"It looks pretty, but it has not a very poetic
origin," she returned. "It is nothing but the quarry
out of which the old house at the top of it was
built."

"I must venture to differ from you entirely in
the aspect such an origin assumes to me," I said.
"It seems to me a more poetic origin than any con-
vulsion of nature whatever would have been; for,
look you," I said — being as a young man too
much inclined to the didactic, "for, look you," I
said — and she did look at me — "from that buried
mass of rock has arisen this living house with its
histories of ages and generations; and" —

Here I saw a change pass upon her face: it
grew almost pallid. But her large blue eyes were
still fixed on mine.

"And it seems to me," I went on, "that such a
chasm made by the uplifting of a house therefrom,
is therefore in itself more poetic than if it were even
the mouth of an extinct volcano. For, grand as
the motions and deeds of Nature are, terrible as is
the idea of the fiery heart of the earth breaking out
in convulsions, yet here is something greater; for

human will, human thought, human hands in human labour and effort, have all been employed to build this house, making not only the house beautiful, but the place whence it came beautiful too. It stands on the edge of what Shelley would call its 'ante-natal tomb' — now beautiful enough to be its mother — filled from generation to generation —"

Her face had grown still paler, and her lips moved as if she would speak; but no sound came from them. I had gone on, thinking it best to take no notice of her paleness; but now I could not help expressing concern.

"I am afraid you feel ill, Miss Oldcastle."

"Not at all," she answered, more quickly than she had yet spoken.

"This place must be damp," I said. "I fear you have taken cold."

She drew herself up a little haughtily, thinking no doubt that after her denial I was improperly pressing the point. So I drew back to the subject of our conversation.

"But I can hardly think," I said, "that all this mass of stone could be required to build the house, large as it is. A house is not solid, you know."

"No," she answered. "The original building was more of a castle, with walls and battlements. I can show you the foundations of them still; and the picture, too, of what the place used to be. We are not what we were then. Many a cottage, too, has been built out of this old quarry. Not a stone has been taken from it for the last fifty years, though.

Just let me show you one thing, Mr. Walton, and then I must leave you."

"Do not let me detain you a moment. I will go at once," I said; "though, if you would allow me, I should be more at ease if I might see you safe at the top of the stair first."

She smiled.

"Indeed, I am not ill," she answered; "but I have duties to attend to. Just let me show you this, and then you shall go with me back to mamma."

She led the way to the edge of the pond and looked into it. I followed, and gazed down into its depths, till my sight was lost in them. I could see no bottom to the rocky shaft."

"There is a strong spring down there," she said. "Is it not a dreadful place? Such a depth!"

"Yes," I answered; "but it has not the horror of dirty water; it is as clear as crystal. How does the surplus escape?"

"On the opposite side of the hill you came up, there is a well with a strong stream from it into the river."

"I almost wonder at your choosing such a place to read in. I should hardly like to be so near this pond," said I, laughing.

"Judy has taken all that away. Nothing in nature, and everything out of it, is strange to Judy, poor child! But just look down a little way into the water on this side. Do you see anything?"

"Nothing," I answered.

"Look again, against the wall of the pond," she said.

"I see a kind of arch or opening in the side," I answered.

"That is what I wanted you to see. Now, do you see a little barred window, there, in the face of the rock, through the trees?"

"I cannot say I do," I replied.

"No. Except you know where it is — and even then it is not·so easy to find it. I find it by certain trees."

"What is it?"

"It is the window of a little room in the rock, from which a stair leads down through the rock ·to a sloping passage. That is the end of it you see under the water."

"Provided, no doubt," I said, "in case of siege, to procure water."

"Most likely; but not, therefore, confined to that purpose. There are more dreadful stories than I can bear to think of —"

Here she paused abruptly, and began anew.

"— As if that house had brought death and doom out of the earth with it. There was an old burial-ground here before the Hall was built."

"Have you ever been down the stair you speak of?" I asked.

"Only part of the way," she answered. "But Judy knows every step of it. If it were not that the door at the top is locked, she would have dived through that archway now, and been in her own room in half the time. The child does not know what fear means."

We now moved away from the pond, towards the side of the quarry and the open-air staircase, which I thought must be considerably more pleasant than the other. I confess I longed to see the gleam of that water at the bottom of the dark sloping passage, though.

Miss Oldcastle accompanied me to the room where I had left her mother, and took her leave with merely a bow of farewell. I saw the old lady glance sharply from her to me as if she were jealous of what we might have been talking about.

"Grannie, are you afraid Mr. Walton has been saying pretty things to Aunt Winnie? I assure you he is not of that sort. He doesn't understand that kind of thing. But he would have jumped into the pond after me and got his death of cold if auntie would have let him. It *was* cold. I think I see you dripping now, Mr. Walton."

There she was in her dark corner, coiled up on a couch, and laughing heartily; but all as if she had done nothing extraordinary. And, indeed, estimated either by her own notions or practices, what she had done was not in the least extraordinary.

Disinclined to stay any longer, I shook hands with the grandmother, with a certain invincible sense of slime, and with the grandchild with a feeling of mischievous health, as if the girl might soon corrupt the clergyman into a partnership in pranks as well as in friendship. She followed me out of the room, and danced before me down the oak staircase, clearing the portion from the first landing at a bound. Then she turned and waited for me, who came very deliberately, feeling the unsure contact of sole and wax. As soon as I reached her, she said, in a half-whisper, reaching up towards me on tiptoe —

"Isn't she a beauty?"

"Who? your grandmamma?" I returned.

She gave me a little push, her face glowing with fun. But I did not expect she would take her revenge as she did.

"Yes, of course," she answered, quite gravely. "Isn't she a beauty?"

And then, seeing that she had put me *hors de combat*, she burst into loud laughter, and, opening the hall-door for me, let me go without another word.

I went home very quietly, and, as I said, stepping with curious care — of which, of course, I did not think at the time — over the yellow and brown leaves that lay in the middle of the road.

CHAPTER VII.

The Bishop's Basin.

I WENT home very quietly, as I say, thinking about the strange elements that not only combine to make life, but must be combined in our idea of life, before we can form a true theory about it. Now-a-days, the vulgar notion of what is lifelike in any annals is to be realized by sternly excluding everything but the commonplace; and the means at least are often attained, with this much of the end as well — that the appearance life bears to vulgar minds is represented with a wonderful degree of success. But I believe that this is at least quite as unreal a mode of representing life as the other extreme, wherein the unlikely, the romantic, and the uncommon predominate. I doubt whether there is a single history — if one could only get at the whole of it — in which there is not a considerable admixture of the unlikely become fact, including a few strange coincidences; of the uncommon, which, although striking at first, has grown common from familiarity with its presence as our own; with even at least some one more or less rosy touch of what we call the romantic. My own conviction is, that the poetry is far the deepest in us, and that the prose is only broken-down poetry; and likewise that to this our lives correspond. The poetic region is the true one, and just *therefore* the incredible one to the lower order of mind; for although every mind is capable of the truth, or rather capable of becoming capable of the truth, there may lie ages between its capacity and the truth. As you will hear some people read poetry so that no mortal could tell it was poetry, so do some people read their own lives and those of others.

I fell into these reflections from comparing in my own mind my former experiences in visiting my parishioners with those of that day. True, I had never sat down to talk with one of them without finding that that man or that woman had actually a *history*, the most marvellous and important fact to a human being; nay, I had found something more or less remarkable in every one of their histories, so that I was more than barely interested in each of them. And as I made more acquaintance with them, (for I had not been in the position, or the disposition either, before I came to Marshmallows, necessary to the gathering of such experiences,) I came to the conclusion — not that I had got into an extraordinary parish of characters — but that every parish must be more or less extraordinary from the same cause. Why did I not use to see such people about me before? Surely I had undergone a change of some sort. Could it be, that the trouble I had been going through of late, had opened the eyes of my mind to the understanding, or rather the simple *seeing*, of my fellow-men?

But the people among whom I had been to-day belonged rather to such as might be put into a romantic story. Certainly I could not see much that was romantic in the old lady; and yet, those

7*

eyes and that tight-skinned face — what might they not be capable of in the working out of a story? And then the place they lived in! Why, it would hardly come into my ideas of a nineteenth-century country parish at all. I was tempted to try to per-suade myself that all that had happened, since I rose to look out of the window in the old house, had been but a dream. For how could that wooded dell have come there after all? It was much too large for a quarry. And that madcap girl — she never flung herself into the pond! — it could not be. And what could the book have been that the lady with the sea-blue eyes was reading? Was that a real book at all? No. Yes. Of course it was. But what was it? What had that to do with the matter? It might turn out to be a very commonplace book after all. No; for commonplace books are generally new, or at least in fine bindings. And here was a shabby little old book, such as, if it had been com-monplace, would not have been likely to be the monpanion of a young lady at the bottom of a quarry—

"A savage place, as holy and enchanted
As e'ver beneath a waning moon was haunted
By woman wailing for her demon lover."

I know all this will sound ridiculous, especially that quotation from *Kubla Khan* coming after the close of the preceding sentence; but it is only so much the more like the jumble of thoughts that made a chaos of my mind as I went home. And then for that terrible pool, and subterranean passage, and all that — what had it all to do with this broad daylight, and these dying autumn leaves? No doubt

there had been such places. No doubt there were
such places somewhere yet. No doubt this was one
of them. But, somehow or other, it would not come
in well. I had no intention of *going in for* — that
is the phrase now — going in for the romantic. I
would take the impression off by going to see Weir
the carpenter's old father. Whether my plan was
successful or not, I shall leave my reader to judge.

I found Weir busy as usual, but not with a
coffin this time. He was working at a window-sash.
"Just like life," I thought — tritely perhaps. "The
other day he was closing up in the outer darkness,
and now he is letting in the light."

"It's a long time since you was here last, sir,"
he said, but without a smile.

Did he mean a reproach? If so, I was more glad
of that reproach than I would have been of the
warmest welcome, even from Old Rogers. The fact
was that, having a good deal to attend to besides,
and willing at the same time to let the man feel that
he was in no danger of being bored by my visits, I
had not made use even of my reserve in the shape
of a visit to his father.

"Well," I answered, "I wanted to know something about all my people, before I paid a second
visit to any of them."

"All right, sir. Don't suppose I meant to
complain. Only to let you know you was welcome, sir."

"I've just come from my first visit to Oldcastle
Hall. And, to tell the truth, for I don't like pretences,
my visit to-day was not so much to you as to your

father, whom, perhaps, I ought to have called upon
before, only I was afraid of seeming to intrude upon
you, seeing we don't exactly think the same way
about some things," I added — with a smile, I know,
which was none the less genuine that I remember
it yet.

And what makes me remember it yet? It is the
smile that lighted up his face in response to mine.
For it was more than I looked for. And his answer
helped to fix the smile in my memory.

"You made me think, sir, that perhaps, after all,
we were much of the same way of thinking, only
perhaps you was a long way ahead of me."

Now the man was not right in saying that we
were much of the same way of *thinking;* for our
opinions could hardly do more than come within
sight of each other; but what he meant was right
enough. For I was certain, from the first, that the
man had a regard for the downright, honest way of
things, and I hoped that I too had such a regard.
How much of selfishness and of pride in one's own
judgment might be mixed up with it, both in his
case and mine, I had been too often taken in — by
myself, I mean — to be at all careful to discriminate,
provided there was a proportion of real honesty
along with it, which, I felt sure, would ultimately
eliminate the other. For in the moral nest, it is not
as with the sparrow and the cuckoo. The right, the
original inhabitant is the stronger; and, however unlikely at any given point in the history it may be,
the sparrow will grow strong enough to heave the
intruding cuckoo overboard. So I was pleased that

the man should do me the honour of thinking I was
right as far as he could see, which is the greatest
honour one man can do another; for it is setting him
on his own steed, as the eastern tyrants used to do.
And I was delighted to think that the road lay open
for further and more real communion between us in
time to come.

"Well," I answered, "I think we shall understand each other perfectly before long. But now
I must see your father, if it is convenient and
agreeable."

"My father will be delighted to see you, I know,
sir. He can't get so far as the church on Sundays; but you'll find him much more to your mind
than me. He's been putting ever so many questions
to me about the new parson, wanting me to try
whether I could not get more out of you than the
old parson. That's the way we talk about you, you
see, sir. You'll understand. And I've never told
him that I'd been to church since you came — I
suppose from a bit of pride, because I had so long
refused to go; but I don't doubt some of the neighbours have told him, for he never speaks about it
now. And I know he's been looking out for you;
and I fancy he's begun to wonder that the parson
was going to see everybody but him. It *will* be a
pleasure to the old man, sir, for he don't see a great
many to talk to; and he's fond of a bit of gossip, is
the old man, sir."

So saying, Weir led the way through the shop
into a lobby behind, and thence, up what must have
been a back stair of the old house, into a large room

over the workshop.   There were bits of old carving
about the walls of the room yet, but, as in the shop
below, all had been whitewashed.   At one end stood
a bed with chintz curtains and a warm-looking coun-
terpane of rich faded embroidery.   There was a bit
of carpet by the bedside, and another bit in front of
the fire; and there the old man sat, on one side, in
a high-backed not very easy-looking chair.   With a
great effort he managed to rise as I approached him,
notwithstanding my entreaties that he would   not
move.   He looked much older when on his feet, for
he was bent nearly double, in which posture the
marvel was how he could walk at all.   For he did
totter a few steps to meet me, without even the aid
of a stick, and, holding out a thin, shaking hand,
welcomed me with an air of breeding rarely to be
met with in his station in society.   But the chief
part of this polish sprung from the inbred kindliness
of his nature, which was manifest in the expression
of his noble old countenance.   Age is such a different thing in different natures!   One man seems to
grow more and more selfish as he grows older; and
in another the slow fire of time seems only to con-
sume, with fine, imperceptible gradations, the yet
lingering selfishness in him, letting the light of the
kingdom, which the Lord says is within, shine out
more and more, as the husk grows thin and is ready
to fall off, that the man, like the seed sown, may
pierce the earth of this world and rise into the pure
air and wind and dew of the second life.   The face
of a loving old man is always to me like a morning
moon, reflecting the yet unrisen sun of the other

world, yet fading before its approaching light, until, when it does rise, it pales and withers away from our gaze, absorbed in the source of its own beauty. This old man, you may see, took my fancy wonderfully; for even at this distance of time, when I am old myself, the recollection of his beautiful old face makes me feel as if I could write poetry about him.

"I'm blithe to see ye, sir," said he. "Sit ye down, sir."

And, turning, he pointed to his own easy-chair; and I then saw his profile. It was delicate as that of Dante, which in form it marvellously resembled. But all the sternness which Dante's evil times had generated in his prophetic face was in this old man's replaced by a sweetness of hope that was lovely to behold.

"No, Mr. Weir," I said, "I cannot take your chair. The Bible tells us to rise up before the aged, not to turn them out of their seats."

"It would do me good to see you sitting in my cheer, sir. The pains that my son Tom there takes to keep it up as long as the old man may want it! It's a good thing I bred him to the joiner's trade, sir. Sit ye down, sir. The cheer'll hold ye, though I warrant it won't last that long after I be gone home. Sit ye down, sir."

Thus entreated, I hesitated no longer, but took the old man's seat. His son brought another chair for him, and he sat down opposite the fire and close to me. Thomas then went back to his work, leaving us alone.

"Ye've had some speech wi' my son Tom," said the old man, the moment he was gone, leaning a little towards me. "It's main kind o' you, sir, to take up kindly wi' poor folks like us."

"You don't say it's kind of a person to do what he likes best," I answered. "Besides, it's my duty to know all my people."

"Oh yes, sir, I know that. But there's a thousand ways ov doin' the same thing. I ha' seen folks, parsons and others, 'at made a great show ov being friendly to the poor, ye know, sir; and all the time you could see, or if you couldn't see you could tell without seein', that they didn't much regard them in their hearts; but it was a sort of accomplishment to be able to talk to the poor, like, after their own fashion. But the minute an ould man sees you, sir, he believes that you *mean* it, sir, whatever it is. For an ould man somehow comes to know things like a child. They call it a second childhood, don't they, sir? And there are some things worth growin' a child again to get a hould ov again."

"I only hope what you say may be true — about me, I mean."

"Take my word for it, sir. You have no idea how that boy of mine, Tom there, did hate all the clergy till you come. Not that he's anyway favourable to them yet, only he'll say nothin' again' you, sir. He's got an unfortunate gift o' seein' all the faults first, sir; and when a man is that way given, the faults always hides the other side, so that there's nothing but faults to be seen."

"But I find Thomas quite open to reason."

"That's because you understand him, sir, and know how to give him head. He tould me of the talk you had with him. You don't bait him. You don't say, 'You must come along wi' me,' but you turns and goes along wi' him. He's not a bad fellow at all, is Tom; but he will have the reason for everythink. Now I never did want the reason for everythink. I was content to be tould a many things. But Tom, you see, he was born with a sore bit in him somewheres, I don't rightly know wheres; and I don't think he rightly knows what's the matter with him himself."

"I dare say you have a guess though, by this time, Mr. Weir," I said; "and I think I have a guess too."

"Well, sir, if he'd only give in, I think he would be far happier. But he can't see his way clear."

"You must give him time, you know. The fact is, he doesn't feel at home yet. And how can he, so long as he doesn't know his own father?"

"I'm not sure that I rightly understand you," said the old man, looking bewildered and curious.

"I mean," I answered, "that till a man knows that he is one of God's family, living in God's house, with God up-stairs, as it were, while he is at his work or his play in a nursery below-stairs, he can't feel comfortable. For a man could not be made that should stand alone, like some of the beasts. A man must feel a head over him, because he's not enough to satisfy himself, you know. Thomas just wants faith; that is, he wants to feel that there is a loving Father over him, who is doing things all well and right, if we could only understand them, though it really does not look like it sometimes."

"Ah, sir, I might have understood you well enough, if my poor old head hadn't been started on a wrong track. For I fancied for the moment that you were just putting your finger upon the sore place in Tom's mind. There's no use in keeping family misfortunes from a friend like you, sir. That boy has known his father all his life; but I was nearly half his age before I knew mine."

"Strange!" I said, involuntarily almost.

"Yes, sir; strange you may well say. A strange story it is. The Lord help my mother! I beg yer pardon, sir. I'm no Catholic. But that prayer will come of itself sometimes. As if it could be of any use now! God forgive me!"

"Don't you be afraid, Mr. Weir, as if God was ready to take offence at what comes naturally, as you say. An ejaculation of love is not likely to offend Him who is so grand that he is always meek and lowly of heart, and whose love is such that ours is a mere faint light — 'a little glooming light much like a shade' — as one of our own poets says, beside it."

"Thank you, Mr. Walton. That's a real comfortable word, sir. And I am heart-sure it's true, sir. God be praised for evermore! He *is* good, sir; as I have known in my poor time, sir. I don't believe there ever was one that just lifted his eyes and looked up'ards, instead of looking down to the ground, that didn't get some comfort, to go on with, as it were — the ready-money of comfort, as it were — though it might be none to put in the bank, sir."

"That's true enough," I said. "Then your father and mother —?"

And here I hesitated.

"Were never married, sir," said the old man promptly, as if he would relieve me from an embarrassing position. "*I* couldn't help it. And I'm no less the child of my Father in heaven for it. For if He hadn't made me, I couldn't ha' been their son, you know, sir. So that He had more to do wi' the makin' o' me than they had; though mayhap, if He had had his way all out, I might ha' been the son o' somebody else. But, now that things be so, I wouldn't have liked that at all, sir; and bein' once born so, I would not have e'er another couple of parents in all England, sir, though I ne'er knew one o' them. And I do love my mother. And I'm so sorry for my father that I love him too, sir. And if I could only get my boy Tom to think as I do, I would die like a psalm-tune on an organ, sir."

"But it seems to me strange," I said, "that your son should think so much of what is so far gone by. Surely he would not want another father than you, now. He is used to his position in life. And there can be nothing cast up to him about his birth or descent."

"That's all very true, sir, and no doubt it would be as you say. But there has been other things to keep his mind upon the old affair. Indeed, sir, we

have had the same misfortune all over again among
the young people. And I mustn't say anything
more about it; only my boy Tom has a sore heart."

I knew at once to what he alluded; for I could
not have been about in my parish all this time without learning that the strange handsome woman in
the little shop was the daughter of Thomas Weir,
and that she was neither wife nor widow. And it
now occurred to me for the first time that it was a
likeness to her little boy that had affected me so
pleasantly when I first saw Thomas, his grandfather.
The likeness to his great-grandfather, which I saw
plainly enough, was what made the other fact clear
to me. And at the same moment I began to be
haunted with a flickering sense of a third likeness
which I could not in the least fix or identify.

"Perhaps," I said, "he may find some good
come out of that too."

"Well, who knows, sir?"

"I think," I said, "that if we do evil that good
may come, the good we looked for will never come
thereby. But once evil is done, we may humbly
look to Him who bringeth good out of evil, and
wait. Is your grand-daughter Catherine in bad
health? She looks so delicate!"

"She always had an uncommon look. But what
she looks like now, I don't know. I hear no com-
plaints; but she has never crossed this door since we
got her set up in that shop. She never comes near
her father or her sister, though she lets them, leastways her sister, go and see her. I'm afraid Tom
has been rayther unmerciful with her. And if ever

he put a bad name upon her in her hearing, I know from what that lass used to be as a young one, that she wouldn't be likely to forget it, and as little likely to get over it herself or pass it over to another, even her own father. I don't believe they do more nor nod to one another when they meet in the village. It's well even if they do that much. It's my belief there's some people made so hard that they never can forgive anythink."

"How did she get into the trouble? Who is the father of her child?"

"Nay, that no one knows for certain; though there be suspicions, and one of them no doubt correct. But I believe fire wouldn't drive his name out at her mouth. I know my lass. When she says a thing she'll stick to it."

I asked no more questions. But after a short pause the old man went on.

"I shan't soon forget the night I first heard about my father and mother. That was a night! The wind was roaring like a mad beast about the house, — not this house, sir, but the great house over the way."

"You don't mean Oldcastle Hall?" I said.

"'Deed I do, sir," returned the old man. "This house here belonged to the same family at one time; though when I was born it was another branch of the family, second cousins or something, that lived in it. But even then it was something on to the downhill road, I believe."

"But," I said, fearing my question might have turned the old man aside from a story worth hearing, "never mind all that now, if you please. I am anxious to hear all about that night. Do go on. You were saying the wind was blowing about the old house."

"Eh, sir, it was roaring! — roaring as if it was mad with rage! And every now and then it would come down the chimley like out of a gun, and blow the smoke and a'most the fire into the middle of the housekeeper's room. For the housekeeper had been giving me my supper. I called her auntie, then; and didn't know a bit that she wasn't my aunt really. I was at that time a kind of a under-game-keeper upon the place, and slept over the stable. But I fared of the best, for I was a favourite with the old woman — I suppose because I had given her plenty of trouble in my time. That's always the way, sir. — Well, as I was a-saying, when the wind stopped for a moment, down came the rain with a noise that sounded like a regiment of cavalry on the turnpike road t'other side of the hill. And then up the wind got again and swept the rain away, and took it all in its own hand again, and went on roaring worse than ever. 'You'll be wet afore you get across the yard, Samuel,' said auntie, looking very prim in her long white apron, as she sat on the other side of the little round table before the fire, sipping a drop of hot rum and water, which she always had before she went to bed. 'You'll be wet to the skin, Samuel,' she said. 'Never mind,' says I. 'I'm not salt nor yet sugar; and I'll be going, auntie, for you'll be wanting your bed.' — 'Sit ye still,' said she. 'I don't want my bed yet.'

And there she sat, sipping at her rum and water; and there I sat, o' the other side, drinking the last of a pint of October she had gotten me from the cellar — for I had been out in the wind all day. 'It was just such a night as this,' said she, and then stopped again. — But I'm wearying you, sir, with my long story."

"Not in the least," I answered. "Quite the contrary. Pray tell it out your own way. You won't tire me, I assure you."

So the old man went on.

"'It was just such a night as this,' she began again — 'leastways it was snow and not rain that was coming down, as if the Almighty was a-going to spend all His winter-stock at oncet.' — 'What happened such a night, auntie?' I said. 'Ah, my lad!' said she, 'ye may well ask what happened. None has a better right. You happened. That's all.' —'Oh, that's all, is it, auntie?' I said, and laughed. 'Nay, nay, Samuel,' said she, quite solemn, 'what is there to laugh at, then? I assure you, you was anything but welcome.' — "And why wasn't I welcome?' I said. 'I couldn't help it, you know. I'm very sorry to hear I intruded,' I said, still making game of it, you see; for I always did like a joke. 'Well,' she said, 'you certainly was't wanted. But I don't blame you, Samuel, and I hope you won't blame me.' — 'What *do* you mean, Auntie?' 'I mean this, that it's my fault, if so be that fault it is, that you're sitting there now, and not lying, in less bulk by a good deal, at the bottom of the Bishop's Basin.' That's what they call a deep pond at the

foot of the old house, sir; though why or wherefore, I'm sure I don't know. 'Most extraordinary,
Auntie!' I said, feeling very queer, and as if I
really had no business to be there. 'Never you
mind, my dear,' says she; 'there you are, and you
can take care of yourself now as well as anybody.'
— 'But who wanted to drown me?' 'Are you sure
you can forgive him, if I tell you?' — 'Sure enough,
suppose he was sitting where you be now,' I answered. 'It was, I make no doubt, though I can't
prove it, — I am morally certain it was your own
father.' I felt the skin go creepin' together upon
my head, and I couldn't speak. 'Yes, it was, child;
and it's time you knew all about it. Why, you
don't know who your own father was!' — 'No more
I do,' I said; 'and I never cared to ask, somehow.
I thought it was all right, I suppose. But I wonder
now that I never did.' — 'Indeed you did many a
time, when you was a mere boy, like; but I suppose, as you never was answered, you give it up for
a bad job, and forgot all about it, like a wise man.
You always was a wise child, Samuel.' So the old
lady always said, sir. And I was willing to believe
she was right, if I could. 'But now,' said she, 'it's
time you knew all about it. — Poor Miss Wallis!
— I'm no aunt of yours, my boy, though I love
you nearly as well, I think, as if I was; for dearly
did I love your mother. She was a beauty, and
better than she was beautiful, whatever folks may
say. The only wrong thing, I'm certain, that she
ever did, was to trust your father too much. But I
must see and give you the story right through from

beginning to end. — Miss Wallis, as I came to know from her own lips, was the daughter of a country attorney, who had a good practice, and was likely to leave her well off. Her mother died when she was a little girl. It's not easy getting on without a mother, my boy. So she wasn't taught much of the best sort, I reckon. When her father died early, and she was left alone, the only thing she could do was to take a governess's place, and she came to us. She never got on well with the children, for they were young and self-willed and rude, and would not learn to do as they were bid. I never knew one o' them shut the door when they went out of this room. And, from having had all her own way at home, with plenty of servants, and money to spend, it was a sore change to her. But she was a sweet creature, that she was. She did look sorely tried when Master Freddy would get on the back of her chair, and Miss Gusta would lie down on the rug, and never stir for all she could say to them, but only laugh at her. — To be sure!' And then Auntie would take a sip at her rum and water, and sit considering old times like a statie. And I sat as if all my head was one great ear, and I never spoke a word. And Auntie began again. 'The way I came to know so much about her was this. Nobody, you see, took any notice or care of her. For the children were kept away with her in the old house, and my lady wasn't one to take trouble about anybody till once she stood in her way, and then she would just shove her aside or crush her like a spider, and ha' done with her.' —

8*

They have always been a proud and a fierce race,
the Oldcastles, sir," said Weir, taking up the speech
in his own person, "and there's been a deal o'
breedin' in-and-in amongst them, and that has kept
up the worst of them. The men took to the women
of their own sort somehow, you see. The lady up
at the old Hall now is a Crowfoot. I'll just tell
you one thing the gardener told me about her years
ago, sir. She had a fancy for hyacinths in her
rooms in the spring, and she had some particular
fine ones; and a lady of her acquaintance begged
for some of them. And what do you think she
did? She couldn't refuse them, and she couldn't
bear any one to have them as good as she. And so
she sent the hyacinth-roots — but she boiled 'em
first. The gardener told me himself, sir. — 'And
so, when the poor thing,' said Auntie, 'was taken
with a dreadful cold, which was no wonder if you
saw the state of the window in the room she had to
sleep in, and which I got old Jones to set to rights
and paid him for it out of my own pocket, else he
wouldn't ha' done it at all, for the family wasn't too
much in the way or the means either of paying their
debts — well, there she was, and nobody minding
her, and of course it fell to me to look after her. It
would have made your heart bleed to see the poor
thing flung all of a heap on her bed, blue with cold
and coughing. "My dear!" I said; and she burst
out crying, and from that moment there was confidence between us. I made her as warm and as
comfortable as I could, but I had to nurse her for a
fortnight before she was able to do anything again.

She didn't shirk her work though, poor thing. It was a heartsore to me to see the poor young thing with her sweet eyes and her pale face, talking away to those children that were more like wild cats than human beings. She might as well have talked to wild cats, I'm sure. But I don't think she was ever so miserable again as she must have been before her illness; for she used often to come and see me of an evening, and she would sit there where you are sitting now for an hour at a time, without speaking, her thin white hands lying folded in her lap, and her eyes fixed on the fire. I used to wonder what she could be thinking about, and I had made up my mind she was not long for this world; when all at once it was announced that Miss Oldcastle, who had been to school for some time, was coming home; and then we began to see a great deal of company, and for month after month the house was more or less filled with visitors, so that my time was constantly taken up, and I saw much less of poor Miss Wallis than I had seen before. But when we did meet on some of the back stairs, or when she came to my room for a few minutes before going to bed, we were just as good friends as ever. And I used to say, "I wish this scurry was over, my dear, that we might have our old times again." 'And she would smile and say something sweet. But I was surprised to see that her health began to come back — at least so it seemed to me, for her eyes grew brighter and a flush came upon her pale face, and though the children were as tiresome as ever, she didn't seem to mind it so much. But indeed she

had not very much to do with them out of school
hours now; for when the spring came on, they
would be out and about the place with their sister
or one of their brothers; and indeed, out of doors
it would have been impossible for Miss Wallis to
do anything with them.   Some of the visitors would
take to them too, for they behaved so badly to
nobody as to Miss Wallis, and indeed they were
clever children, and could be engaging enough when
they pleased. — But then I had a blow, Samuel.
It was a lovely spring night, just after the sun was
down, and I wanted a drop of milk fresh from the
cow for something that I was making for dinner
the next day; so I went through the kitchen-
garden and through the belt of young larches to go
to the shippen.   But when I got among the trees,
who should I see at the other end of the path that
went along, but Miss Wallis walking arm-in-arm
with Captain Crowfoot, who was just home from
India, where he had been with Lord Clive.   The
captain was a man about two or three and thirty, a
relation of the family, and the son of Sir Giles
Crowfoot' — who lived then in this old house, sir,
and had but that one son, my father, you see, sir.
— 'And it did give me a turn,' said my aunt, 'to
see her walking with him, for I felt as sure as
judgment that no good could come of it.   For the
captain had not the best of characters — that is,
when people talked about him in chimney-corners,
and such like, though he was a great favourite with
everybody that knew nothing about him.   He was a
fine, manly, handsome fellow, with a smile that, as

people said; no woman could resist, though I'm sure
it would have given me no trouble to resist it, whatever they may mean by that, for I saw that that
same smile was the falsest thing of all the false
things about him. All the time he was smiling, you
would have thought he was looking at himself in a
glass. He was said to have gathered a power of
money in India, somehow or other. But I don't
know, only I don't think he would have been the
favourite he was with my lady if he hadn't. And
reports were about, too, of the ways and means by
which he had made the money; some said by rob-
bing the poor heathen creatures; and some said it
was only that his brother officers didn't quite approve of his speculating as he did in horses and
other things. I don't know whether officers are so
particular. At all events, this was a fact, for it was
one of his own servants that told me, not thinking
any harm or any shame of it. He had quarrelled
with a young ensign in the regiment. On which
side the wrong was, I don't know. But he first
thrashed him most unmercifully, and then called
him out, as they say. And when the poor fellow
appeared, he could scarcely see out of his eyes, and
certainly couldn't take anything like an aim. And
he shot him dead, did Captain Crowfoot.' — Think
of hearing that about one's own father, sir! But I
never said a word, for I hadn't a word to say. —
'Think of that, Samuel,' said my aunt, 'else you
won't believe what I am going to tell you. And
you won't even then, I dare say. But I must tell
you, nevertheless and notwithstanding. — Well, I

felt as if the earth was sinking away from under
the feet of me, and I stood and stared at them. And
they came on, never seeing me, and actually went
close past me and never saw me; at least, if he saw
me he took no notice, for I don't suppose that the
angel with the flaming sword would have put him
out. But for her, I know she didn't see me, for her
face was down, burning and smiling at once.' — I'm
an old man now, sir, and I never saw my mother;
but I can't tell you the story without feeling as if
my heart would break for the poor young lady. —
'I went back to my room,' said my aunt, 'with my
empty jug in my hand, and I sat down as if I had
had a stroke, and I never moved till it was pitch
dark and my fire out. It was a marvel to me afterwards that nobody came near me, for everybody was
calling after me at that time. And it was days before I caught a glimpse of Miss Wallis again, at
least to speak to her. At last, one night she came
to my room; and without a moment of parley, I said
to her, "Oh, my dear! what was that wretch saying
to you?" — "What wretch?" says she, quite sharp
like. "Why, Captain Crowfoot," says I, "to be
sure." — "What have you to say against Captain
Crowfoot?" says she, quite scornful like. So I
tumbled out all I had against him in one breath.
She turned awful pale, and she shook from head to
foot, but she was able for all that to say, "Indian
servants are known liars, Mrs. Prendergast," says
she, "and I don't believe one word of it all. But
I'll ask him, the next time I see him." — "Do so,
my dear," I said, not fearing for myself, for I knew

he would not make any fuss that might bring the
thing out into the air, and hoping that it might
lead to a quarrel between them. And the next time
I met her, Samuel — it was in the gallery that
takes to the west turret, she passed' me with a nod
just, and a blush instead of a smile on her sweet
face. And I didn't blame her, Samuel; but I knew
that that villain had gotten a hold of her. And so
I could only cry, and that I did. Things went on
like this for some months. The captain came and
went, stopping a week at a time. Then he stopped
for a whole month, and this was in the first of the
summer; and then he said he was ordered abroad
again, and went· away. But he didn't go abroad.
He came again in the autumn for the shooting, and
began to make up to Miss Oldcastle, who had grown
a fine young woman by that time. And then Miss
Wallis began to pine. The captain went away again.
Before long I was certain that if ever young creature
was in a consumption, she was; but she never said
a word to me. How ever the poor thing got on
with her work, I can't think, but she grew weaker
and weaker. I took the best care of her she would
let me, and contrived that she should have her meals
in her own room; but something was between her
and me that she never spoke a word about herself,
and never alluded to the captain. By and by came
the· news that the captain and Miss Oldcastle were
to be married in the spring. And Miss Wallis took
to her bed after that; and my lady said she had
never been of much use, and wanted to send her
away. But Miss Oldcastle, who was far superior to

any of the rest in her disposition, spoke up for her.
She had been to ask me about her, and I told her
the poor thing must go to a hospital if she was sent
away, for she had ne'er a home to go to. And then
she went to see the governess, poor thing! and spoke
very kindly to her; but never a word would Miss
Wallis answer; she only stared at her with great,
big, wild-like eyes. And Miss Oldcastle thought she
was out of her mind, and spoke of an asylum. But
I said she hadn't long to live, and if she would get
my lady her mother to consent to take no notice, I
would take all the care and trouble of her. And
she promised, and the poor thing was left alone. I
began to think myself her mind must be going, for
not a word would she speak, even to me, though
every moment I could spare I was up with her in
her room. Only I was forced to be careful not to
be out of the way when my lady wanted me, for
that would have tied me more. At length one day,
as I was settling her pillow for her, she all at once
threw her arms about my neck, and burst into a
terrible fit of crying. She sobbed and panted for
breath so dreadfully, that I put my arms round her
and lifted her up to give her relief; and when I laid
her down again, I whispered in her ear, "I know
now, my dear. I'll do all I can for you." She
caught hold of my hand and held it to her lips, and
then to her bosom, and cried again, but more quietly,
and all was right between us once more. It was
well for her, poor thing, that she could go to her bed.
And I said to myself, "Nobody need ever know
about it; and nobody ever shall if I can help it."

To tell the truth, my hope was that she would die before there was any need for further concealment. But people in that condition seldom die, they say, till all is over; and so she lived on and on, though plainly getting weaker and weaker. — At the captain's next visit, the wedding-day was fixed. And after that a circumstance came about that made me uneasy. A Hindoo servant — the captain called him his *nigger* always — had been constantly in attendance upon him. I never could abide the snake-look of the fellow, nor the noiseless way he went about the house. But this time the captain had a Hindoo woman with him as well. He said that his man had fallen in with her in London; that he had known her before; that she had come home as nurse with an English family, and it would be very nice for his wife to take her back with her to India, if she could only give her house-room, and make her useful till after the wedding. This was easily arranged, and he went away to return in three weeks, when the wedding was to take place. Meantime poor Emily grew fast worse, and how she held out with that terrible cough of hers I never could understand — and spitting blood, too, every other hour or so, though not very much. And now, to my great trouble, with the preparations for the wedding, I could see yet less of her than before; and when Miss Oldcastle sent the Hindoo to ask me if she might not sit in the room with the poor girl, I did not know how to object, though I did not at all like her being there. I felt a great mistrust of the woman somehow or other. I never did like blacks, and I never shall. So she went, and sat by her, and waited on her very kindly — at least poor Emily said so. I called her Emily because she had begged me, that she might feel as if her mother were with her, and she was a child again. I had tried before to find out from her when greater care would be necessary, but she couldn't tell me anything. I doubted even if she understood me. I longed to have the wedding over that I might get rid of the black woman, and have time to take her place, and get everything prepared. The captain arrived, and his man with him. And twice I came upon the two blacks in close conversation. — Well, the wedding-day came. The people went to church; and while they were there a terrible storm of wind and snow came on, such that the horses would hardly face it. The captain was going to take his bride home to his father, Sir Giles's; but, short as the distance was, before the time came the storm got so dreadful that no one could think of leaving the house that night. The wind blew for all the world just as it blows this night, only it was snow in its mouth, and not rain. Carriage and horses and all would have been blown off the road for certain. It did blow, to be sure! After dinner was over and the ladies were gone to the drawing-room, and the gentlemen had been sitting over their wine for some time, the butler, William Weir — an honest man, whose wife lived at the lodge — came to my room looking scared. "Lawks, William!" says I,' said my aunt, sir, '"what ever is the matter with you?" — "Well, Mrs. Prendergast!" says he, and said no more.

"Lawks, William," says I, "speak out." — "Well,"
says he, "Mrs. Prendergast, it's a strange wedding,
it is! There's the ladies all alone in the with-
drawing-room, and there's the gentlemen calling for
more wine, and cursing and swearing that it's awful
to hear. It's my belief that swords 'll be drawn
afore long." — "Tut!" says I, "William, it 'll come
the sooner if you don't give them what they want.
Go and get it as fast as you can." — "I don't
a'most like goin' down them stairs alone, in sich a
night, ma'am," says he. "Would you mind coming
with me?" — "Dear me, William," says I, "a
pretty story to tell your wife" — she was my own
half-sister, and younger than me — "a pretty story
to tell your wife, that you wanted an old body like
me to go and take care of you in your own cellar,"
says I. "But I'll go with you, if you like; for, to
tell the truth, it's a terrible night." And so down
we went, and brought up six bottles more of the
best port. And I really didn't wonder, when I was
down there, and heard the dull roar of the wind
against the rock below, that William didn't much
like to go alone. — When he went back with the
wine, the captain said, "William, what kept you so
long? Mr. Centlivre says that you were afraid to
go down into the cellar." Now, wasn't that odd,
for it was a real fact? Before William could reply,
Sir Giles said, "A man might well be afraid to go
anywhere alone in a night like this." Whereupon
the captain cried, with an oath, that he would go
down the underground stair, and into every vault
on the way, for the wager of a guinea. And there

the matter, according to William, dropped, for the
fresh wine was put on the table. But after they had
drunk the most of it — the captain, according to
William, drinking less than usual — it was brought
up again, he couldn't tell by which of them. And
in five minutes after, they were all at my door, de-
manding the key of the room at the top of the stair.
I was just going up to see poor Emily when I heard
the noise of their unsteady feet coming along the
passage to my door; and I gave the captain the key
at once, wishing with all my heart he might get a
good fright for his pains. He took a jug with him,
too, to bring some water up from the well, as a
proof he had been down. The rest of the gentlemen
went with him into the little cellar-room; but they
wouldn't stop there till he came up again, they said
it was so cold. They all came into my room, where
they talked as gentlemen wouldn't do if the wine
hadn't got uppermost. It was some time before the
captain returned. It's a good way down and back.
When he came in at last, he looked as if he had got
the fright I wished him, he had such a scared look.
The candle in his lantern was out, and there was no
water in the jug. "There's your guinea, Centlivre,"
says he, throwing it on the table. "You needn't
ask me any questions, for I won't answer one of
them." — "Captain," says I, as he turned to leave
the room, and the other gentlemen rose to follow
him, "I'll just hang up the key again." — "By all
means," says he. "Where is it, then?" says I. He
started and made as if he searched his pockets all
over for it. "I must have dropped it," says he;

"but it's of no consequence; you can send William to look for it in the morning. It can't be lost, you know." — "Very well, captain," said I. But I didn't like being without the key, because of course he hadn't locked the door, and that part of the house has a bad name, and no wonder. It wasn't exactly pleasant to have the door left open. All this time I couldn't get to see how Emily was. As often as I looked from my window, I saw her light in the old west turret out there, Samuel. You know the room where the bed is still. The rain and the wind will be blowing right through it to-night. That's the bed you was born upon, Samuel.' — It's all gone now, sir, turret and all, like a good deal more about the old place; but there's a story about that turret afterwards, only I mustn't try to tell you two things at once. — 'Now I had told the Indian woman that if anything happened, if she was worse, or wanted to see me, she must put the candle on the right side of the window, and I should always be looking out, and would come directly, whoever might wait. For I was expecting you some time soon, and nobody knew anything about when you might come. But there the blind continued drawn down as before. So I thought all was going on right. And what with the storm keeping Sir Giles and so many more ˙that would have gone home that night, there was no end of work, and some contrivance necessary, I can tell you, to get them all bedded for the night, for we were nothing too well provided with blankets and linen in the house. There was always more room than money in it. So it was past twelve o'clock before

I had a minute to myself, and that was only after
they had all gone to bed — the bride and bride·
groom in the crimson chamber of course.   Well, at
last I crept quietly into Emily's room.   I ought to
have told you that I had not let her know anything
about the wedding being that day, and had enjoined
the heathen woman not to say a word; for I thought
she might as well die without hearing about it.   But
I believe the vile wretch did tell her.   When I
opened the room-door, there was no light there.   I
spoke, but no one answered.   I had my own candle
in my hand, but it had been blown out as I came
up the stair.   I turned and ran along the corridor
to reach the main stair, which was the nearest way
to my room, when all at once I heard such a shriek
from the crimson chamber as I never heard in my
life.   It made me all creep like worms.   And in a
moment doors and doors were opened, and lights
came out, everybody looking terrified; and what with
drink, and horror, and sleep, some of the gentlemen
were awful to look upon.   And the door of the
crimson chamber opened too, and the captain appeared in his dressing-gown, bawling out to know
what was the matter; though I'm certain, to this
day, the cry did come from that room, and that he
knew more about it than any one else did.   As soon
as I got a light, however, which I did from Sir
Giles's candle, I left them to settle it amongst them,
and ran back to the west turret.   When I entered
the room, there was my dear girl lying white and
motionless.   There could be no doubt a baby had
been born, but no baby was to be seen.   I rushed

to the bed; but though she was still warm, your poor mother was quite dead. There was no use in thinking about helping her; but what could have become of the child? As if by a light in my mind, I saw it all. I rushed down to my room, got my lantern, and, without waiting to be afraid, ran to the underground stairs, where I actually found the door standing open. I had not gone down more than three turnings, when I thought I heard a cry, and I sped faster still. And just about half-way down, there lay a bundle in a blanket. And how ever you got over the state I found you in, Samuel, I can't think. But I caught you up as you was, and ran to my own room with you; and I locked the door, and there being a kettle on the fire, and some conveniences in the place, I did the best for you I could. For the breath wasn't out of you, though it well might have been. And then I laid you before the fire, and by that time you had begun to cry a little, to my great pleasure, and then I got a blanket off my bed, and wrapt you up in it; and, the storm being abated by this time, made the best of my way with you through the snow to the lodge, where William's wife lived. It was not so far off then as it is now. But in the midst of my trouble the silly body did make me laugh when he opened the door to me, and saw the bundle in my arms. "Mrs. Prendergast," says he, "I didn't expect it of you." — "Hold your tongue," I said. "You would never have talked such nonsense if you had had the grace to have any of your own," says I. And with that I into the bedroom and shut the door, and left

him out there in his shirt. My sister and I soon
got everything arranged, for there was no time to
lose. And before morning I had all made tidy, and
your poor mother lying as sweet a corpse as ever
angel saw. And no one could say a word against
her. And it's my belief that that villain made her
believe somehow or other that she was as good as
married to him. She was buried down there in the
churchyard, close by the vestry-door,' said my aunt,
sir; and all of our family have been buried there
ever since, my son Tom's wife among them, sir."

"But what was that cry in the house?" I asked.
"And what became of the black woman?"

"The woman was never seen again in our quarter; and what the cry was my aunt never would say.
She seemed to know though; notwithstanding, as she
said, that Captain and Mrs. Crowfoot denied all
knowledge of it. But the lady looked dreadful, she
said, and never was well again, and died at the
birth of her first child. That was the present Mrs.
Oldcastle's father, sir."

"But why should the woman have left you on
the stair, instead of drowning you in the well at the
bottom?"

"My aunt evidently thought there was some
mystery about that as well as the other, for she had
no doubt about the woman's intention. But all she
would ever say concerning it was, 'The key was
never found, Samuel. You see I had to get a new
one made.' And she pointed to where it hung on
the wall. 'But that doesn't look new now,' she
would say. 'The lock was very hard to fit again.'

And so you see, sir, I was brought up as her
nephew, though people were surprised, no doubt,
that William Weir's wife should have a child, and
nobody know she was expecting. — Well, with all
the reports of the captain's money, none of it showed
in this old place, which from that day began, as it
were, to crumble away. There's been little repair
done upon it since then. If it hadn't been a well-
built place to begin with, it wouldn't be standing
now, sir. But it's a very different place, I can tell
you. Why, all behind was a garden with terraces,
and fruit trees, and gay flowers, to no end. I remember it as well as yesterday; nay, a great deal
better, for the matter of that. For I don't remember
yesterday at all, sir."

I have tried a little to tell the story as he told
it. But I am aware that I have succeeded very
badly; for I am not like my friend in London, who,
I verily believe, could give you an exact represen-
tation of any dialect he ever heard. I wish I had
been able to give a little more of the form of the
old man's speech; all I have been able to do is to
show a difference from my own way of telling a
story. But in the main, I think, I have reported it
correctly. I believe if the old man was correct in
representing his aunt's account, the story is very
little altered between us.

But why should I tell such a story 'at all?

I am willing to allow, at once, that I have very
likely given it more room than it deserves in these
poor Annals of mine; but the reason why I tell it
at all is simply this, that, as it came from the old

9*

man's lips, it interested me greatly. It certainly did not produce the effect I had hoped to gain from an interview with him, namely, *a reduction to the common and present.* For all this ancient tale tended to keep up the sense of distance between my day's experience at the Hall and the work I had to do amongst my cottagers and tradespeople. Indeed it came very strangely upon that experience.

"But surely you did not believe such an extravagant tale? The old man was in his dotage, to begin with."

Had the old man been in his dotage, which he was not, my answer would have been a more triumphant one. For when was dotage consistently and imaginatively inventive? But why should I not believe the story? There are people who can never believe anything that is not (I do not say merely in accordance with their own character, but) in accordance with the particular mood they may happen to be in at the time it is presented to them. They know nothing of human nature beyond their own immediate preference at the moment for port or sherry, for vice or virtue. To tell me there could not be a man so lost to shame, if to rectitude, as Captain Crowfoot, is simply to talk nonsense. Nay, gentle reader, if you — and let me suppose I address a lady — if you will give yourself up for thirty years to doing just whatever your lowest self and not your best self may like, I will warrant you capable, by the end of that time, of child-murder at least. I do not think the descent to Avernus is always easy; but it is always possible. Many and many such a story was fact in old times; and human nature being the same still, though under different restraints, equally horrible things are constantly in progress towards the windows of the newspapers.

"But the whole tale has such a melodramatic air!"

That argument simply amounts to this: that, because such subjects are capable of being employed with great dramatic effect, and of being at the same time very badly represented, therefore they cannot take place in real life. But ask any physician of your acquaintance, whether a story is unlikely simply because it involves terrible things such as do not occur every day. The fact is, that such things, occurring monthly or yearly only, are more easily hidden away out of sight. Indeed we can have no sense of security for ourselves except in the knowledge that we are striving up and away, and therefore cannot be sinking nearer to the region of such awful possibilities.

Yet, as I said before, I am afraid I have given it too large a space in my narrative. Only it so forcibly reminded me at the time of the expression I could not understand upon Miss Oldcastle's face, and since then has been so often recalled by circumstances and events, that I felt impelled to record it in full. And now I have done with it.

I left the old man with thanks for the kind reception he had given me, and walked home, revolving many things with which I shall not detain the attention of my reader. Indeed my thoughts were confused and troubled, and would ill bear analysis

or record. I shut myself up in my study, and tried
to read a sermon of Jeremy Taylor. But it would
not do. I fell fast asleep over it at last, and woke
refreshed.

CHAPTER VIII.

What I Preached.

DURING the suffering which accompanied the disappointment at which I have already hinted, I did not think it inconsistent with the manly spirit in which I was resolved to endure it, to seek consolation from such a source as the New Testament — if mayhap consolation for such a trouble was to be found there. Whereupon, a little to my surprise, I discovered that I could not read the Epistles at all. For I did not then care an atom for the theological discussions in which I had been interested before, and for the sake of which I had read those epistles. Now that I was in trouble, what to me was that philosophical theology staring me in the face from out the sacred page? Ah! reader, do not misunderstand me. All reading of the Book is not reading of the Word. And many that are first shall be last and the last first. I know *now* that it was Jesus Christ and not theology that filled the hearts of the men that wrote those epistles — Jesus Christ, the living, loving God-Man, whom I found — not in the Epistles, but in the Gospels. The Gospels contain what the apostles preached — the Epistles what they wrote after the preaching. And until we understand the Gospel, the good news of Jesus Christ our brother-king — until we understand Him, until we

have His Spirit, promised so freely to them that ask
it — all the Epistles, the words of men who were
full of Him, and wrote out of that fulness, who loved
Him so utterly that by that very love they were
lifted into the air of pure reason and right, and would
die for Him, and did die for Him, without two
thoughts about it, in the very simplicity of *no choice*
— the Letters, I say, of such men are to us a sealed
book.   Until we love the Lord so as to do what He
tells us, we have no right to have an opinion about
what one of those men meant; for all they wrote is
about things beyond us.   The simplest woman who
tries not to judge her neighbour, or not to be anxious
for the morrow, will better know what is best to
know, than the best-read bishop without that one
simple outgoing of his highest nature in the effort
to do the will of Him who thus spoke.

   But I have, as is too common with me, been led
away by my feelings from the path to the object before me.   What I wanted to say was this: that, although I could make nothing of the epistles, could
see no possibility of consolation for my distress
springing from them, I found it altogether different
when I tried the Gospel once more.   Indeed, it then
took such a hold of me as it had never taken before.
Only that is simply saying nothing.   I found out
that I had known nothing at all about it; that I had
only a certain surface-knowledge, which tended rather
to ignorance, because it fostered the delusion that I
did know.   Know that man, Christ Jesus! Ah! Lord,
I would go through fire and water to sit the last at
Thy table in Thy kingdom; but dare I say now I

know Thee! — But Thou art the Gospel, for Thou
art the Way, the Truth, and the Life; and I have
found Thee the Gospel. For I found, as I read,
that Thy very presence in my thoughts, not as the
theologians show Thee, but as Thou showedst thy-
self to them who report Thee to us, smoothed the
troubled waters of my spirit, so that, even while the
storm lasted, I was able to walk upon them to go to
Thee. And when those waters became clear, I most
rejoiced in their clearness because they mirrored Thy
form — because Thou wert there to my vision — the
one Ideal, the perfect man, the God perfected as
king of men by working out his Godhood in the
work of man; revealing that God and man are one;
that to serve God, a man must be partaker of the
Divine nature; that for a man's work to be done
thoroughly, God must come and do it first himself;
that to help men, He must be what He is — man in
God, God in man — visibly before their eyes, or to
the hearing of their ears. So much I saw.

And therefore, when I was once more in a position to help my fellows, what could I want to give
them but that which was the very bread and water
of life to me — the Saviour himself? And how was
I to do this? — By trying to represent the man in
all the simplicity of his life, of his sayings and doings,
of his refusals to say or do. — I took the story from
the beginning, and told them about the Baby; trying to make the fathers and mothers, and all whose
love for children supplied the lack of fatherhood and
motherhood, feel that it was a real baby-boy. And
I followed the life on and on, trying to show them

how He felt, as far as one might dare to touch such
sacred things, when He did so and so, or said so and
so; and what His relation to His father and mother
and brothers and sisters was, and to the different
kinds of people who came about Him.   And I tried
to show them what His sayings meant, as far as I
understood them myself, and where I could not understand them I just told them so, and said I hoped for
more light by and by to enable me to understand
them; telling them that that hope was a sharp goad
to my resolution, driving me on to do my duty, because I knew that only as I did my duty would
light go up in my heart, making me wise to understand the precious words of my Lord.   And I told
them that if they would try to do their duty, they
would find more understanding from that than from
any explanation I could give them.

And so I went on from Sunday to Sunday. And
the number of people that slept grew less and less,
until at last it was reduced to the churchwarden, Mr.
Brownrigg, and an old washerwoman, who, poor
thing, stood so much all the week, that sitting down
with her was like going to bed, and she never could
do it, as she told me, without going to sleep.   I,
therefore, called upon her every Monday morning,
and had five minutes' chat with her as she stood at
her wash-tub, wishing to make up to her for her
drowsiness; and thinking that if I could once get her
interested in anything, she might be able to keep
awake a little while at the beginning of the sermon;
for she gave me no chance of interesting her on
Sundays — going fast asleep the moment I stood up

to preach. I never got so far as that, however; and
the only fact that showed me I had made any impression upon her, beyond the pleasure she always
manifested when I appeared on the Monday, was,
that, whereas all my linen had been very badly
washed at first, a decided improvement took place
after a while, beginning with my surplice and bands,
and gradually extending itself to my shirts and handkerchiefs; till at last even Mrs. Pearson was unable
to find any fault with the poor old sleepy woman's
work. For Mr. Brownrigg, I am not sure that the
sense of any one sentence I ever uttered, down to
the day of his death, entered into his brain — I dare
not say his mind or heart. With regard to him, and
millions besides, I am more than happy to obey my
Lord's command, and not judge.

But it was not long either before my congrega-
tions began to improve, whatever might be the cause.
I could not help hoping that it was really because
they liked to hear the Gospel, that is, the good news
about Christ himself. And I always made use of
the knowledge I had of my individual hearers, to
say what I thought would do them good. Not that
I ever preached *at* anybody; I only sought to explain the principles of things in which I knew action
of some sort was demanded from them. For I re-
membered how our Lord's sermon against covetousness, with the parable of the rich man with the little
barn, had for its occasion the request of a man that
our Lord would interfere to make his brother share
with him; which He declining to do, yet gave both
brothers a lesson such as, if they wished to do what

was right, would help them to see clearly what was
the right thing to do in this and every such matter.
Clear the mind's eye, by washing away the covetousness, and the whole nature would be full of light,
and the right walk would speedily follow.

Before long, likewise, I was as sure of seeing
the pale face of Thomas Weir perched, like that of
a man beheaded for treason, upon the apex of the
gablet of the old tomb, as I was of hearing the
wonderful playing of that husky old organ, of which
I have spoken once before. I continued to pay him
a visit every now and then; and I assure you, never
was the attempt to be thoroughly honest towards a
man better understood or more appreciated than my
attempt was by the *atheistical* carpenter. The man
was no more an atheist than David was when he
saw the wicked spreading like a green bay-tree, and
was troubled at the sight. He only wanted to see a
God in whom he could trust. And if I succeeded at
all in making him hope that there might be such a
God, it is to me one of the most precious seals of
my ministry.

But it was now getting very near Christmas, and
there was one person whom I had never yet seen at
church: that was Catherine Weir. I thought, at first,
it could hardly be that she shrunk from being seen;
for how then could she have taken to keeping a
shop, where she must be at the beck of every one?
I had several times gone and bought tobacco of her
since that first occasion; and I had told my housekeeper to buy whatever she could from her, instead
of going to the larger shop in the place; at which

Mrs. Pearson had grumbled a good deal, saying how could the things be so good out of a poky shop like that? But I told her I did not care if the things were not quite as good; for it would be of more consequence to Catherine to have the custom, than it would be to me to have the one lump of sugar I put in my tea of a morning one shade or even two shades whiter. So I had contrived to keep up a kind of connexion with her, although I saw that any attempt at conversation was so distasteful to her, that it must do harm until something should have brought about a change in her feelings; though what feeling wanted changing, I could not at first tell. I came to the conclusion that she had been wronged grievously, and that this wrong operating on a nature similar to her father's, had drawn all her mind to brood over it. The world itself, the whole order of her life, everything about her, would seem then to have wronged her; and to speak to her of religion would only rouse her scorn, and make her feel as if God himself, if there were a God, had wronged her too. Evidently, likewise, she had that peculiarity of strong undeveloped natures, of being unable, once possessed by one set of thoughts, to get rid of it again, or to see anything except in the shadow of those thoughts. I had no doubt, however, at last, that she was ashamed of her position in the eyes of society, although a hitherto indomitable pride had upheld her to face it so far as was necessary to secure her independence; both of which — pride and shame — prevented her from appearing where it was unnecessary, and especially in church. I could do nothing more than wait for a favourable opportunity. I could invent no way of reaching her yet, for I had soon found that kindness to her boy was regarded rather in the light of an insult to her. I should have been greatly puzzled to account for his being such a sweet little fellow, had I not known that he was a great deal with his aunt and grandfather. A more attentive and devout worshipper was not in the congregation than that little boy.

Before going on to speak of another of the most remarkable of my parishioners, whom I have just once mentioned I believe already, I should like to say that on three several occasions before Christmas I had seen Judy look grave. She was always quite well-behaved in church, though restless, as one might expect. But on these occasions she was not only attentive, but grave, as if she felt something or other. I will not mention what subjects I was upon at those times, because the mention of them would not, in the minds of my readers, at all harmonize with the only notion of Judy they can yet by possibility have.

For Mrs. Oldcastle, I never saw her change countenance or even expression at anything — I mean in church.

CHAPTER IX.

The Organist.

On the afternoon of my second Sunday at Marsh-mallows, I was standing in the churchyard, casting a long shadow in the light of the declining sun. I was reading the inscription upon an old headstone, for I thought everybody was gone; when I heard a door open, and shut again before I could turn. I saw at once that it must have been a little door in the tower, almost concealed from where I stood by a deep buttress. I had never seen the door open, and I had never inquired anything about it, supposing it led merely into the tower.

After a moment it opened again, and, to my surprise, out came, stooping his tall form to get his gray head clear of the low archway, a man whom no one could pass without looking after him. Tall, and strongly built, he had the carriage of a military man, without an atom of that sternness which one generally finds in the faces of those accustomed to command. He had a large face, with large regular features, and large clear gray eyes, all of which united to express an exceeding placidity or repose. It shone with intelligence — a mild intelligence — no way suggestive of profundity, although of geniality. Indeed, there was a little too much expression. The face seemed to express *all* that lay beneath it.

I was not satisfied with the countenance; and yet
it looked quite good.   It was somehow a too well-
ordered face.   It was quite Greek in its outline; and
marvellously well kept and smooth, considering that
the beard, to which razors were utterly strange, and
which descended half-way down his breast, would
have been as white as snow except for a slight yel-
lowish tinge.   His eyebrows were still very dark,
only just touched with the frost of winter. His hair,
too, as I saw when he lifted his hat, was still
wonderfully dark for the condition of his beard. —
It flashed into my mind, that this must be the
organist who played so remarkably. Somehow I had
not happened yet to inquire about him.   But there
was a stateliness in this man amounting almost to
consciousness of dignity; and I was a little bewildered.   His clothes were all of black, very neat
and clean, but old-fashioned and threadbare.   They
bore signs of use, but more signs of time and careful
keeping.   I would have spoken to him, but something in the manner in which he bowed to me as
he passed, prevented me, and I let him go un-
accosted.

The sexton coming out directly after, and proceeding to lock the door, I was struck by the action.
"What *is* he locking the door for?" I said to myself.
But I said nothing to him, because I had not answered
the question myself yet.

"Who is that gentleman," I asked, "who came
out just now?"

"That is Mr. Stoddart, sir," he answered.

I thought I had heard the name in the neighbourhood before.

"Is it he who plays the organ?" I asked.

"That he do, sir. He's played our organ for the last ten year, ever since he come to live at the Hall."

"What Hall?"

"Why the Hall, to be sure, — Oldcastle Hall, you know."

And then it dawned on my recollection that I had heard Judy mention her uncle Stoddart. But how could he be her uncle?

"Is he a relation of the family?" I asked.

"He's a brother-in-law, I believe, of the old lady, sir, but how ever he come to live there I don't know. It's no such binding connexion, you know, sir. He's been in the milintairy line, I believe, sir, in the Ingies, or somewheres."

I do not think I shall have any more strange parishioners to present to my readers; at least I do not remember any more just at this moment. And this one, as the reader will see, I positively could not keep out.

A military man from India! a brother-in-law of Mrs. Oldcastle, choosing to live with her! an entrancing performer upon an old, asthmatic, dry-throated church organ! taking no trouble to make the clergyman's acquaintance, and passing him in the churchyard with a courteous bow, although his face was full of kindliness, if not of kindness! I could not help thinking all this strange. And yet — will the reader cease to accord me credit when I assert it? — although I had quite intended to inquire after him when I left the vicarage to go to the Hall, and had even thought of him when sitting with Mrs. Oldcastle, I never thought of him again after going with Judy, and left the house without having made a single inquiry after him. Nor did I think of him again till just as I was passing under the outstretched neck of one of those serpivolants on the gate; and what made me think of him then, I cannot in the least imagine; but I resolved at once that I would call upon him the following week, lest he should think that the fact of his having omitted to call upon me had been the occasion of such an apparently pointed omission on my part. For I had long ago determined to be no further guided by the rules of society than as they might aid in bringing about true neighbourliness, and if possible friendliness and friendship. Wherever they might interfere with these, I would disregard them — as far on the other hand as the disregard of them might tend to bring about the results I desired.

When, carrying out this resolution, I rang the door-bell at the Hall, and inquired whether Mr. Stoddart was at home, the butler stared; and, as I simply continued gazing in return, and waiting, he answered at length, with some hesitation, as if he were picking and choosing his words:

"Mr. Stoddart never calls upon any one, sir."

"I am not complaining of Mr. Stoddart," I answered, wishing to put the man at his ease.

"But nobody calls upon Mr. Stoddart," he returned.

"That's very unkind of somebody, surely," I
said.

"But he doesn't want anybody to call upon
him, sir."

"Ah! that's another matter. I didn't know that.
Of course, nobody has a right to intrude upon anybody. However, as I happen to have come without
knowing his dislike to being visited, perhaps you
will take him my card, and say that if it is not disagreeable to him, I should like exceedingly to thank
him in person for his sermon on the organ last
Sunday."

He had played an exquisite voluntary in the
morning.

"Give my message exactly, if you please," I said,
as I followed the man into the hall.

"I will try, sir," he answered. "But won't you
come up-stairs to mistress's room, sir, while I take
this to Mr. Stoddart?"

"No, I thank you," I answered. "I came to call
upon Mr. Stoddart only, and I will wait the result
of your mission here in the hall."

The man withdrew, and I sat down on a bench,
and amused myself with looking at the portraits
about me. I learned afterwards that they had hung,
till some thirty years before, in a long gallery connecting the main part of the house with that portion
to which the turret referred to so often in Old Weir's
story was attached. One particularly pleased me. It
was the portrait of a young woman — very lovely
— but with an expression both sad and — scared, I
think, would be the readiest word to communicate

10 *

what I mean. It was indubitably, indeed remarkably, like Miss Oldcastle. And I learned afterwards that it was the portrait of Mrs. Oldcastle's grandmother, that very Mrs. Crowfoot mentioned in Weir's story. It had been taken about six months after her marriage, and about as many before her death.

The butler returned, with the request that I would follow him. He led me up the grand staircase, through a passage at right angles to that which led to the old lady's room, up a narrow circular staircase at the end of the passage, across a landing, then up a straight steep narrow stair, upon which two people could not pass without turning sideways and then squeezing. At the top of this I found myself in a small cylindrical lobby, papered in blocks of stone. There was no door to be seen. It was lighted by a conical skylight. My conductor gave a push against the wall. Certain blocks yielded, and others came forward. In fact a door revolved on central pivots, and we were admitted to a chamber crowded with books from floor to ceiling, arranged with wonderful neatness and solidity. From the centre of the ceiling, whence hung a globular lamp, radiated what I took to be a number of strong beams supporting a floor above; for our ancestors put the ceiling above the beams, instead of below them as we do, and gained in space if they lost in quietness. But I soon found out my mistake. Those radiating beams were in reality book-shelves. For on each side of those I passed under I could see the gilded backs of books standing closely ranged together. I had never seen the contrivance before, nor, I presume, was it to be seen anywhere else.

"How does Mr. Stoddart reach those books?" I asked my conductor.

"I don't exactly know, sir," whispered the butler. "His own man could tell you, I dare say. But he has a holiday to-day; and I do not think he would explain it either; for he says his master allows no interference with his contrivances. I believe, however, he does not use a ladder."

There was no one in the room, and I saw no entrance but that by which we had entered. The next moment, however, a nest of shelves revolved in front of me, and there Mr. Stoddart stood with out-stretched hand.

"You have found me at last, Mr. Walton, and I am glad to see you," he said.

He led me into an inner room, much larger than the one I had passed through.

"I am glad," I replied, "that I did not know, till the butler told me, your unwillingness to be in-truded upon; for I fear, had I known it, I should have been yet longer a stranger to you."

"You are no stranger to me. I have heard you read prayers, and I have heard you preach."

"And I have heard you play; so you are no stranger to me either."

"Well, before we say another word," said Mr. Stoddart, "I must just say one word about this report of my unsociable disposition. — I encourage it; but am very glad to see you notwithstanding. — Do sit down."

I obeyed, and waited for the rest of his word.

"I was so bored with visits after I came, visits which were to me utterly uninteresting, that I was only too glad when the unusual nature of some of my pursuits gave rise to the rumour that I was mad. The more people say I am mad, the better pleased I am, so long as they are satisfied with my own mode of shutting myself up, and do not attempt to carry out any fancies of their own in regard to my personal freedom."

Upon this followed some desultory conversation, during which I took some observations of the room. Like the outer room, it was full of books from floor to ceiling. But the ceiling was divided into compartments, harmoniously coloured.

"What a number of books you have!" I observed.

"Not a great many," he answered. "But I think there is hardly one of them with which I have not some kind of personal acquaintance. I think I could almost find you any one you wanted in the dark, or in the twilight at least, which would allow me to distinguish whether the top edge was gilt, red, marbled, or uncut. I have bound a couple of hundred or so of them myself. I don't think you could tell the work from a tradesman's. I'll give you a guinea for the poor-box if you pick out three of my binding consecutively."

I accepted the challenge; for although I could not bind a book, I considered myself to have a keen eye for the outside finish. After looking over the backs of a great many, I took one down, examined a little further, and presented it.

"You are right. Now try again."

Again I was successful, although I doubted.

"And now for the last," he said.

Once more I was right.

"There is your guinea," said he, a little mortified.

"No," I answered. "I do not feel at liberty to take it, because, to tell the truth, the last was a mere guess, nothing more."

Mr. Stoddart looked relieved.

"You are more honest than most of your profession," he said. "But I am far more pleased to offer you the guinea upon the smallest doubt of your having won it."

"I have no claim upon it."

"What! Couldn't you swallow a small scruple like that for the sake of the poor even? Well, I don't believe *you* could. — Oblige me by taking this guinea for some one or other of your poor people. But I *am* glad you weren't sure of that last book. I am indeed."

I took the guinea, and put it in my purse.

"But," he resumed, "you won't do, Mr. Walton. You're not fit for your profession. You won't tell a lie for God's sake. You won't dodge about a little to keep all right between Jove and his weary parishioners. You won't cheat a little for the sake of the poor! You wouldn't even bamboozle a little at a bazaar!"

"I should not like to boast of my principles," I

answered; "for the moment one does so, they become
as the apples of Sodom. But assuredly I would not
favour a fiction to keep a world out of hell. The
hell that a lie would keep any man out of is doubtless the very best place for him to go to. It is truth,
yes, *The Truth* that saves the world."

"You are right, I daresay. You are more sure
about it than I am though."

"Let us agree where we can," I said, "first of
all; and that will make us able to disagree, where
we must, without quarrelling."

"Good," he said — "Would you like to see my
workshop?"

"Very much, indeed," I answered, heartily.

"Do you take any pleasure in applied mechanics?"

"I used to do so as a boy. But of course I have
little time now for anything of the sort."

"Ah! of course."

He pushed a compartment of books. It yielded,
and we entered a small closet. In another moment
I found myself leaving the floor, and in yet a moment we were on the floor of an upper room.

"What a nice way of getting up stairs!" I said.

"There is no other way of getting to this room,"
answered Mr. Stoddart. "I built it myself; and
there was no room for stairs. This is my shop. In
my library I only read my favourite books. Here
I read anything I want to read; write anything I
want to write; bind my books; invent machines; and
amuse myself generally. Take a chair."

I obeyed, and began to look about me.

The room had many books in detached book-cases. There were various benches against the walls between, — one a bookbinder's; another a carpenter's; a third had a turning-lathe; a fourth had an iron vice fixed on it, and was evidently used for working in metal. Besides these, for it was a large room, there were several tables with chemical apparatus upon them, Florence-flasks, retorts, sand-baths, and such like; while in a corner stood a furnace.

"What an accumulation of ways and means you have about you!" I said; "and all, apparently, to different ends."

"All to the same end, if my object were understood."

"I presume I must ask no questions as to that object?"

"It would take time to explain. I have theories of education. I think a man has to educate himself into harmony. Therefore he must open every possible window by which the influences of the All may come in upon him. I do not think any man complete without a perfect development of his mechanical faculties, for instance, and I encourage them to develop themselves into such windows."

"I do not object to your theory, provided you do not put it forward as a perfect scheme of human life. If you did, I should have some questions to ask you about it, lest I should misunderstand you."

He smiled what I took for a self-satisfied smile.

There was nothing offensive in it, but it left me without anything to reply to. No embarrassment followed, however, for a rustling motion in the room the same instant attracted my attention, and I saw, to my surprise, and I must confess, a little to my confusion, Miss Oldcastle. She was seated in a corner, reading from a quarto lying upon her knees.

"Oh! you didn't know my niece was here? To tell the truth, I forgot her when I brought you up, else I would have introduced you."

"That is not necessary, uncle," said Miss Oldcastle, closing her book.

I was by her instantly. She slipped the quarto from her knee, and took my offered hand.

"Are you fond of old books?" I said, not having anything better to say.

"Some old books," she answered.

"May I ask what book you were reading?"

"I will answer you — under protest," she said, with a smile.

"I withdraw the question at once," I returned.

"I will answer it notwithstanding. It is a volume of Jacob Behmen."

"Do you understand him?"

"Yes. Don't you?"

"Well, I have made but little attempt," I answered. "Indeed, it was only as I passed through London last that I bought his works; and I am sorry to find that one of the plates is missing from my copy."

"Which plate is it? It is not very easy, I un-

derstand, to procure a perfect copy. One of my
uncle's copies has no two volumes bound alike. Each
must have belonged to a different set."

"I can't tell you what the plate is. But there
are only three of those very curious unfolding
ones in my third volume, and there should be
four."

"I do not think so. Indeed, I am sure you are
wrong."

"I am glad to hear it — though to be glad that
the world does not possess what I thought I only
was deprived of, is selfishness, cover it over as one
may with the fiction of a perfect copy."

"I don't know," she returned, without any response to what I said. "I should always like things
perfect myself."

"Doubtless," I answered; and thought it better
to try another direction.

"How is Mrs. Oldcastle?" I asked, feeling in its
turn the reproach of hypocrisy; for though I could
have suffered, I hope, in my person and goods and
reputation, to make that woman other than she was,
I could not say that I cared one atom whether she
was in health or not. Possibly I should have pre-
ferred the latter member of the alternative; for the
suffering of the lower nature is as a fire that drives
the higher nature upwards. So I felt rather hypo-
critical when I asked Miss Oldcastle after her.

"Quite well, thank you," she answered, in a
tone of indifference, which implied either that she
saw through me, or shared in my indifference. I
could not tell which.

"And how is Miss Judy?" I inquired.

"A little savage, as usual."

"Not the worse for her wetting, I hope."

"Oh! dear no. There never was health to equal that child's. It belongs to her savage nature."

"I wish some of us were more of savages, then," I returned; for I saw signs of exhaustion in her eyes which moved my sympathy.

"You don't mean me, Mr. Walton, I hope. For if you do, I assure you your interest is quite thrown away. Uncle will tell you I am as strong as an elephant."

But here came a slight elevation of her person; and a shadow, at the same moment, passed over her face. I saw that she felt she ought not to have allowed herself to become the subject of conversation.

Meantime her uncle was busy at one of his benches filing away at a piece of brass fixed in the vice. He had thick gloves on. And indeed it had puzzled me before to think how he could have so many kinds of work and yet keep his hands so smooth and white as they were. I could not help thinking the results could hardly be of the most useful description if they were all accomplished without some loss of whiteness and smoothness in the process. Even the feet that keep the garments clean must be washed themselves in the end.

When I glanced away from Miss Oldcastle in the embarrassment produced by the repulsion of her last manner, I saw Judy in the room. At the same moment Miss Oldcastle rose.

"What is the matter, Judy?" she said.

"Grannie wants you," said Judy.

Miss Oldcastle left the room, and Judy turned to me.

"How do you do, Mr. Walton?" she said.

"Quite well, thank you, Judy," I answered. "Your uncle admits you to his workshop, then?"

"Yes, indeed. He would feel rather dull, sometimes, without me. Wouldn't you, Uncle Stoddart?"

"Just as the horses in the field would feel dull without the gad-fly, Judy," said Mr. Stoddart, laughing.

Judy, however, did not choose to receive the laugh as a scholium explanatory of the remark, and was gone in a moment, leaving Mr. Stoddart and myself alone. I must say he looked a little troubled at the precipitate retreat of the damsel; but he recovered himself with a smile, and said to me,

"I wonder what speech I shall make next to drive you away, Mr. Walton."

"I am not so easily got rid of, Mr. Stoddart," I answered. "And as for taking offence, I don't like it, and therefore I never take it. But tell we what you are doing now."

"I have been working for some time at an attempt after a perpetual motion, but, I must confess, more from a metaphysical or logical point of view than a mechanical one."

Here he took a drawing from a shelf, explanatory of his plan.

"You see," he said, "here is a top, made of platinum, the heaviest of metals, except iridium — which it would be impossible to procure enough of, and which would be difficult to work into the proper shape. It is surrounded, you will observe, by an air-tight receiver, communicating by this tube with a powerful air-pump. The plate upon which the point of the top rests and revolves is a diamond; and I ought to have mentioned that the peg of the top is a diamond likewise. This is of course for the sake of reducing the friction. By this apparatus communicating with the top, through the receiver, I set the top in motion — after exhausting the air as far as possible. Still there is the difficulty of the friction of the diamond point upon the diamond plate, which must ultimately occasion repose. To obviate this, I have constructed here, underneath, a small steam-engine, which shall cause the diamond plate to revolve at precisely the same rate of speed as the top itself. This, of course, will prevent all friction."

"Not that with the unavoidable remnant of air, however," I ventured to suggest.

"That is just my weak point," he answered. "But that will be so very small!"

"Yes; but enough to deprive the top of *perpetual* motion."

"But suppose I could get over that difficulty, would the contrivance have a right to the name of a perpetual motion? For you observe that the steam-

engine below would not be the cause of the motion.
That comes from above, here, and is withdrawn,
finally withdrawn."

"I understand perfectly," I answered. "At least
I think I do. But I return the question to you: Is
a motion which, although not caused, is *enabled* by
another motion, worthy of the name of a perpetual
motion; seeing the perpetuity of motion has not to
do merely with time, but with the indwelling of self-
generative power — renewing itself constantly with
the process of exhaustion?"

He threw down his file on the bench.

"I fear you are right," he said. "But you will
allow it would have made a very pretty machine."

"Pretty, I will allow," I answered, "as distinguished from beautiful. For I can never dissociate
beauty from use."

"You say that! with all the poetic things you
say in your sermons! For I am a sharp listener,
and none the less such that you do not see me. I
have a loophole for seeing you. And I flatter myself, therefore, I am the only person in the congregation on a level with you in respect of balancing
advantages. I cannot contradict you, and you cannot address me."

"Do you mean, then, that whatever is poetical
is useless?" I asked.

"Do you assert that whatever is useful is beautiful?" he retorted.

"A full reply to your question would need a
ream of paper and a quarter of quills," I answered;
"but I think I may venture so far as to say that

whatever subserves a noble end must in itself be beautiful."

"Then a gallows must be beautiful because it subserves the noble end of ridding the world of malefactors?" he returned promptly.

I had to think for a moment before I could reply.

"I do not see anything noble in the end," I answered. "If the machine got rid of malefaction, it would indeed have a noble end. But if it only compels it to move on, as a constable does — from this world into another — I do not, I say, see anything so noble in that end. The gallows cannot be beautiful."

"Ah, I see. You don't approve of capital punishments."

"I do not say that. An inevitable necessity is something very different from a noble end. To cure the diseased mind is the noblest of ends; to make the sinner forsake his ways, and the unrighteous man his thoughts, the loftiest of designs; but to punish him for being wrong, however necessary it may be for others, cannot, if dissociated from the object of bringing good out of evil, be called in any sense a *noble* end. I think now, however, it would be but fair in you to give me some answer to my question. Do you think the poetic useless?"

"I think it is very like my machine. It may exercise the faculties without subserving any immediate progress."

"It is so difficult to get out of the region of the poetic, that I cannot think it other than useful: it is so wide-spread. The useless could hardly be so nearly universal. But I should like to ask you another question: What is the immediate effect of anything poetic upon your mind?"

"Pleasure," he answered.

"And is pleasure good or bad?"

"Sometimes the one, sometimes the other."

"In itself?"

"I should say so."

"I should not."

"Are you not, then, by your very profession, more or less an enemy of pleasure?"

"On the contrary, I believe that pleasure is good, and does good, and urges to good. *Care* is the evil thing."

"Strange doctrine for a clergyman."

"Now, do not misunderstand me, Mr. Stoddart. That might not hurt you, but it would distress me. Pleasure, obtained by wrong, is poison and horror. But it is not the pleasure that hurts, it is the wrong that is in it that hurts; the pleasure hurts only as it leads to more wrong. I almost think myself, that if you could make everybody happy, half the evil would vanish from the earth."

"But you believe in God?"

"I hope in God I do."

"How can you then think that He would not destroy evil at such a cheap and pleasant rate?"

"Because he wants to destroy *all* the evil, not the half of it; and destroy it so that it shall not grow again; which it would be sure to do very soon if it had no antidote but happiness. As soon as men got used to happiness, they would begin to sin again, and so lose it all. But care is distrust. I wonder, now if ever there was a man who did his duty, and *took no thought*. I wish I could get the testimony of such a man. Has anybody actually tried the plan?"

But here I saw that I was not taking Mr. Stoddart with me (as the old phrase was). The reason I supposed to be, that he had never been troubled with much care. But there remained the question, whether he trusted in God or the Bank?

I went back to the original question.

"But I should be very sorry you should think, that to give pleasure was my object in saying poetic things in the pulpit. If I do so, it is because true things come to me in their natural garments of poetic forms. What you call the *poetic* is only the outer beauty that belongs to all inner or spiritual beauty — just as a lovely face — mind, I say *lovely*, not *pretty*, not *handsome* — is the outward and visible presence of a lovely mind. Therefore, saying I cannot dissociate beauty from use, I am free to say as many poetic things — though, mind, I don't claim them: you attribute them to me — as shall be of the highest use, namely, to embody and reveal the true. But a machine has material use for its end. The most grotesque machine I ever saw that *did* something, I felt to be in its own kind beautiful; as God called many fierce and grotesque things good when He made the world — good for their good end. But your machine does nothing more than raise the metaphysical doubt and ques-

tion, whether it can with propriety be called a perpetual motion or not?"

To this Mr. Stoddart making no reply, I take
the opportunity of the break in our conversation to
say to my readers, that I know there was no satisfactory following out of an argument on either side
in the passage of words I have just given. Even
the closest reasoner finds it next to impossible to
attend to all the suggestions in his own mind, not
one of which he is willing to lose, to attend at the
same time to everything his antagonist says or sug-
gests, that he may do him justice, and to keep an
even course towards his goal — each having the
opposite goal in view. In fact, an argument, however simply conducted and honourable, must just
resemble a game at football; the unfortunate question being the ball, and the numerous and sometimes conflicting thoughts which arise in each mind
forming the two parties whose energies are spent in
a succession of kicks. In fact, I don't like argument, and I don't care for the victory. If I had my
way, I would never argue at all. I would spend
my energy in setting forth what I believe — as
like itself as I could represent it, and so leave it to
work its own way, which, if it be the right way,
it must work in the right mind, — for Wisdom is
justified of her children; while no one who loves
the truth can be other than anxious, that if he has
spoken the evil thing it may return to him void:
that is a defeat he may well pray for. To succeed
in the wrong is the most dreadful punishment to a
man who, in the main, is honest. But I beg to

11*

assure my reader I could write a long treatise on the matter between Mr. Stoddart and myself; therefore, if he is not yet interested in such questions, let him be thankful to me for considering such a treatise out of place here. I will only say in brief, that I believe with all my heart that the true is the beautiful, and that nothing evil can be other than ugly. If it seems not so, it is in virtue of some good mingled with the evil, and not in the smallest degree in virtue of the evil.

I thought it was time for me to take my leave. But I could not bear to run away with the last word, as it were: so I said,

"You put plenty of poetry yourself into that voluntary you played last Sunday. I am so much obliged to you for it!"

"Oh! that fugue. You liked it, did you?"

"More than I can tell you."

"I am very glad."

"Do you know those two lines of Milton in which he describes such a performance on the organ?"

"No. Can you repeat them?"

" 'His volant touch,
Instinct through all proportions, low and high,
Fled and pursued transverse the resonant fugue.' "

"That is wonderfully fine. Thank you. That is better than my fugue by a good deal. You have cancelled the obligation."

"Do you think doing a good turn again is cancelling an obligation? I don't think an obligation can ever be *returned* in the sense of being got rid of. But I am being hypercritical."

"Not at all. — Shall I tell you what I was thinking of while playing that fugue?"

"I should like much to hear."

"I had been thinking, while you were preaching, of the many fancies men had worshipped for the truth; now following this, now following that; ever believing they were on the point of laying hold upon her, and going down to the grave empty-handed as they came."

"And empty-hearted, too?" I asked; but he went on without heeding me.

"And I saw a vision of multitudes following, following where nothing was to be seen, with arms outstretched in all directions, some clasping vacancy to their bosoms, some reaching on tiptoe over the heads of their neighbours, and some with hanging heads, and hands clasped behind their backs, retiring hopeless from the chase."

"Strange!" I said; "for I felt so full of hope while you played, that I never doubted it was hope you meant to express."

"So I do not doubt I did; for the multitude was full of hope, vain hope, to lay hold upon the truth. And you, being full of the main expression, and in sympathy with it, did not heed the undertones of disappointment, or the sighs of those who turned their backs on the chase. Just so it is in life."

"I am no musician," I returned, "to give you a musical counter to your picture. But I see a grave man tilling the ground in peace, and the form of Truth standing behind him, and folding her wings

closer and closer over and around him as he works
on at his day's labour."

"Very pretty," said Mr. Stoddart, and said no
more.

"Suppose," I went on, "that a person knows
that he has not laid hold on the truth, is that sufficient ground for his making any further assertion
than that he has not found it?"

"No. But if he has tried hard and has not
found *anything* that he can say is true, he cannot
help thinking that most likely there is no such
thing."

"Suppose," I said, "that nobody has found the
truth, is that sufficient ground for saying that nobody
ever will find it? or that there is no such thing as
truth to be found? Are the ages so nearly done that
no chance yet remains? Surely if God has made us
to desire the truth, He has got some truth to cast
into the gulf of that desire. Shall God create hunger
and no food? But possibly a man may be looking
the wrong way for it. You may be using the micro-
scope, when you ought to open both eyes and lift up
your head. Or a man may be finding some truth
which is feeding his soul, when he does not think
he is finding any. You know the *Fairy Queen*.
Think how long the Redcross Knight travelled with
the Lady Truth — Una, you know — without learning to believe in her; and how much longer still
without ever seeing her face. For my part, may God
give me strength to follow till I die. Only I will
venture to say this, that it is not by any agony of
the intellect that I expect to discover her."

Mr. Stoddart sat drumming silently with his fingers, a half-smile on his face, and his eyes raised at an angle of forty-five degrees. I felt that the enthusiasm with which I had spoken was thrown away upon him. But I was not going to be ashamed therefore. I would put some faith in his best nature.

"But does not," he said, gently lowering his eyes upon mine after a moment's pause — "does not your choice of a profession imply that you have not to give chase to a fleeting phantom? Do you not profess to have, and hold, and therefore teach the truth?"

"I profess only to have caught glimpses of her white garments, — those, I mean, of the abstract truth of which you speak. But I have seen that which is eternally beyond her: the ideal in the real, the living truth, not the truth that I can *think*, but the truth that thinks itself, that thinks me, that God has thought, yea, that God is, the truth *being* true to itself and to God and to man — Christ Jesus, my Lord, who knows, and feels, and does the truth. I have seen Him, and I am both content and unsatisfied. For in Him are hid all the treasures of wisdom and knowledge. Thomas à Kempis says: 'Cui æternum Verbum loquitur, ille a multis opinionibus expeditur.'" (He to whom the eternal Word speaks, is set free from a press of opinions.)

I rose, and held out my hand to Mr. Stoddart. He rose likewise, and took it kindly, conducted me to the room below, and ringing the bell, committed me to the care of the butler.

As I approached the gate, I met Jane Rogers coming back from the village. I stopped and spoke to her. Her eyes were very red.

"Nothing amiss at home, Jane?" I said.

"No, sir, thank you," answered Jane, and burst out crying.

"What is the matter, then? Is your——"

"Nothing's the matter with nobody, sir."

"Something is the matter with you."

"Yes, sir. But I'm quite well."

"I don't want to pry into your affairs; but if you think I can be of any use to you, mind you come to me."

"Thank you kindly, sir," said Jane; and, dropping a courtesy, walked on with her basket.

I went to her parents' cottage. As I came near the mill, the young miller was standing in the door with his eyes fixed on the ground, while the mill went on hopping behind him. But when he caught sight of me, he turned, and went in, as if he had not seen me.

"Has he been behaving ill to Jane?" thought I.

As he evidently wished to avoid me, I passed the mill without looking in at the door, as I was in the habit of doing, and went on to the cottage, where I lifted the latch, and walked in. Both the old people were there, and both looked troubled, though they welcomed me none the less kindly.

"I met Jane," I said, "and she looked unhappy; so I came on to hear what was the matter."

"You oughtn't to be troubled with our small affairs," said Mrs. Rogers.

"If the parson wants to know, why, the parson must be told," said Old Rogers, smiling cheerily, as if he at least would be relieved by telling me.

"I don't want to know," I said, "if you don't want to tell me. But can I be of any use?"

"I don't think you can, sir, — leastways, I'm afraid not," said the old woman.

"I am sorry to say, sir, that Master Brownrigg and his son has come to words about our Jane; and it's not agreeable to have folk's daughter quarrelled over in that way," said Old Rogers. "What'll be the upshot on it, I don't know, but it looks bad now. For the father he tells the son that if ever he hear of him saying one word to our Jane, out ov the mill he goes, as sure as his name's Dick. Now, it's rather a good chance, I think, to see what the young fellow's made of, sir. So I tells my old 'oman here; and so I told Jane. But neither on 'em seems to see the comfort of it somehow. But the New Testament do say a man shall leave father and mother, and cleave to his wife."

"But she ain't his wife yet," said Mrs. Rogers to her husband, whose drift was not yet evident.

"No more she can be, 'cept he leaves his father for her."

"And what'll become of them then, without the mill?"

"You and me never had no mill, old 'oman," said Rogers; "yet here we be, very nearly ripe now, — ain't us, wife?"

"Medlar-like, Old Rogers, I doubt, — rotten before we're ripe," replied his wife, quoting a more humorous than refined proverb.

"Nay, nay, old 'oman. Don't 'e say so. The Lord won't let us rot before we're ripe, anyhow. That I be sure on."

"But, anyhow, it's all very well to talk. Thou knows how to talk, Rogers. But how will it be when the children comes, and no mill?"

"To grind 'em in, old 'oman?"

Mrs. Rogers turned to me, who was listening with real interest, and much amusement.

"I wish you would speak a word to Old Rogers, sir. He never will speak as he's spoken to. He's always over merry, or over serious. He either takes me up short with a sermon, or he laughs me out of countenance that I don't know where to look."

Now I was pretty sure that Rogers's conduct was simple consistency, and that the difficulty arose from his always acting upon one or two of the plainest principles of truth and right; whereas his wife, good woman — for the bad, old leaven of the Pharisees could not rise much in her somehow — was always reminding him of certain precepts of behaviour to the oblivion of principles. "A bird in the hand," &c. — "Marry in haste," &c. — "When want comes in at the door, love flies out at the window," were amongst her favourite sayings; although not one of them was supported by her own experience. For instance, she had married in haste herself, and never, I believe, had once thought of repenting of it, although she had had far more than the requisite leisure for doing so. And many was the time that want had come in at her door, and the first thing it always did was to clip the wings of Love and make him less flighty, and more tender and serviceable. So I could not even pretend to read her husband a lecture.

"He's a curious man, Old Rogers," I said. "But as far as I can see, he's in the right, in the main. Isn't he now?"

"Oh, yes, I daresay. I think he's always right about the rights of the thing, you know. But a body may go too far that way. It won't do to starve, sir."

Strange confusion — or, ought I not rather to say? — ordinary and common-place confusion of ideas!

"I don't think," I said, "any one can go too far in the right way."

"That's just what I want my old 'oman to see, and I can't get it into her, sir. If a thing's right, it's right, and if a thing's wrong, why, wrong it is. The helm must either be to starboard or port, sir."

"But why talk of starving?" I said. "Can't Dick work? Who could think of starting that nonsense?"

"Why, my old 'oman here. She wants 'em to give it up and wait for better times. The fact is, she don't want to lose the girl."

"But she hasn't got her at home now."

"She can have her when she wants her, though

— leastways after a bit of warning. Whereas if
she was married, and the consequences a follerin' at
her heels, like a man-o'-war with her convoy, she
would find she was chartered for another port, she
would."

"Well, you see, sir, Rogers and me's not so
young as we once was, and we're likely to be
growing older every day. And if there's a difficulty
in the way of Jane's marriage, why, I take it as a
Godsend."

"How would you have liked such a Godsend,
Mrs. Rogers, when you were going to be married
to your sailor here? What would you have done?"

"Why, whatever he liked, to be sure. But then,
you see, Dick's not my Rogers."

"But your daughter thinks about him much in
the same way as you did about this dear old man
here when he was young."

"Young people may be in the wrong. *I* see no·
thing in Dick Brownrigg."

"But young people may be right sometimes, and
old people may be wrong sometimes."

"I can't be wrong about Rogers."

"No, but you may be wrong about Dick."

"Don't you trouble yourself about my old 'oman,
sir. She allus was awk'ard in stays, but she never
missed them yet. When she's said her say, round
she comes in the wind like a bird, sir."

"There's a good old man to stick up for your
old wife! Still I say, they may as well wait a bit.
It would be a pity to anger the old gentleman."

"What does the young man say to it?"

"Why, he says like a man, he can work for her as well's the mill, and he's ready, if she is."

"I am very glad to hear such a good account of him. I shall look in, and have a little chat with him. I always liked the look of him. Good morning, Mrs. Rogers."

"I'll see you across the stream, sir," said the old man, following me out of the house.

"You see, sir," he resumed, as soon as we were outside, "I'm always afeard of taking things out of the Lord's hands. It's the right way, surely, that when a man loves a woman, and has told her so, he should act like a man, and do as is right. And isn't that the Lord's way? And can't He give them what's good for them. Mayhap they won't love each other the less in the end if Dick has a little bit of the hard work that many a man that the Lord loved none the less has had before him. I wouldn't like to anger the old gentleman, as my wife says; but if I was Dick, I know what I would do. But dont 'e think hard of my wife, sir, for I believe there's a bit of pride in it. She's afeard of bein' supposed to catch at Richard Brownrigg, because he's above us, you know, sir. And I can't altogether blame her, only we ain't got to do with the look o' things, but with the things themselves."

"I understand you quite, and I'm very much of your mind. You can trust me to have a little chat with him, can't you?"

"That I can, sir."

Here we had come to the boundary of his garden —the busy stream that ran away as if it was scared

at the labour it had been compelled to go through,
and was now making the best of its speed back to
its mother-ocean, to tell sad tales of a world where
every little brook must do some work ere it gets
back to its rest.   I bade him good day, jumped
across it, and went into the mill, where Richard was
tying the mouth of a sack as gloomily as the brothers
of Joseph must have tied their sacks after his silver
cup had been found.

"Why did you turn away from me, as I passed
half-an-hour ago, Richard?" I said, cheerily.

"I beg your pardon, sir. I didn't think you
saw me."

"But supposing I hadn't? — But I won't tease
you. I know all about it. Can I do anything for
you?"

"No, sir. You can't move my father. It's no
use talking to him. He never hears a word anybody
says. He never hears a word you say o' Sundays,
sir. He won't even believe the *Mark Lane Express*
about the price of corn. It's no use talking to him,
sir."

"You wouldn't mind if I were to try?"

"No, sir. You can't make matters worse. No
more can you make them any better, sir."

"I don't say I shall talk to him; but I may try
it, if I find a fitting opportunity."

"He's always worse — more obstinate, that is,
when he's in a good temper. So you may choose
your opportunity wrong. But it's all the same. It
can make no difference."

"What are you going to do, then?"

"I would let him do his worst. But Jane doesn't like to go against her mother. I'm sure I can't think how she should side with my father against both of us. He never laid her under any such obligation, I'm sure."

"There may be more ways than one of accounting for that. You must mind, however, and not be too hard upon your father. You're quite right in holding fast to the girl; but mind that vexation does not make you unjust."

"I wish my mother were alive. She was the only one that ever could manage him. How she contrived to do it nobody could think; but manage him she did, somehow or other. There's not a husk of use in talking to *him*."

"I daresay he prides himself on not being moved by talk. But has he ever had a chance of knowing Jane — of seeing what kind of a girl she is?"

"He's seen her over and over."

"But seeing isn't always believing."

"It certainly isn't with him."

"If he could only know her! But don't you be too hard upon him. And don't do anything in a hurry. Give him a little time, you know. Mrs. Rogers won't interfere between you and Jane, I am pretty sure. But don't push matters till we see. Good-bye."

"Good-bye, and thank you kindly, sir. — Ain't I to see Jane in the meantime?"

"If I were you, I would make no difference. See her as often as you used, which I suppose was as often as you could. I don't think, I say, that

her mother will interfere.   Her father is all on your
side."

I called on Mr. Brownrigg; but, as his son had
forewarned me, I could making nothing of him.   He
didn't see, when the mill was his property, and Dick
was his son, why he shouldn't have his way with
them.   And he was going to have his way with
them.   His son might marry any lady in the land;
and he wasn't going to throw himself away that
way.

I will not weary my readers with the conversation we had together.   All my missiles of argument
were lost as it were in a bank of mud, the weight
and resistance of which they only increased.   My
experience in the attempt, however, did a little to
reconcile me to his going to sleep in church; for I
saw that it could make little difference whether he
was asleep or awake.   He, and not Mr. Stoddart in
his organ sentry-box, was the only person whom it
was absolutely impossible to preach to.   You might
preach *at* him; but *to* him? — no.

CHAPTER X.

My Christmas Party.

As Christmas Day drew nearer and nearer, my heart glowed with the more gladness; and the question came more and more pressingly — Could I not do something to make it more really a holiday of the Church for my parishioners? That most of them would have a little more enjoyment on it than they had had all the year through, I had ground to hope; but I wanted to connect this gladness — in their minds, I mean, for who could dissever them in fact? — with its source, the love of God, that love manifested unto men in the birth of the Human Babe, the Son of Man. But I would not interfere with the Christmas Day at home. I resolved to invite as many of my parishioners as would come, to spend Christmas Eve at the Vicarage.

I therefore had a notice to that purport affixed to the church door; and resolved to send out no personal invitations whatever, so that I might not give offence by accidental omission. The only person thrown into perplexity by this mode of proceeding was Mrs. Pearson.

"How many am I to provide for, sir?" she said, with an injured air.

"For as many as you ever saw in church at one time," I said. "And if there should be too much, why so much the better. It can go to make Christmas Day the merrier at some of the poorer houses."

She looked discomposed, for she was not of an easy temper. But she never *acted* from her temper; she only *looked* or *spoke* from it.

"I shall want help," she said, at length.

"As much as you like, Mrs. Pearson. I can trust you entirely."

Her face brightened; and the end showed that I had not trusted her amiss.

I was a little anxious about the result of the invitation — partly as indicating the amount of confidence my people placed in me. But although no one said a word to me about it beforehand except Old Rogers, as soon as the hour arrived, the people began to come. And the first I welcomed was Mr. Brownrigg.

I had had all the rooms on the ground-floor prepared for their reception. Tables of provision were set out in every one of them. My visitors had tea or coffee, with plenty of bread and butter, when they arrived; and the more solid supplies were reserved for a later part of the evening. I soon found myself with enough to do. But before long, I had a very efficient staff. For after having had occasion, once or twice, to mention something of my plans for the evening, I found my labours gradually diminish, and yet everything seemed to go right; the fact being that good Mr. Boulderstone, in one part, had cast himself into the middle of the flood, and stood there immovable both in face and person, turning its waters into the right channel, namely, towards the barn, which I had fitted up for their reception in a body; while in another quarter, namely, in the barn, Dr. Duncan was doing his best, and that was simply something first-rate, to entertain the people till all should be ready. From a kind of instinct these gentlemen had taken upon them to be my staff, almost without knowing it, and very grateful I was. I found, too, that they soon gathered some of the young and more active spirits about them, whom they employed in various ways for the good of the community.

When I came in and saw the goodly assemblage, for I had been busy receiving them in the house, I could not help rejoicing that my predecessor had been so fond of farming that he had rented land in the neighbourhood of the vicarage, and built this large barn, of which I could make a hall to entertain my friends. The night was frosty — the stars shining brilliantly overhead — so that, especially for country people, there was little danger in the short passage to be made to it from the house. But, if necessary, I resolved to have a covered-way built before next time. For how can a man be *the person* of a parish, if he never entertains his parishioners? And really, though it was lighted only with candles round the walls, and I had not been able to do much for the decoration of the place, I thought it looked very well, and my heart was glad that Christmas Eve — just as if the Babe had been coming again to us that same night. And is He not always coming to us afresh in every childlike feeling that awakes in the hearts of His people?

12*

I walked about amongst them, greeting them,
and greeted everywhere in turn with kind smiles
and hearty shakes of the hand. As often as I paused
in my communications for a moment, it was amusing
to watch Mr. Boulderstone's honest, though awkward
endeavours to be at ease with his inferiors; but Dr.
Duncan was just a sight worth seeing. Very tall
and very stately, he was talking now to this old
man, now to that young woman, and every face
glistened towards which he turned. There was no
condescension about him. He was as polite and
courteous to one as to another, and the smile that
every now and then lighted up his old face, was
genuine and sympathetic. No one could have known
by his behaviour that he was not at court. And I
thought — Surely even the contact with such a man
will do something to refine the taste of my people.
I felt more certain than ever that a free mingling of
all classes would do more than anything else towards
binding us all into a wise patriotic nation; would
tend to keep down that foolish emulation which
makes one class ape another from afar, like Ben
Jonson's *Fungoso*, "still lighting short a suit;" would
refine the roughness of the rude, and enable the
polished to see with what safety his just share in
public matters might be committed into the hands of
the honest workman. If we could once leave it to
each other to give what honour is due; knowing that
honour demanded is as worthless as insult unde-
served is hurtless! What has one to do to honour
himself? That is and can be no honour. When
one has learned to seek the honour that cometh from

God only, he will take the withholding of the honour
that comes from men very quietly indeed.

The only thing that disappointed me was, that
there was no one there to represent Oldcastle Hall.
But how could I have everything a success at once?
— And Catherine Weir was likewise absent.

After we had spent a while in pleasant talk, and
when I thought nearly all were with us, I got up on
a chair at the end of the barn and said: —

"Kind friends, — I am very grateful to you for
honouring my invitation as you have done. Permit
me to hope that this meeting will be the first of
many, and that from it may grow the yearly custom
in this parish of gathering in love and friendship
upon Christmas Eve. When God comes to man,
man looks round for his neighbour. When man departed from God in the Garden of Eden, the only
man in the world ceased to be the friend of the only
woman in the world; and, instead of seeking to bear
her burden, became her accuser to God, in whom he
saw only the Judge, unable to perceive that the infinite love of the Father had come to punish him in
tenderness and grace. But when God in Jesus
comes back to men, brothers and sisters spread forth
their arms to embrace each other, and so to embrace
Him. This is, when He is born again in our souls.
For, dear friends, what we all need is just to become little children like Him; to cease to be careful
about many things, and trust in Him, seeking only
that He should rule, and that we should be made
good like Him. What else is meant by 'Seek ye
first the kingdom of God and his righteousness, and

all these things shall be added unto you?' Instead
of doing so, we seek the things God has promised
to look after for us, and refuse to seek the thing He
wants us to seek — a thing that cannot be given
us, except we seek it. We profess to think Jesus
the grandest and most glorious of men, and yet
hardly care to be like Him; and so when we are
offered His Spirit, that is, His very nature within us,
for the asking, we will hardly take the trouble to
ask for it. But to-night, at least, let all unkind
thoughts, all hard judgments of one another, all
selfish desires after our own way, be put from us,
that we may welcome the Babe into our very bosoms;
that when He comes amongst us — for is He not
like a child still, meek and lowly of heart? — He
may not be troubled to find that we are quarrel-
some, and selfish, and unjust."

I came down from the chair, and Mr. Brownrigg
being the nearest of my guests and wide awake, for
he had been standing, and had indeed been listening to every word according to his ability, I shook
hands with him. And positively there was some
meaning in the grasp with which he returned mine.

I am not going to record all the proceedings of
the evening; but I think it may be interesting to
my readers to know something of how we spent it.
First of all, we sang a hymn about the Nativity.
And then I read an extract from a book of travels,
describing the interior of an Eastern cottage, probably much resembling the inn in which our Lord
was born, the stable being scarcely divided from the
rest of the house. For I felt that to open the inner

eyes even of the brain, enabling people to *see* in some measure the reality of the old lovely story, to help them to have what the Scotch philosophers call a true *conception* of the external conditions and circumstances of the events, might help to open the yet deeper spiritual eyes which alone can see the meaning and truth dwelling in and giving shape to the outward facts. And the extract was listened to with all the attention I could wish, except, at first, from some youngsters at the further end of the barn, who became, however, perfectly still as I proceeded.

After this followed conversation, during which I talked a good deal to Jane Rogers, paying her particular attention indeed, with the hope of a chance of bringing old Mr. Brownrigg and her together in some way.

"How is your mistress, Jane?" I said.

"Quite well, sir, thank you. I only wish she was here."

"I wish she were. But perhaps she will come next year."

"I think she will. I am almost sure she would have liked to come to-night; for I heard her say" ——

"I beg your pardon, Jane, for interrupting you; but I would rather not be told anything you may have happened to overhear," I said, in a low voice.

"Oh, sir!" returned Jane, blushing a dark crimson; "it wasn't anything particular."

"Still, if it was anything on which a wrong conjecture might be built" — I wanted to soften it to her — "it is better that one should not be told it. Thank you for your kind intention, though. And now, Jane," I said, "will you do me a favour?"

"That I will, sir, if I can."

"Sing that Christmas carol I heard you sing last night to your mother."

"I didn't know any one was listening, sir."

"I know you did not. I came to the door with your father, and we stood and listened."

She looked very frightened. But I would not have asked her had I not known that she could sing like a bird.

"I am afraid I shall make a fool of myself," she said.

"We should all be willing to run that risk for the sake of others," I answered.

"I will try then, sir."

So she sang, and her clear voice soon silenced the speech all round.

"Babe Jesus lay on Mary's lap;
  The sun shone in his hair;
And so it was she saw, mayhap,
  The crown already there.

"For she sang: 'Sleep on, my little King!
  Bad Herod dares not come;
Before Thee, sleeping, holy thing,
  Wild winds would soon be dumb.

"'I kiss Thy hands, I kiss Thy feet,
  My King, so long desired;
Thy hands shall never be soil'd, my sweet,
  Thy feet shall never be tired.

> "'For Thou art the King of men, my son;
> Thy crown I see it plain;
> And men shall worship Thee, every one,
> And cry, Glory! Amen.'
>
> "Babe Jesus open'd his eyes so wide!
> At Mary look'd her Lord.
> And Mary stinted her song and sigh'd.
> Babe Jesus said never a word."

When Jane had done singing, I asked her where she had learned the carol; and she answered. —

"My mistress gave it me. There was a picture to it of the Baby on his mother's knee."

"I never saw it," I said. "Where did you get the tune?"

"I thought it would go with a tune I knew; and I tried it, and it did. But I was not fit to sing to you, sir."

"You must have quite a gift of song, Jane!" I said.

"My father and mother can both sing."

Mr. Brownrigg was seated on the other side of me, and had apparently listened with some interest. His face was ten degrees less stupid than it usually was. I fancied I saw even a glimmer of some satisfaction in it. I turned to Old Rogers.

"Sing us a song, Old Rogers," I said.

"I'm no canary at that, sir; and besides, my singing days be over. I advise you to ask Dr. Duncan there. He *can* sing."

I rose and said to the assembly:

"My friends, if I did not think God was pleased to see us enjoying ourselves, I should have no heart

for it myself. I am going to ask our dear friend
Dr. Duncan to give us a song. — If you please,
Dr. Duncan."

"I am very nearly too old," said the doctor;
"but I will try."

His voice was certainly a little feeble; but the
song was not much the worse for it. And a more
suitable one for all the company he could hardly
have pitched upon.

> "There is a plough that has no share,
> But a coulter that parteth keen and fair.
> But the furrows they rise
> To a terrible size,
> Or ever the plough hath touch'd them there.
> 'Gainst horses and plough in wrath they shake:
> The horses are fierce; but the plough will break.
>
> "And the seed that is dropt in those furrows of fear,
> Will lift to the sun neither blade nor ear.
> Down it drops plumb,
> Where no spring times come;
> And here there needeth no harrowing gear:
> Wheat nor poppy nor any leaf
> Will cover this naked ground of grief.
>
> "But a harvest-day will come at last
> When the watery winter all is past;
> The waves so gray
> Will be shorn away
> By the angels' sickles keen and fast;
> And the buried harvest of the sea
> Stored in the barns of eternity."

Genuine applause followed the good doctor's
song. I turned to Miss Boulderstone, from whom I
had borrowed a piano, and asked her to play a
country dance for us. But first I said — not getting up on a chair this time: —

"Some people think it is not proper for a clergyman to dance. I mean to assert my freedom from any such law. If our Lord chose to represent, in His parable of the Prodigal Son, the joy in Heaven over a repentant sinner by the figure of 'music and dancing,' I will hearken to Him rather than to men, be they as good as they may."

For I had long thought that the way to make indifferent things bad, was for good people not to do them.

And so saying, I stepped up to Jane Rogers, and asked her to dance with me. She blushed so dreadfully that, for a moment, I was almost sorry I had asked her. But she put her hand in mine at once; and if she was a little clumsy, she yet danced very naturally, and I had the satisfaction of feeling that I had an honest girl near me, who I knew was friendly to me in her heart.

But to see the faces of the people! While I had been talking, Old Rogers had been drinking in every word. To him it was milk and strong meat in one. But now his face shone with a father's gratification besides. And Richard's face was glowing too. Even old Brownrigg looked with a curious interest upon us, I thought.

Meantime Dr. Duncan was dancing with one of his own patients, old Mrs. Trotter, to whose wants he ministered far more from his table than his surgery. I have known that man, hearing of a case of want from his servant, send the fowl he was about to dine upon, untouched, to those whose necessity was greater than his.

And Mr. Boulderstone had taken out old Mrs.
Rogers; and young Brownrigg had taken Mary Weir.
Thomas Weir did not dance at all, but looked on
kindly.

"Why don't you dance, Old Rogers?" I said, as
I placed his daughter in a seat beside him.

"Did your honour ever see an elephant go up
the futtock-shrouds?"

"No. I never did."

"I thought you must, sir, to ask me why I don't
dance. You won't take my fun ill, sir? I'm an
old man-o'-war's man, you know, sir."

"I should have thought, Rogers, that you would
have known better by this time, than make such an
apology to *me*."

"God bless you, sir. An old man's safe with
you — or a young lass, either, sir," he added, turning with a smile to his daughter.

I turned, and addressed Mr. Boulderstone.

"I am greatly obliged to you, Mr. Boulderstone,
for the help you have given me this evening. I've
seen you talking to everybody, just as if you had to
entertain them all."

"I hope I haven't taken too much upon me. But
the fact is, somehow or other, I don't know how, I
got into the spirit of it."

"You got into the spirit of it because you wanted
to help me, and I thank you heartily."

"Well, I thought it wasn't a time to mind one's
peas and cues exactly. And really it's wonderful
how one gets on without them. I hate formality
myself."

The dear fellow was the most formal man I had
ever met.

"Why don't you dance, Mr. Brownrigg?"

"Who'd care to dance with me, sir? I don't
care to dance with an old woman; and a young
woman won't care to dance with me."

"I'll find you a partner, if you will put yourself
in my hands."

"I don't mind trusting myself to you, sir."

So I led him to Jane Rogers. She stood up in
respectful awe before the master of her destiny.
There were signs of calcitration in the churchwarden,
when he perceived whither I was leading him. But
when he saw the girl stand trembling before him,
whether it was that he was flattered by the signs of
his own power, accepting them as homage, or that
his hard heart actually softened a little, I cannot
tell, but, after just a perceptible hesitation, he said:

"Come along, my lass, and let's have a hop
together."

She obeyed very sweetly.

"Don't be too shy," I whispered to her as she
passed me.

And the churchwarden danced very heartily with
the lady's-maid.

I then asked him to take her into the house,
and give her something to eat in return for her
song. He yielded somewhat awkwardly, and what
passed between them I do not know. But when
they returned, she seemed less frightened at him
than when she heard me make the proposal. And

when the company was parting, I heard him take
leave of her with the words —

"Give us a kiss, my girl, and let bygones be
bygones."

Which kiss I heard with delight. For had I
not been a peacemaker in this matter? And had I
not then a right to feel blessed? — But the understanding was brought about simply by making the
people meet — compelling them, as it were, to
know something of each other really. Hitherto this
girl had been a mere name, or phantom at best, to
her lover's father; and it was easy for him to treat
her as such, that is, as a mere fancy of his son's.
The idea of her had passed through his mind; but
with what vividness any idea, notion, or conception
could be present to him, my readers must judge
from my description of him. So that obstinacy was
a ridiculously easy accomplishment to him. For he
never had any notion of the matter to which he was
opposed — only of that which he favoured. It is
very easy indeed for such people to stick to their
point.

But I took care that we should have dancing in
moderation. It would not do for people either to
get weary with recreation, or excited with what was
not worthy of producing such an effect. Indeed we
had only six country dances during the evening.
That was all. And between the dances I read two
or three of Wordsworth's ballads to them, and they
listened even with more interest than I had been
able to hope for. The fact was that the happy and
free-hearted mood they were in "enabled the judg-

ment." I wish one knew always by what musical spell to produce the right mood for receiving and reflecting a matter as it really is. Every true poem carries this spell with it in its own music, which it sends out before it as a harbinger, or properly a *herberger*, to prepare a harbour or lodging for it. But then it needs a quiet mood first of all, to let this music be listened to.

For I thought with myself, if I could get them to like poetry and beautiful things in words, it would not only do them good, but help them to see what is in the Bible, and therefore to love it more. For. I never could believe that a man who did not find God in other places as well as in the Bible ever found Him there at all. And I always thought, that to find God in other books enabled us to see clearly that he was *more* in the Bible than in any other book, or all other books put together.

After supper we had a little more singing. And to my satisfaction nothing came to my eyes or ears, during the whole evening, that was undignified or ill-bred. Of course, I knew that many of them must have two behaviours, and that now they were on their good behaviour. But I thought the oftener such were put on their good behaviour, giving them the opportunity of finding out how nice it was, the better. It might make them ashamed of the other at last

There were many little bits of conversation I overheard, which I should like to give my readers; but I cannot dwell longer upon this part of my Annals. Especially I should have enjoyed recording one piece of talk, in which Old Rogers was evidently

trying to move a more directly religious feeling in
the mind of Dr. Duncan.   I thought I could see
that *the* difficulty with the noble old gentleman was
one of expression.   But after all the old fore-mast-
man was a seer of the Kingdom; and the other,
with all his refinement, and education, and goodness
too, was but a child in it.

Before we parted, I gave to each of my guests
a sheet of Christmas Carols, gathered from the older
portions of our literature.   For most of the modern
hymns are to my mind neither milk nor meat —
mere wretched imitations.   There were a few curious
words and idioms in these, but I thought it better
to leave them as they were; for they might set
them inquiring, and give me an opportunity of interesting them further, some time or other, in the
history of a word; for, in their ups and downs of
fortune, words fare very much like human beings.

And here is my sheet of Carols: —

AN HYMNE OF HEAVENLY LOVE.

O blessed Well of Love! O Floure of Grace!
O glorious Morning-Starre! O Lampe of Light!
Most lively image of thy Father's face,
Eternal King of Glorie, Lord of Might,
Meeke Lambe of God, before all worlds behight,
How can we Thee requite for all this good?
Or what can prize that Thy most precious blood?

Yet nought Thou ask'st in lieu of all this love,
But love of us, for guerdon of Thy paine:
Ay me! what can us lesse than that behove?
Had He required life of us againe,
Had it beene wrong to ask His owne with gaine?
He gave us life, He it restored lost;
Then life were least, that us so little cost.

But He our life hath left unto us free,
Free that was thrall, and blessed that was bann'd;
Ne ought demaunds but that we loving boe,
As He himselfe hath lov'd us afore-hand,
And bound therto with an eternall band,
Him first to love that us so dearely bought,
And next our brethren, to His image wrought.

Him first to love great right and reason is,
Who first to us our life and being gave,
And after, when we fared bad amisse,
Us wretches from the second death did save;
And last, the food of life, which now we have,
Even He Himselfe, in His dear sacrament,
To feede our hungry soules, unto us lent.

Then next, to love our brethren, that were made
Of that selfe mould, and that self Maker's hand,
That we, and to the same againe shall fade,
Where they shall have like heritage of land,
However here on higher steps we stand,
Which also were with selfe-same price redeemed
That we, however of us light esteemed.

Then rouze thy selfe, O Earth! out of thy soyle,
In which thou wallowest like to filthy swyne,
And doest thy mynd in durty pleasures moyle,
Unmindfull of that dearest Lord of thyne;
Lift up to Him thy heavie clouded eyne,
That thou this soveraine bountie mayst behold,
And read, through love, His mercies manifold.

Beginne from first, where He encradled was
In simple cratch, wrapt in a wad of hay,
Betweene the toylfull oxe and humble asse,
And in what rags, and in how base array,
The glory of our heavenly riches lay,
When Him the silly shepheards came to see,
Whom greatest princes sought on lowest knee.

From thence reade on the storie of His life,
His humble carriage, His unfaulty wayes,
His cancred foes, His fights, His toyle, His strife,
His paines, His povertie, His sharpe assayes,
Through which He past His miserable dayes,
Offending noue, and doing good to all,
Yet being malist both by great and small.

With all thy hart, with all thy soule and mind,
Thou must Him love, and His beheasts embrace;
All other loves, with which the world doth blind
Weake fancies, and stirre up affections base,
Thou must renounce and utterly displace,
And give thy selfe unto Him full and free,
That full and freely gave Himselfe to thee.

Then shall thy ravisht soul inspired bee
With heavenly thoughts farre above humane skil,
And thy bright radiant eyes shall plainly see
Th' idee of His pure glorie present still
Before thy face, that all thy spirits shall fill
With sweete enragement of celestial love,
Kindled through sight of those faire things above.

SPENSER.

NEW PRINCE, NEW POMP.

Behold a silly tender Babe,
  In freezing winter night,
In homely manger trembling lies;
  Alas! a piteous sight.

The inns are full, no man will yield
  This little Pilgrim bed;
But forced He is with silly beasts
  In crib to shroud His head.

Despise Him not for lying there,
  First what He is inquire;
An orient pearl is often found
  In depth of dirty mire.

Weigh not His crib, His wooden dish,
  Nor beast that by Him feed;
Weigh not His mother's poor attire,
  Nor Joseph's simple weed.

This stable is a Prince's court,
  The crib His chair of state;
The beasts are parcel of His pomp,
  The wooden dish His plate.

The persons in that poor attire
　　His royal liveries wear;
The Prince himself is come from heaven —
　　This pomp is praised there.

With joy approach, O Christian wight!
　　Do homage to thy King;
And highly praise this humble pomp
　　Which He from heaven doth bring.
　　　　　　　　　　　　SOUTHWELL.

A DIALOGUE BETWEEN THREE SHEPHERDS.

1. Where is this blessed Babe
　　　　That hath made
　All the world so full of joy
　　　　And expectation;
　That glorious Boy
　　　　That crowns each nation
　With a triumphant wreath of blessedness?

2. Where should He be but in the throng,
　　　　　　　And among
　His angel-ministers, that sing
　　　　　　　And take wing
　Just as may echo to His voice,
　　　　　　　And rejoice,
　When wing and tongue and all
　May so procure their happiness?

3. But He hath other waiters now.
　　　　　　　A poor cow,
　An ox and mule stand and behold,
　　　　　　　And wonder,
　That a stable should enfold
　　　　　　　Him that can thunder.
Chorus.　O what a gracious God have we!
　How good! How great! Even as our misery.
　　　　　　　　　　　　JEREMY TAYLOR.

13*

A SONG OF PRAISE FOR THE BIRTH OF CHRIST.

Away, dark thoughts; awake, my joy;
  Awake, my glory; sing;
Sing songs to celebrate the birth
  Of *Jacob's* God and King.
O happy night, that brought forth light,
  Which makes the blind to see!
The day spring from on high came down
  To cheer and visit thee.

The wakeful shepherds, near their flocks,
  Were watchful for the morn;
But better news from heaven was brought,
  Your Saviour Christ is born.
In *Bethlem*-town the infant lies,
  Within a place obscure,
O little *Bethlem*, poor in walls,
  But rich in furniture!

Since heaven is now come down to earth,
  Hither the angels fly!
Hark, how the heavenly choir doth sing
  Glory to God on High!
The news is spread, the church is glad,
  Simeon, o'ercome with joy,
Sings with the infant in his arms,
  Now let thy servant die.

Wise men from far beheld the star,
  Which was their faithful guide,
Until it pointed forth the Babe,
  And Him they glorified.
Do heaven and earth rejoice and sing —
  Shall we our Christ deny?
He's born for us, and we for Him:
  Glory to God on High.

JOHN MASON.

CHAPTER XI.

Sermon on God and Mammon.

I NEVER asked questions about the private affairs of any of my parishioners, except of themselves individually upon occasion of their asking me for advice, and some consequent necessity for knowing more than they told me. Hence, I believe, they became the more willing that I should know. But I heard a good many things from others, notwithstanding, for I could not be constantly closing the lips of the communicative as I had done those of Jane Rogers. And amongst other things, I learned that Miss Oldcastle went most Sundays to the neighbouring town of Addicehead to church. Now I had often heard of the ability of the rector, and although I had never met him, was prepared to find him a cultivated if not an original man. Still, if I must be honest, which I hope I must, I confess that I heard the news with a pang, in analysing which I discovered the chief component to be jealousy. It was no use asking myself why I should be jealous: there the ugly thing was. So I went and told God I was ashamed, and begged Him to deliver me from the evil, because His was the kingdom and the power and the glory. And He took my part against myself, for He waits to be gracious. Perhaps the reader may, however, suspect a deeper cause for this

feeling (to which I would rather not give the true
name again) than a merely professional one.

But there was one stray sheep of my flock that
appeared in church for the first time on the morning
of Christmas Day — Catherine Weir.   She did not
sit beside her father, but in the most shadowy corner
of the church — near the organ loft, however.   She
could have seen her father if she had looked up, but
she kept her eyes down the whole time, and never
even lifted them to me.   The spot on one cheek was
much brighter than that on the other, and made her
look very ill.

I prayed to our God to grant me the honour' of
speaking a true word to them all; which honour I
thought I was right in asking, because the Lord re-
proached the Pharisees for not seeking the honour
that cometh from God.   Perhaps I may have put a
wrong interpretation on the passage.   It is, however,
a joy to think that He will not give you a stone,
even if you should take it for a loaf and ask for it
as such.   Nor is He, like the scribes, lying in wait
to catch poor erring men in their words or their
prayers, however mistaken they may be.

I took my text from the Sermon on the Mount.
And as the magazine for which these Annals were
first written was intended chiefly for Sunday reading,
I wrote my sermon just as if I were preaching it to
my unseen readers as I spoke it to my present
parishioners.   And here it is now: —

The Gospel according to St. Matthew, the sixth

chapter, and part of the twenty-fourth and twenty-fifth verses: —

"'*Ye cannot serve God and Mammon. Therefore I say unto you, Take no thought for your life.*'

"When the Child whose birth we celebrate with glad hearts this day, grew up to be a man, He said this.   Did He mean it? — He never said what He did not mean. Did He mean it wholly? — He meant it far beyond what the words could convey. He meant it altogether and entirely.   When people do not understand what the Lord says, when it seems to them that His advice is impracticable, instead of searching deeper for a meaning which will be evidently true and wise, they comfort themselves by thinking He could not have meant it altogether, and so leave it. Or they think that if He did mean it, He could not expect them to carry it out.   And in the fact that they could not do it perfectly if they were to try, they take refuge from the duty of trying to do it at all; or, oftener, they do not think about it at all as anything that in the least concerns them.   The Son of our Father in heaven may have become a child, may have led the one life which belongs to every man to lead, may have suffered because we are sinners, may have died for our sakes, doing the will of His Father in heaven, and yet we have nothing to do with the words He spoke out of the midst of His true, perfect knowledge, feeling, and action! Is it not strange that it should be so? Let it not be so with us this day.   Let us seek to find out what our Lord means, that we may do it; trying and failing and trying again — verily to be victorious at last —

what matter *when*, so long as we are trying, and so coming nearer to our end!

"*Mammon*, you know, means *riches*. Now, riches are meant to be the slave — not even the servant of man, and not to be the master. If a man serve his own servant, or in a word any one who has no just claim to be his master, he is a slave. But here he serves his own slave. On the other hand, to serve God, the source of our being, our own glorious Father, is freedom; in fact, is the only way to get rid of all bondage. So you see plainly enough that a man cannot serve God and Mammon. For how can a slave of his own slave be the servant of the God of freedom, of Him who can have no one to serve Him but a free man? His service is freedom. Do not, I pray you, make any confusion between service and slavery. To serve is the highest, noblest calling in creation. For even the Son of man came not to be ministered unto, but to minister, yea, with Himself.

"But how can a man *serve* riches? Why, when he says to riches, 'Ye are my good.' When he feels he cannot be happy without them. When he puts forth the energies of his nature to get them. When he schemes and dreams and lies awake about them. When he will not give to his neighbour for fear of becoming poor himself. When he wants to have more, and to know he has more, than he can need. When he wants to leave money behind him, not for the sake of his children or relatives, but for the name of the wealth. When he leaves his money, not to those who *need* it, even of his relations, but

to those who are rich like himself, making them yet
more of slaves to the overgrown monster they worship
for his size. When he honours those who have money
because they have money, irrespective of their character; or when he honours in a rich man what he
would not honour in a poor man. Then is he the
slave of Mammon. Still more is he Mammon's slave
when his devotion to his god makes him oppressive
to those over whom his wealth gives him power; or
when he becomes unjust in order to add to his
stores. — How will it be with such a man when on
a sudden he finds that the world has vanished, and
he is alone with God? There lies the body in which
he used to live, whose poor necessities first made
money of value to him, but with which itself and
its fictitious value are both left behind. He cannot
now even try to bribe God with a cheque. The
angels will not bow down to him because his property, as set forth in his will, takes five or six
figures to express its amount. It makes no difference
to them that he has lost it, though; for they never
respected him. And the poor souls of Hades, who
envied him the wealth they had lost before, rise up
as one man to welcome him, not for love of him —
no worshipper of Mammon loves another — but rejoicing in the mischief that has befallen him, and
saying, "Art thou also become one of us?" And
Lazarus in Abraham's bosom, however sorry he may
be for him, however grateful he may feel to him for
the broken victuals and the penny, cannot with one
drop of the water of Paradise cool that man's parched
tongue.

"Alas, poor Dives! poor server of Mammon, whose vile god can pretend to deliver him no longer! Or rather, for the blockish god never pretended anything — it was the man's own doing — Alas for the Mammon-worshipper! he can no longer deceive himself in his riches. And so even in hell he is something nobler than he was on earth; for he worships his riches no longer. He cannot. He curses them.

"Terrible things to say on Christmas Day! But if Christmas Day teaches us anything, it teaches us to worship God and not Mammon; to worship spirit and not matter; to worship love and not power.

"Do I now hear any of my friends saying in their hearts: Let the rich take that! It does not apply to us. We are poor enough? Ah, my friends, I have known a light-hearted, liberal rich man lose his riches, and be liberal and light-hearted still. I knew a rich lady once, in giving a large gift of money to a poor man, say apologetically, "I hope it is no disgrace in me to be rich, as it is none in you to be poor." It is not the being rich that is wrong, but the serving of riches, instead of making them serve your neighbour and yourself — your neighbour for this life, yourself for the everlasting habitations. God knows it is hard for the rich man to enter into the kingdom of heaven; but the rich man does sometimes enter in; for God hath made it possible. And the greater the victory, when it is the rich man that overcometh the world. It is easier for the poor man to enter into the kingdom, yet many of the poor have failed to enter in, and the greater

is the disgrace of their defeat. For the poor have
more done for them, as far as outward things go,
in the way of salvation than the rich, and, have a
beatitude all to themselves besides. For in the
making of this world as a school of salvation, the
poor, as the necessary majority, have been more
regarded than the rich. Do not think, my poor
friend, that God will let you off. He lets nobody
off. You, too, must pay the uttermost farthing. He
loves you too well to let you serve Mammon a whit
more than your rich neighbour. 'Serve Mammon!'
do you say? 'How can I serve Mammon? I have
no Mammon to serve.' — Would you like to have
riches a moment sooner than God gives them?
Would you serve Mammon if you had him? —
'Who can tell?' do you answer? 'Leave those
questions till I am tried.' But is there no bitterness
in the tone of that response? Does it not mean, 'It
will be a long time before I have a chance of trying
that?' — But I am not driven to such questions for
the chance of convicting some of you of Mammon-
worship. Let us look to the text. Read it again.

"'*Ye cannot serve God and Mammon. Therefore I
say unto you, Take no thought for your life.*'

"Why are you to take no thought? Because
you cannot serve God and Mammon. Is taking
thought, then, a serving of Mammon? Clearly. —
Where are you now, poor man? Brooding over the
frost? Will it harden the ground so that the God
of the sparrows cannot find food for His son? Where
are you now, poor woman? Sleepless over the
empty cupboard and to-morrow's dinner? 'It is be-

cause we have no bread?' do you answer? Have
you forgotten the five loaves among the five thousand,
and the fragments that were left? Or do you know
nothing of your Father in heaven, who clothes the
lilies and feeds the birds? O ye of little faith! O
ye poor-spirited Mammon-worshippers! who worship
him not even because he has given you anything,
but in the hope that he may some future day be-
nignantly regard you. But I may be too hard upon
you. I know well that our Father sees a great
difference between the man who is anxious about his
children's dinner, or even about his own, and the
man who is only anxious to add another ten thousand
to his much goods laid up for many years. But you
ought to find it easy to trust in God for such a
matter as your daily bread, whereas no man can by
any possibility trust in God for ten thousand pounds.
The former need is a God-ordained necessity; the
latter desire a man-devised appetite at best — possibly swinish greed. Tell me, do you long to be
rich? Then you worship Mammon. Tell me, do
you think you would feel safer if you had money
in the bank? Then you are Mammon-worshippers;
for you would trust the barn of the rich man rather
than the God who makes the corn to grow. Do you
say — 'What shall we eat? and what shall we drink?
and wherewithal shall we be clothed?' Are ye thus
of doubtful mind? — Then you are Mammon-worshippers.

"But how is the work of the world to be done
if we take no thought? — We are nowhere told not
to take thought. We *must* take thought. The question

is — What are we to take or not to take thought
about? By some who do not know God, little work
would be done if they were not driven by anxiety
of some kind. But you, friends, are you content to
go with the nations of the earth, or do you seek a
better way — *the* way that the Father of the nations
would have you walk in?

"*What* then are we to take thought about? Why,
about our work. What are we not to take thought
about? Why, about our life. The one is our business: the other is God's. But you turn it the other
way. You take no thought of earnestness about the
doing of your duty; but you take thought of care
lest God should not fulfil His part in the goings on
of the world. A man's business is just to do his
duty: God takes upon Himself the feeding and the
clothing. Will the work of the world be neglected
if a man thinks of his work, his duty, God's will to
be done, instead of what he is to eat, what he is to
drink, and wherewithal he is to be clothed? And
remember all the needs of the world come back to
these three. You will allow, I think, that the work
of the world will be only so much the better done;
that the very means of procuring the raiment or the
food will be the more thoroughly used. What, then,
is the only region on which the doubt can settle?
Why, God. He alone remains to be doubted. Shall
it be so with you? Shall the Son of man, the baby
now born, and for ever with us, find no faith in
you? Ah, my poor friend, who canst not trust in
God — I was going to say you *deserve* — but what
do I know of you to condemn and judge you? — I

was going to say, you deserve to be treated like the
child who frets and complains because his mother
holds him on her knee and feeds him mouthful by
mouthful with her own loving hand.   I meant —
you deserve to have your own way for a while; to
be set down, and told to help yourself, and see what
it will come to; to have your mother open the cup-
board-door for you, and leave you alone to your
pleasures. Alas! poor child! When the sweets begin
to pall, and the twilight begins to come duskily into
the chamber, and you look about all at once and see
no mother, how will your cupboard comfort you
then?   Ask it for a smile, for a stroke of the gentle
hand, for a word of love.   All the full-fed Mammon
can give you is what your mother would have given
you without the consequent loathing, with the light
of her countenance upon it all, and the arm of her
love around you. — And this is what God does
sometimes, I think, with the Mammon-worshippers
amongst the poor.   He says to them, Take your
Mammon, and see what he is worth.   Ah, friends,
the children of God can never be happy serving
other than Him.   The prodigal might fill his belly
with riotous living or with the husks that the swine
ate.   It was all one, so long as he was not with his
father.   His soul was wretched.   So would you be
if you had wealth, for I fear you would only be
worse Mammon-worshippers than now, and might
well have to thank God for the misery of any swine-
trough that could bring you to your senses.

"But we do see people die of starvation sometimes? — Yes.   But if you did your work in God's

name and left the rest to Him, that would not trouble
you. You would say, If it be God's will that I
should starve, I can starve as well as another. And
your mind would be at ease. 'Thou wilt keep him
in perfect peace whose mind is stayed upon Thee,
because he trusteth in Thee.' Of that I am sure. It
may be good for you to go hungry and bare-foot;
but it must be utter death to have no faith in God.
It is not, however, in God's way of things that the
man who does his work shall not live by it. We do
not know why here and there a man may be left to
die of hunger, but I do believe that they who wait
upon the Lord shall not lack any good. What it
may be good to deprive a man of till he knows and
acknowledges whence it comes, it may be still better
to give him when he has learned that every good
and every perfect gift is from above, and cometh
down from the Father of lights.

"I *should* like to know a man who just minded
his duty and troubled himself about nothing; who
did his own work and did not interfere with God's.
How nobly he would work — working not for reward,
but because it was the will of God! How happily
he would receive his food and clothing, receiving
them as the gifts of God! What peace would be
his! What a sober gaiety! How hearty and in-
fectious his laughter! What a friend he would be!
How sweet his sympathy! And his mind would be
so clear he would understand everything. His eye
being single, his whole body would be full of light.
No fear of his ever doing a mean thing. He would
die in a ditch rather. It is this fear of want that

makes men do mean things. They are afraid to part
with their precious lord — Mammon. He gives no
safety against such a fear.   One of the richest men
in England is haunted with the dread of the workhouse.   This man whom I should like to know,
would be sure that God would have him liberal,
and he would be what God would have him. Riches
are not in the least necessary to that.   Witness our
Lord's admiration of the poor widow with her great
farthing.

"But I think I hear my troubled friend who
does not love money, and yet cannot trust in God
out and out, though she fain would, — I think I
hear her say, 'I believe I could trust Him for myself, or at least I should be ready to dare the worst
for His sake; but my children — it is the thought of
my children that is too much for me.' Ah, woman!
she whom the Saviour praised so pleasedly, was one
who trusted Him for her daughter. What an honour
she had! 'Be it unto thee even as thou wilt.' Do
you think you love your children better than He
who made them? Is not your love what it is because He put it into your heart first? Have not you
often been cross with them? Sometimes unjust to
them?   Whence came the returning love that rose
from unknown depths in your being, and swept
away the anger and the injustice? You did not
create that love.   Probably you were not good
enough to send for it by prayer. But it came. God
sent it. He makes you love your children; be sorry
when you have been cross with them; ashamed when
you have been unjust to them; and yet you won't

trust Him to give them food and clothes! Depend
upon it, if. He ever refuses to give them food and
clothes, and you knew all about it, the why and the
wherefore, you would not dare to. give them food or
clothes either.   He loves them a thousand times
better than you do — be sure of that — and feels
for their sufferings, too, when He cannot give them
just what he would like to give them — cannot for
their good, I mean.

"But as your mistrust will go further, I can go
further to meet it. You will say, 'Ah! yes' — in
your feeling, I mean, not in words, — you will say,
'Ah! yes — food and clothing of a sort! Enough to
keep life in and too much cold out! But I want
my children to have plenty of *good* food, and *nice*
clothes.'

"Faithless mother! Consider the birds of the air.
They have so much that at least they can sing!
Consider the lilies — they were red lilies, those.
Would you not trust Him who delights in glorious
colours — more at least than you, or He would
never have created them and made us to delight in
them? I do not say that your children shall be
clothed in scarlet and fine linen; but if not, it is not
because God despises scarlet and fine linen or does
not love your children. He loves them, I say, too
much to give them everything all at once. But He
would make them such that they may have everything without being the worse; and with being the
better for it. And if you cannot trust Him yet, it
begins to be a shame, I think.   .

"It has been well said that no man ever sank

under the burden of the day. It is when to-morrow's burden is added to the burden of to-day, that the weight is more than a man can bear. Never load yourselves so, my friends. If you find yourselves so loaded, at least remember this: it is your own doing, not God's. He begs you to leave the future to Him, and mind the present. What more or what else could He do to take the burden off you? Nothing else would do it. Money in the bank wouldn't do it. He cannot do to-morrow's business for you beforehand to save you from fear about it. That would derange everything. What else is there but to tell you to trust in Him, irrespective of the fact that nothing else but such trust can put our heart at peace, from the very nature of our relation to Him as well as the fact that we need these things. We think that we come nearer to God than the lower animals do by our foresight. But there is another side to it. We are like to Him with whom there is no past or future, with whom a day is as a thousand years, and a thousand years as one day, when we live with large bright spiritual eyes, doing our work in the great present, leaving both past and future to Him to whom they are ever present, and fearing nothing, because He is in our future, as much as He is in our past, as much as, and far more than, we can feel Him to be in our present. Partakers thus of the divine nature, resting in that perfect All-in-all in whom our nature is eternal too, we walk without fear, full of hope and courage and strength to do His will, waiting for the endless good which He is always giving as fast as He can get us able to take

it in. Would not this be to be more of gods than
Satan promised to Eve? To live carelessly-divine,
duty-doing, fearless, loving, self-forgetting lives — is
not that more than to know both good and evil —
lives in which the good, like Aaron's rod, has swallowed up the evil, and turned it into good? For
pain and hunger are evils; but if faith in God swal-
lows them up, do they not so turn into good? I say
they do. And I am glad to believe that I am not
alone in my parish in this conviction. · I have never
been too hungry, but I have had trouble which I
would gladly have exchanged for hunger and cold
and weariness. Some of you have known hunger
and cold and weariness. Do you not join with me
to say: It is well, and better than well — whatever
helps us to know the love of Him who is our God?

"But there *has been* just one man who has acted
thus. And it is His Spirit in our hearts that makes
us desire to know or to be another such — who
would do the will of God for God, and let God do
God's will for Him. For His will is all. And this
man is the baby whose birth we celebrate this day.
Was this a condition to choose — that of a baby —
by one who thought it part of a man's high calling
to take care of the morrow? Did He not thus cast
the whole matter at once upon the hands and heart
of His Father? Sufficient unto the baby's day is
the need thereof; he toils not, neither does he spin,
and yet he is fed and clothed, and loved, and rejoiced in. Do you remind me that sometimes even
his mother forgets him — a mother, most likely, to
whose self-indulgence or weakness the child owes his

14*

birth as hers? Ah! but he is not therefore forgotten,
however like it things may look to our half-seeing
eyes, by his Father in heaven.   One of the highest
benefits we can reap from understanding the way of
God with ourselves is, that we become able thus to
trust Him for others with whom we do not understand His ways.

"But let us look at what will be more easily
shown — how, namely, He did the will of His Father,
and took no thought for the morrow after He became
a man.   Remember how He forsook His trade when
the time came for Him to preach.   Preaching was
not a profession then.   There were no monasteries,
or vicarages, or stipends, then.   Yet witness for
the Father the garment woven throughout; the ministering of women; the purse in common! Hard-
working men and rich ladies were ready to help
Him, and did help Him with all that He needed. —
Did He then never want? Yes; once at least — for
a little while only.

"He was a-hungered in the wilderness. 'Make
bread,' said Satan. 'No,' said our Lord. — He could
starve; but He could not eat bread that His Father
did not give Him, even though He could make it
Himself. He had come hither to be tried. But when
the victory was secure, lo! the angels brought Him
food from His Father. — Which was better? To
feed Himself, or be fed by His Father? Judge yourselves, anxious people. He sought the kingdom of
God and His righteousness, and the bread was added
unto Him.

"And this gives me occasion to remark that the

same truth holds with regard to any portion of the
future as well as the morrow.   It is a principle, not
a command, 'or an encouragement, or a promise
merely. In respect of it there is no difference between
next day and next year, next hour and next century.
You will see at once the absurdity of taking no
thought for the morrow, and taking thought for next
year.   But do you see likewise that it is equally
reasonable to trust God for the next moment, and
equally unreasonable not to trust Him?   The Lord
was hungry and needed food now, though He could
still go without for a while. He left it to His Father.
And so He told His disciples to do when they were
called to answer before judges and rulers. 'Take
no thought. It shall be given you what ye shall
say.'   You have a disagreeable duty to do at twelve
o'clock.   Do not blacken nine and ten and eleven,
and all between, with the colour of twelve.   Do the
work of each, and reap your reward in peace.   So
when the dreaded moment in the future becomes the
present, you shall meet it walking in the light, and
that light will overcome its darkness. How often do
men who have made up their minds what to say and
do under certain expected circumstances, forget the
words and reverse the actions! The best preparation
is the present well seen to, the last duty done. For
this will keep the eye so clear and the body so full
of light that the right action will be perceived at
once, the right words will rush from the heart to the
lips, and the man, full of the spirit of God because
he cares for nothing but the will of God, will trample
on the evil thing in love, and be sent, it may be, in

a chariot of fire to the presence of his Father, or
stand unmoved amid the cruel mockings of the men
he loves.

"Do you feel inclined to say in your hearts: 'It
was easy for Him to take no thought, for He had
the matter in His own hands?' But observe there is
nothing very noble in a man's taking no thought except it be from faith.   If there were no God to take
thought for us, we should have no right to blame
any one for taking thought.   You may fancy the
Lord had His own power to fall back upon.   But
that would have been to Him just the one dreadful
thing.   That His Father should forget Him! — no
power in Himself could make up for that.   He feared
nothing for Himself; and never once employed His
divine power to save Him from His human fate.   Let
God do that for Him if He saw fit.   He did not
come into the world to take care of Himself.   That
would not be in any way divine.   To fall back on
Himself, God failing Him — how could that make
it easy for Him to avoid care?   The very idea would
be torture.   That would be to declare heaven void,
and the world without a God.   He would not even
pray to His Father for what He knew He should
have if He did ask it.   He would just wait His
will.

"But see how the fact of His own power adds
tenfold significance to the fact that He trusted in
God.   We see that this power would not serve His
need — His need not being to be fed and clothed,
but to be one with the Father, to be fed by His
hand, clothed by His care.   This was what the Lord

wanted — and we need, alas! too often without
wanting it. He never once, I repeat, used His
power for Himself. That was not His business.
He did not care about it. His life was of no value
to Him but as His Father cared for it. God would
mind all that was necessary for Him, and He would
mind the work His Father had given Him to do.
And, my friends, this is just the one secret of a
blessed life, the one thing every man comes into
this world to learn. With what authority it comes
to us from the lips of Him who knew all about it,
and ever did as He said!

"Now you see that He took no thought for the
morrow. And in the name of the holy child Jesus,
I call upon you, this Christmas Day, to cast care to
the winds, and trust in God; to receive the message
of peace and good-will to men; to yield yourselves
to the spirit of God, that you may be taught what
He wants you to know; to remember that the one
gift promised without reserve to those who ask it —
the one gift worth having — the gift which makes
all other gifts a thousand-fold in value, is the gift
of the Holy Spirit, the spirit of the child Jesus, who
will take of the things of Jesus and show them to
you — make you understand them, that is — so
that you shall see them to be true, and love Him
with all your heart and soul, and your neighbour as
yourselves."

And here, having finished my sermon, I will
give my reader some lines with which he may not
be acquainted, from a writer of the Elizabethan

time. I had meant to introduce them into my sermon, but I was so carried away with my subject that I forgot them. For I always preached *extempore*, which phrase I beg my reader will not misinterpret as meaning *on the spur of the moment*, or *without the due preparation of much thought.*

> "O man! thou image of thy Maker's good,
> What canst thou fear, when breathed into thy blood
> His Spirit is that built thee? What dull sense
> Makes thee suspect, in need, that Providence
> Who made the morning, and who placed the light
> Guide to thy labours; who called up the night,
> And bid her fall upon thee like sweet showers,
> In hollow murmurs, to lock up thy powers;
> Who gave thee knowledge; who so trusted thee
> To let thee grow so near Himself, the Tree?
> Must He then be distrusted? Shall His frame
> Discourse with Him why thus and thus I am?
> He made the Angels thine, thy fellows all;
> Nay even thy servants, when devotions call.
> Oh! canst thou be so stupid then, so dim,
> To seek a saving* influence, and lose Him?
> Can stars protect thee? Or can poverty,
> Which is the light to heaven, put out His eye?
> He is my star; in Him all truth I find,
> All influence, all fate. And when my mind
> Is furnished with His fulness, my poor story
> Shall outlive all their age, and all their glory.
> The hand of danger cannot fall amiss,
> When I know what, and in whose power, it is.
> Nor want, the curse of man, shall make me groan:
> A holy hermit is a mind alone.
>   *   *   *
> Affliction, when I know it, is but this,
> A deep alloy whereby man tougher is
> To bear the hammer; and the deeper still,
> We still arise more image of His will;
> Sickness, an humorous cloud 'twixt us and light;
> And death, at longest, but another night."

* Many, in those days, believed in astrology.

I had more than ordinary attention during my discourse, at one point in which I saw the down-bent head of Catherine Weir sink yet lower upon her hands. After a moment, however, she sat more erect than before, though she never lifted her eyes to meet mine. I need not assure my reader that she was not present to my mind when I spoke the words that so far had moved her. Indeed, had I thought of her, I could not have spoken them.

As I came out of the church, my people crowded about me with outstretched hands and good wishes. One woman, the aged wife of a more aged labourer,. who could not get near me, called from the outskirts of the little crowd —

"May the Lord come and see ye every day, sir. And may ye never know the hunger and cold as me and Tomkins has come through."

"Amen to the first of your blessing, Mrs. Tomkins, and hearty thanks to you. But I daren't say *Amen* to the other part of it after what I've been preaching, you know."

"But there'll be no harm if I say it for ye, sir?"

"No, for God will give me what is good, even if your kind heart should pray against it."

"Ah, sir, ye don't know what it is to be hungry *and* cold."

"Neither shall you any more, if I can help it."

"God bless ye, sir. But we're pretty tidy just in the meantime."

I walked home, as usual on Sunday mornings, by the road. It was a lovely day. The sun shone so warm that you could not help thinking of what

he would be able to do before long — draw prim-
roses and buttercups out of the earth by force of
sweet persuasive influences. But in the shadows lay
fine webs and laces of ice, so delicately lovely that
one could not but be glad of the cold that made
the water able to please itself by taking such graceful forms. And I wondered over again for the hun-
dredth time what could be the principle which,
in the wildest, most lawless, fantastically chaotic,
apparently capricious work of nature, always kept it
beautiful. The beauty of holiness must be at the
heart of it somehow, I thought. Because our God
is so free from stain, so loving, so unselfish, so
good, so altogether what He wants us to be, so
holy, therefore all His works declare Him in beauty;
His fingers can touch nothing but to mould it into
loveliness; and even the play of His elements is in
grace and tenderness of form.

And then I thought how the sun, at the farthest
point from us, had begun to come back towards us;
looked upon us with a hopeful smile; was like the
Lord when He visited His people as a little one of
themselves, to grow upon the earth till it should
blossom as the rose in the light of His presence.
"Ah! Lord," I said, in my heart, "draw near unto
Thy people. It is spring-time with Thy world, but
yet we have cold winds and bitter hail, and pinched
voices forbidding them that follow Thee and follow
not with us. Draw nearer, Sun of Righteousness,
and make the trees bourgeon, and the flowers blossom, and the voices grow mellow and glad, so that
all shall join in praising Thee, and find thereby

that harmony is better than unison.   Let it be summer, O Lord, if it ever may be summer in this court
of the Gentiles.   But Thou hast told us that Thy
kingdom cometh within us, and so Thy joy must
come within us too.   Draw nigh then, Lord, to those
to whom Thou wilt draw nigh; and others beholding
their welfare will seek to share therein too, and
seeing their good works will glorify their Father in
heaven."

So I walked home, hoping in my Saviour, and
wondering to think how pleasant I had found it to
be His poor servant to this people.   Already the
doubts which had filled my mind on that first evening of gloom, doubts as to whether I had any right
to the priest's office, had utterly vanished, slain by
the effort to perform the priest's duty.   I never
thought about the matter now. — And how can
doubt ever be fully met but by action?   Try your
theory; try your hypothesis; or if it is not worth
trying, give it up, pull it down.   And I hoped that
if ever a cloud should come over me again, however
dark and dismal it might be, I might be able notwithstanding to rejoice that the sun was shining
on others though not on me, and to say with all
my heart to my Father in heaven, "Thy will be
done."

When I reached my own study, I sat down by
a blazing fire, and poured myself out a glass of
wine; for I had to go out again to see some of my
poor friends, and wanted some luncheon first. — It
is a great thing to have the greetings of the universe
presented in fire and food.   Let me, if I may, be

ever welcomed to my room in winter by a glowing
hearth, in summer by a vase of flowers; if I may
not, let me then think how nice they would be, and
bury myself in my work. I do not think that the
road to contentment lies in despising what we have
not got. Let us acknowledge all good, all delight
that the world holds, and be content without it. But
this we can never be except by possessing the one
thing, without which I do not merely say no man
ought to be content, but no man *can* be content —
the Spirit of the Father.

If any young people read my little chronicle,
will they not be inclined to say, "The vicar has already given us in this chapter hardly anything but
a long sermon; and it is too bad of him to go on
preaching in his study after we saw him safe out of
the pulpit?" Ah, well! just one word, and I drop
the preaching for a while. My word is this: I may
speak long-windedly, and even inconsiderately as
regards my young readers; what I say may fail utterly to convey what I mean; I may be actually
stupid sometimes, and not have a suspicion of it;
but what I mean is true; and if you do not know it
to be true yet, some of you at least suspect it to be
true, and some of you hope it is true; and when you
all see it as I mean it and as you can take it, you
will rejoice with a gladness you know nothing about
now. There, I have done for a little while. I won't
pledge myself for more, I assure you. For to speak
about such things is the greatest delight of my age,
as it was of my early manhood, next to that of loving God and my neighbour. For as these are *the*

two commandments of life, so they are in themselves *the* pleasures of life. But there I am at it again. I beg your pardon now, for I have already inadvertently broken my promise.

I had allowed myself a half-hour before the fire with my glass of wine and piece of bread, and I soon fell into a dreamy state called *reverie*, which I fear not a few, mistake for *thinking*, because it is the nearest approach they ever make to it. And in this reverie I kept staring about my book-shelves. — I am an old man now, and you do not know my name; and if you should ever find it out, I shall very soon hide it under some daisies, I hope, and so escape; and therefore I am going to be egotistic in the most unpardonable manner. I am going to tell you one of my faults, for it continues, I fear, to be one of my faults still, as it certainly was at the period of which I am now writing. I am very fond of books. Do not mistake me. I do not mean that I love reading. I hope I do. That is no fault — a virtue rather than a fault. But, as the old meaning of the word *fond* was *foolish*, I use that word: I am foolishly fond of the bodies of books as distinguished from their souls, or thought-element. I do not say I love their bodies as *divided* from their souls; I do not say I should let a book stand upon my shelves for which I felt no respect, except indeed it happened to be useful to me in some inferior way. But I delight in seeing books about me, books even of which there seems to be no prospect that I shall have time to read a single chapter before I lay this old head down for the last time. Nay, more: I confess that if they are nicely bound, so as to glow and shine in such a fire-light as that by which I was then sitting, I like them ever so much the better. Nay, more yet — and this comes very near to showing myself worse than I thought I was when I began to tell you my fault: there are books upon my shelves which certainly at least would not occupy the place of honour they do occupy, had not some previous owner dressed them far beyond their worth, making modern apples of Sodom of them. Yet there I let them stay, because they are pleasant to the eye, although certainly not things to be desired to make one wise. I could say a great deal more about the matter, *pro* and *con*, but it would be worse than a sermon, I fear. For I suspect that by the time books, which ought to be loved for the truth that is in them, of one sort or another, come to be loved as articles of furniture, the mind has gone through a process more than analogous to that which the miser's mind goes through — namely, that of passing from the respect of money because of what it can do, to the love of money because it is money. I have not yet reached the furniture stage, and I do not think I ever shall. I would rather burn them all. Meantime, I think one safeguard is to encourage one's friends to borrow one's books — not to offer individual books, which is much the same as *offering* advice. That will probably take some of the shine off them, and put a few thumb-marks in them, which both are very wholesome towards the arresting of the furniture declension. For my part, thumbmarks I find very obnoxious — far more so

than the spoiling of the binding. — I know that
some of my readers, who have had sad experience
of the sort, will be saying in themselves, "He might
have mentioned a surer antidote resulting from this
measure, than either rubbed Russia or dirty *glove*-
marks even — that of utter disappearance and irre-
parable loss." But no; that has seldom happened to
me — because I trust my pocket-book, and never
my memory, with the names of those to whom the
individual books are committed. — There, then, is a
little bit of practical advice in both directions for
young book-lovers.

Again I am reminded that I am getting old.
What digressions!

Gazing about on my treasures, the thought suddenly struck me that I had never done as I had
promised Judy; had never found out what her
aunt's name meant in Anglo-Saxon. I would do so
now. I got down my dictionary, and soon discovered that *Ethelwyn* meant *Home-joy*, or *Inhe-
ritance*.

"A lovely meaning," I said to myself.

And then I went off into another reverie, with
the composition of which I shall not trouble my
reader; and with the mention of which I had perhaps no right to occupy the fragment of his time
spent in reading it, seeing I did not intend to tell
him how it was made up. I will tell him something else instead.

Several families had asked me to take my Christmas dinner with them; but, not liking to be thus

limited, I had answered each that I would not, if
they would excuse me, but would look in some time
or other in the course of the evening.

When my half-hour was out, I got up and filled
my pockets with little presents for my poor people,
and set out to find them in their own homes.

I was variously received, but unvaryingly with
kindness; and my little presents were accepted, at
least in most instances, with a gratitude which made
me ashamed of them and of myself too for a few
moments. Mrs. Tomkins looked as if she had never
seen so much tea together before, though there was
only a couple of pounds of it; and her husband received a pair of warm trousers none the less cordially
that they were not quite new, the fact being that I
found I did not myself need such warm clothing this
winter as I had needed the last. I did not dare to
offer Catherine Weir anything, but I gave her little
boy a box of water-colours — in remembrance of
the first time I saw him, though I said nothing about
that. His mother did not thank me. She told little
Gerard to do so, however, and that was something.
And indeed the boy's sweetness would have been
enough for both.

Gerard — an unusual name in England; specially
not to be looked for in the class to which she belonged.

When I reached Old Rogers's cottage, whither I
carried a few yards of ribbon, bought by myself, I
assure my lady friends, with the special object that
the colour should be bright enough for her taste,
and pure enough of its kind for mine, as an offering

to the good dame, and a small hymn-book, in which
were some hymns of my own making, for the good
man —

But do forgive me, friends, for actually describing my paltry presents. I can dare to assure you
it comes from a talking old man's love of detail,
and from no admiration of such small givings as
those. You see I trust you, and I want to stand
well with you. I never could be indifferent to what
people thought of me; though I have had to fight
hard to act as freely as if I were indifferent, especially when upon occasion I found myself approved
of. It is more difficult to walk straight then, than
when men are all against you. — As I have already
broken a sentence, which will not be past setting
for a while yet, I may as well go on to say here,
lest any one should remark that a clergyman ought
not to show off his virtues, nor yet teach his people
bad habits by making them look out for presents
— that my income not only seemed to me dispro-
portioned to the amount of labour necessary in the
parish, but certainly was larger than I required to
spend upon myself; and the miserly passion for
books I contrived to keep a good deal in check; for
I had no fancy for gliding devil-wards for the sake
of a few books after all. So there was no great
virtue — was there? — in easing my heart by giving
a few of the good things people give their children
to my poor friends, whose kind reception of them
gave me as much pleasure as the gifts gave them.
They valued the kindness in the gift, and to look
out for kindness will not make people greedy.

When I reached the cottage, I found not merely
Jane there with her father and mother, which was
natural on Christmas Day, seeing there seemed to
be no company at the Hall, but my little Judy as
well, sitting in the old woman's arm-chair (not that
she used it much, but it was called hers), and looking as much at home as — as she did in the
pond.

"Why, Judy!" I exclaimed, "you here?"

"Yes. Why not, Mr. Walton?" she returned,
holding out her hand without rising, for the chair
was such a large one, and she was set so far back
in it that the easier way was not to rise, which, seeing she was not greatly overburdened with reverence,
was not, I presume, a cause of much annoyance to
the little damsel.

"I know no reason why I shouldn't see a Sand-
wich Islander here. Yet I might express surprise
if I did find one, might I not?"

Judy pretended to pout, and muttered something
about comparing her to a cannibal. But Jane took
up the explanation.

"Mistress had to go off to London with her
mother to-day, sir, quite unexpected, on some bank-
ing business, I fancy, from what I — I beg your
pardon, sir. They're gone anyhow, whatever the
reason may be; and so I came to see my father and
mother, and Miss Judy would come with me."

"She's very welcome," said Mrs. Rogers.

"How could I stay up there with nobody but
Jacob, and that old wolf Sarah? I wouldn't be left
alone with her for the world. She'd have me

in the Bishop's Pool before you came back, Janey dear."

"That wouldn't matter much to you, would it, Judy?" I said.

"She's a white wolf, that old Sarah, I know!" was all her answer.

"But what will the old lady say when she finds you brought the young lady here?" asked Mrs. Rogers.

"I didn't bring her, mother. She would come."

"Besides she'll never know it," said Judy.

I did not see that it was my part to read Judy a lecture here, though perhaps I might have done so if had had more influence over her than I had. I wanted to gain some influence over her, and knew that the way to render my desire impossible of fulfilment would be, to find fault with what in her was a very small affair, whatever it might be in one who had been properly brought up. Besides, a clergyman is not a moral policeman. So I took no notice of the impropiety.

"Had they actually to go away on the morning of Christmas Day?" I said.

"They went anyhow, whether they had to do it or not, sir," answered Jane.

"Aunt Ethelwyn didn't want to go till to-morrow," said Judy. "She said something about coming to church this morning. But grannie said they must go at once. It was very cross of old grannie. Think what a Christmas Day to me without auntie, and with Sarah! But I don't mean to go home till it's

15*

quite dark. I mean to stop here with dear Old
Rogers — that I do."

The latch was gently lifted, and in came young
Brownrigg. So I thought it was time to leave my
best Christmas wishes and take myself away. Old
Rogers came with me to the mill-stream as usual.

"It 'mazes me, sir," he said, "a gentleman o'
your age and bringin' up to know all that you tould
us this mornin'. It 'ud be no wonder now for a man
like me, come to be the shock o' corn fully ripe —
leastways yellow and white enough outside if there
bean't much more than milk inside it yet, — it 'ud
be no mystery for a man like me who'd been brought
up hard, and tossed about well nigh all the world
over — why, there's scarce a wave on the Atlantic
but knows Old Rogers!"

He made the parenthesis with a laugh, and began anew.

"It 'ud be a shame of a man like me not to
know all as you said this morning, sir — leastways I don't mean able to say it right off as you
do, sir; but not to know it, after the Almighty had
been at such pains to beat it into my hard head
just to trust in Him and fear no thing and nobody
— captain, bosun, devil, sunk rock, or breakers
ahead; but just to mind Him and stand by halliard,
brace, or wheel, or hang on by the leeward earing
for that matter. For, you see, what does it signify
whether I go to the bottom or not, so long as I
didn't skulk? or rather," and here the old man took
off his hat and looked up, "so long as the Great
Captain has His way, and things is done to His

mind? But how ever a man like you, goin' to the
college and readin' books, and warm o' nights, and
never, by your own confession this blessed mornin',
sir, knowin' what it was to be downright hungry,
how ever you come to know all those things, is just
past my comprehension, except by a double portion
o' the Spirit, sir. And that's the way I account for
it, sir."

Although I knew enough about a ship to understand the old man, I am not sure that I have properly represented his sea-phrase. But that is of small
consequence, so long as I give his meaning. And a
meaning can occasionally be even better *conveyed* by
less accurate words.

"I will try to tell you how I come to know
about these things as I do," I returned. "How my
knowledge may stand the test of further and severer
trials remains to be seen. But if I should fail any
time, old friend, and neither trust in God nor do
my duty, what I have said to you remains true all
the same."

"That it do, sir, whoever may come short."

"And more than that: failure does not necessarily prove any one to be a hypocrite of no faith.
He may be still a man of little faith."

"Surely, surely, sir. I remember once that my
faith broke down — just for one moment, sir. And
then the Lord gave me my way lest I should blas-
pheme Him in my wicked heart."

"How was that, Rogers?"

"A scream came from the quarter-deck, and then
the cry: 'Child overboard!' There was but one

child, the captain's, aboard. I was sitting just aft the foremast, herring-boning a split in a spare jib. I sprang to the bulwark, and there, sure enough, was the child, going fast astarn, but pretty high in the water. How it happened I can't think to this day, sir, but I suppose my needle, in the hurry, had got into my jacket, so as to skewer it to my jersey, for we were far south of the line at the time, sir, and it was cold. However that may be, as soon as I was overboard, which you may be sure didn't want the time I take tellin' of it, I found that I ought to ha' pulled my jacket off afore I gave the bulwark the last kick. So I rose on the water, and began to pull it over my head — for it was wide, and that was the easiest way, I thought, in the water. But when I had got it right over my head, there it stuck. And there was I, blind as a Dutchman in a fog, and in as strait a jacket as ever poor wretch in Bedlam, for I could only just wag my flippers. Mr. Walton, I believe I swore — the Lord forgive me! — but it was trying. And what was far worse, for one moment I disbelieved in Him; and I do say that's worse than swearing — in a hurry I mean. And that moment something went, the jacket was off, and there was I feelin' as if every stroke I took was as wide as the mainyard. I had no time to repent, only to thank God. And wasn't it more than I deserved, sir? Ah! He can rebuke a man for unbelief by giving him the desire of his heart. And that's a better rebuke than tying him up to the gratings."

"And did you save the child?"

"Oh yes, sir."

"And wasn't the captain pleased?"

"I believe he was, sir. He gave me a glass o' grog, sir. But you was a sayin' of something, sir, when I interrupted of you."

"I am very glad you did interrupt me."

"I'm not though, sir. I've lost summat I'll never hear more."

"No, you shan't lose it. I was going to tell you how I think I came to understand a little about the things I was talking of to-day."

"That's it, sir; that's it. Well, sir, if you please?"

"You've heard of Sir Philip Sidney, haven't you, Old Rogers?"

"He was a great joker, wasn't he, sir?"

"No, no; you're thinking of Sydney Smith, Rogers."

"It may be, sir. I am an ignorant man."

"You are no more ignorant than you ought to be. — But it is time you should know him, for he was just one of your sort. I will come down some evening and tell you about him."

I may as well mention here that this led to week-evening lectures in the barn, which, with the help of Weir the carpenter, was changed into a comfortable room with fixed seats all round it, and plenty of cane-chairs besides — for I always disliked forms in the middle of a room. The object of these lectures was to make the people acquainted with the true heroes of their own country — men great in themselves. And the kind of choice I made

may be seen by those who know about both, from
the fact that, while my first two lectures were on
Philip Sidney, I did not give one whole lecture even
to Walter Raleigh, grand fellow as he was. I wanted
chiefly to set forth the men that could rule themselves, first of all, after a noble fashion. But I have
not finished these lectures yet, for I never wished to
confine them to the English heroes; I am going on
still, old man as I am — not however without re-
tracing passed ground sometimes, for a new generation has come up since I came here, and there is a
new one behind coming up now which I may be
honoured to present in its turn to some of this grand
company — this cloud of witnesses to the truth in
our own and other lands, some of whom subdued
kingdoms, and others were tortured to death, for the
same cause and with the same result.

"Meantime," I went on, "I only want to tell
you one little thing he says in a letter to a younger
brother whom he wanted to turn out as fine a fellow
as possible. It is about horses, or rather, riding, —
for Sir Philip was the best horseman in Europe in
his day, as, indeed, all things taken together, he
seems to have really been the most accomplished
man generally of his time in the world. Writing to
this brother he says —"

I could not repeat the words exactly to Old
Rogers, but I think it better to copy them exactly,
in writing this account of our talk:

"At horsemanship, when you exercise it, read
Crison Claudio, and a book that is called *La Gloria
del' Cavallo*, withal that you may join the thorough

contemplation of it with the exercise; and so shall
you profit more in a month than others in a year."

"I think I see what you mean, sir. I had got
to learn it all without book, as it were, though you
know I had my old Bible, that my mother gave
me, and without that I should not have learned it
at all."

"I only mean it comparatively, you know. You
have had more of the practice, and I more of the
theory. But if we had not both had both, we should
neither of us have known anything about the matter.
I never was content without trying at least to understand things; and if they are practical things, and
you try to practise them at the same time as far as
you do understand them, there is no end to the way
in which the one lights up the other. I suppose
that is how, without your experience, I have more
to say about such things than you could expect.
You know besides that a small matter in which a
principle is involved will reveal the principle, if attended to, just as well as a great one containing the
same principle. The only difference, and that a
most important one, is that though I've got my clay
and my straw together, and they stick pretty well as
yet, my brick, after all, is not half so well baked as
yours, old friend, and it may crumble away yet,
though I hope not."

"I pray God to make both our bricks into stones
of the New Jerusalem, sir. I think I understand
you quite well. To know about a thing is of no
use, except you do it. Besides, as I found out when
I went to sea, you never can know a thing till you

do do it, though I thought I had a tidy fancy about some things beforehand. It's better not to be quite sure that all your seams are calked, and so to keep a look-out on the bilge-pump; isn't it, sir?"

During the most of this conversation, we were standing by the mill-water, half frozen over. The ice from both sides came towards the middle, leaving an empty space between, along which the dark water showed itself, hurrying away as if in fear of its life from the white death of the frost. The wheel stood motionless, and the drip from the thatch of the mill over it in the sun, had frozen in the shadow into icicles, which hung in long spikes from the spokes and the floats, making the wheel — soft green and mossy when it revolved in the gentle sun-mingled summer-water — look like its own gray skeleton now. The sun was getting low, and I should want all my time to see my other friends before dinner, for I would not willingly offend Mrs. Pearson on Christmas Day by being late, especially as I guessed she was using extraordinary skill to prepare me a more than comfortable meal.

"I must go, Old Rogers," I said; "but I will leave you something to think about till we meet again. Find out why our Lord was so much displeased with the disciples, whom He knew to be ignorant men, for not knowing what He meant when He warned them against the leaven of the Pharisees. I want to know what you think about it. You'll find the story told both in the sixteenth chapter of St. Matthew and the eighth of St. Mark."

"Well, sir, I'll try; that is, if you will tell me

what you think about it afterwards, so as to put me right, if I'm wrong."

"Of course I will, if I can find out an explanation to satisfy me. But it is not at all clear to me now. In fact, I do not see the connecting links of our Lord's logic in the rebuke He gives them." ·

"How am I to find out then, sir — knowing nothing of logic at all?" said the old man, his rough worn face summered over with his childlike smile.

"There are many things which a little learning, while it cannot really hide them, may make you less ready to see all at once," I answered, shaking hands with Old Rogers, and then springing across the brook with my carpet-bag in my hand.

By the time I had got through the rest of my calls, the fogs were rising from the streams and the meadows to close in upon my first Christmas Day in my own parish. How much happier I was than when I came such a few months before! The only pang I felt that day was as I passed the monsters on the gate leading to Oldcastle Hall. Should I be honoured to help only the poor of the flock? Was I to do nothing for the rich, for whom it is, and has been, and doubtless will be so hard to enter into the kingdom of heaven? And it seemed to me at the moment that the world must be made for the poor: they had so much more done for them to enable them to inherit it than the rich had. — To these people at the Hall, I did not seem acceptable. I might in time do something with Judy, but the old lady was still so dreadfully repulsive to me that it

troubled my conscience to feel how I disliked her.
Mr. Stoddart seemed nothing more than a dilettante
in religion as well as in the arts and sciences —
music always excepted; while for Miss Oldcastle, I
simply did not understand her yet. And she was
so beautiful! I thought her more beautiful every
time I saw her. But I never appeared to make the
least progress towards any real acquaintance with
her thoughts and feelings. — It seemed to me, I
say, for a moment, coming from the houses of the
warm-hearted poor, as if the rich had not quite fair
play, as it were — as if they were sent into the
world chiefly for the sake of the cultivation of the
virtues of the poor, and without much chance for the
cultivation of their own. I knew better than this
you know, my reader; but the thought came, as
thoughts will come sometimes. It vanished the moment I sought to lay hands upon it, as if it knew
quite well it had no business there. But certainly I
did believe that it was more like the truth to say
the world was made for the poor than to say that it
was made for the rich. And therefore I longed the
more to do something for these whom I considered
the rich of my flock; for it was dreadful to think of
their being poor inside instead of outside.

Perhaps my reader will say, and say with justice,
that I ought to have been as anxious about poor
Farmer Brownrigg as about the beautiful lady. But
the farmer had given me good reason to hope some
progress in him after the way he had given in about
Jane Rogers. Positively I had caught his eye during
the sermon that very day. And, besides — but I

will not be a hypocrite; and seeing I did not certainly take the same interest in Mr. Brownrigg, I
will at least be honest and confess it. As far as regards the discharge of my duties, I trust I should
have behaved impartially had the necessity for any
choice arisen. But my feelings were not quite under
my own control. And we are nowhere told to love
everybody alike, only to love every one who comes
within our reach as ourselves.

I wonder whether my old friend Dr. Duncan
was right. He had served on shore in Egypt under
General Abercromby, and had of course, after the
fighting was over on each of the several occasions —
the French being always repulsed — exercised his
office amongst the wounded left on the field of
battle. — "I do not know," he said, "whether I
did right or not; but I always took the man I came to
first — French or English." — I only know that
my heart did not wait for the opinion of my head
on the matter. I loved the old man the more that
he did as he did. But as a question of casuistry, I
am doubtful about its answer.

This digression is, I fear, unpardonable.

I made Mrs. Pearson sit down with me to dinner,
for Christmas Day was not one to dine alone upon.
And I have ever since had my servants to dine with
me on Christmas Day.

Then I went out again, and made another round
of visits, coming in for a glass of wine at one table,
an orange at another, and a hot chestnut at a third.
Those whom I could not see that day, I saw on the

following days between it and the new year. And so ended my Christmas holiday with my people.

But there is one little incident which I ought to relate before I close this chapter, and which I am ashamed of having so nearly forgotten.

When we had finished our dinner, and I was sitting alone drinking a glass of claret before going out again, Mrs. Pearson came in and told me that little Gerard Weir wanted to see me. I asked her to show him in; and the little fellow entered, looking very shy, and clinging first to the door and then to the wall.

"Come, my dear boy," I said, "and sit down by me."

He came directly and stood before me.

"Would you like a little wine and water?" I said; for unhappily there was no dessert, Mrs. Pearson knowing that I never eat such things.

"No, thank you, sir; I never tasted wine."

I did not press him to take it.

"Please, sir," he went on after a pause, putting his hand in his pocket, "mother gave me some goodies, and I kept them till I saw you come back, and here they are, sir."

Does any reader doubt what I did or said upon this?

I said, "Thank you, my darling," and I ate them up every one of them, that he might see me eat them before he left the house. And the dear child went off radiant.

If anybody cannot understand why I did so, I beg him to consider the matter. If then he cannot come to a conclusion concerning it, I doubt if any explanation of mine would greatly subserve his enlightenment. Meantime, I am forcibly restraining myself from yielding to the temptation to set forth my reasons, which would result in a half-hour's sermon on the Jewish dispensation, including the burnt offering, and the wave and heave offerings, with an application to the ignorant nurses and mothers of English babies, who do the best they can to make original sin an actual fact by training children down in the way they should not go.

CHAPTER XII.

The Avenue.

It will not appear strange that I should linger so long upon the first few months of my association with a people who, now that I am an old man, look to me like my own children. For those who were then older than myself are now "old dwellers in those high countries" where there is no age, only wisdom; and I shall soon go to them. How glad I shall be to see my Old Rogers again, who, as he taught me upon earth, will teach me yet more, I thank my God, in heaven! But I must not let the reverie which always gathers about the feather-end of my pen the moment I take it up to write these recollections, interfere with the work before me.

After this Christmas-tide, I found myself in closer relationship to my parishioners. No doubt I was always in danger of giving unknown offence to those who were ready to fancy that I neglected them, and did not distribute my *favours* equally. But as I never took offence, the offence I gave was easily got rid of. A clergyman, of all men, should be slow to take offence, for if he does, he will never be free or strong to reprove sin. And it must sometimes be his duty to speak severely to those, especially the good who are turning their faces the wrong way. It is of little use to reprove the sinner, but it is worth

while sometimes to reprove those who have a regard
for righteousness, however imperfect they may be.
"Reprove not a scorner, lest he hate thee; rebuke a
wise man, and he will love thee."

But I took great care about *interfering;* though
I would interfere upon request — not always, however, upon the side whence the request came, and
more seldom still upon either side. The clergyman
must never be a partisan. When our Lord was re-
quested to act as umpire between two brothers, He
refused. But He spoke and said, "Take heed, and
beware of covetousness." Now, though the best of
men is unworthy to loose the latchet of His shoe,
yet the servant must be as his Master. Ah me!
while I write it, I remember that the sinful woman
might yet do as she would with His sacred feet. I
bethink me: Desert may not touch His shoe-tie: Love
may kiss His feet.

I visited, of course, at the Hall, as at the farm-
houses in the country, and the cottages in the village.
I did not come to like Mrs. Oldcastle better. And
there was one woman in the house whom I disliked
still more: that Sarah whom Judy had called in my
hearing a white wolf. Her face was yet whiter than
that of her mistress, only it was not smooth like hers;
for its whiteness came apparently from the small-
pox, which had so thickened the skin that no blood,
if she had any, could shine through. I seldom saw
her — only indeed caught a glimpse of her now and
then as I passed through the house.

Nor did I make much progress with Mr. Stoddart. He had always something friendly to say, and

often some theosophical theory to bring forward,
which, I must add, never seemed to me to mean, or
at least to reveal, anything. He was a great reader
of mystical books, and yet the man's nature seemed
cold. It was sunshiny, but not sunny. His intellect
was rather a lambent flame than a genial warmth.
He could make things, but he could not grow anything.
And when I came to see that he had had more than
any one else to do with the education of Miss Oldcastle, I understood her a little better, and saw that
her so-called e-ducation had been in a great measure
re-pression — of a negative sort, no doubt, but not
therefore the less mischievous. For to teach specu-
lation instead of devotion, mysticism instead of love,
word instead of deed, is surely ruinously repressive
to the nature that is meant for sunbright activity
both of heart and hand. My chief perplexity continued to be how he could play the organ as he did.

My reader will think that I am always coming
round to Miss Oldcastle; but if he does, I cannot
help it. I began, I say, to understand her a little
better. She seemed to me always like one walking
in a "watery sunbeam," without knowing that it was
but the wintry pledge of a summer sun at hand. She
took it, or was trying to take it, for *the* sunlight;
trying to make herself feel all the glory people said
was in the light, instead of making haste towards
the perfect day. I found afterwards that several
things had combined to bring about this condition;
and I know she will forgive me, should I, for the
sake of others, endeavour to make it understood by
and by.

I have not much more to tell my readers about this winter. As out of a whole changeful season only one day, or, it may be, but one moment in which the time seemed to burst into its own blossom, will cling to the memory; so of the various interviews with my friends, and the whole flow of the current of my life, during that winter, nothing more of nature or human nature occurs to me worth recording. I will pass on to the summer season as rapidly as I may, though the early spring will detain me with the relation of just a single incident.

I was on my way to the Hall to see Mr. Stoddart. I wanted to ask him whether something could not be done beyond his exquisite playing to rouse the sense of music in my people. I believed that nothing helps you so much to feel as the taking of what share may, from the nature of the thing, be possible to you; because, for one reason, in order to feel, it is necessary that the mind should rest upon the matter, whatever it is. The poorest success, provided the attempt has been genuine, will enable one to enter into any art ten times better than before. Now I had, I confess, little hope of moving Mr. Stoddart in the matter; but if I should succeed, I thought it would do himself more good to mingle with his humble fellows in the attempt to do them a trifle of good, than the opening of any number of intellectual windows towards the circumambient truth.

It was just beginning to grow dusk. The wind was blustering in gusts among the trees, swaying them suddenly and fiercely like a keen passion, now

16*

sweeping them all one way as if the multitude of tops would break loose and rush away like a wild river, and now subsiding as suddenly, and allowing them to recover themselves and stand upright, with tones and motions of indignant expostulation. There was just one cold bar of light in the west, and the east was one gray mass, while overhead the stars were twinkling. The grass and all the ground about the trees were very wet. The time seemed more dreary somehow than the winter. Rigour was past, and tenderness had not come. For the wind was cold without being keen, and bursting from the trees every now and then with a roar as of a sea breaking on distant sands, whirled about me as if it wanted me to go and join in its fierce play.

Suddenly I saw, to my amazement, in a walk that ran alongside of the avenue, Miss Oldcastle, struggling against the wind, which blew straight down the path upon her. The cause of my amazement was twofold. First, I had supposed her with her mother in London, whither their journeys had been not infrequent since Christmas-tide; and next — why should she be fighting with the wind, so far from the house, with only a shawl drawn over her head?

The reader may wonder how I should know her in this attire in the dusk, and where there was not the smallest probability of finding her. Suffice it to say that I did recognise her at once; and passing between two great tree-trunks, and through an opening in some underwood, was by her side in a moment. But the noise of the wind had prevented her from hearing my approach, and when I uttered

her name, she started violently, and, turning, drew
herself up very haughtily, in part, I presume, to
hide her tremor. — She was always a little haughty
with me, I must acknowledge. Could there have
been anything in my address, however unconscious
of it I was, that made her fear I was ready to become intrusive? Or might it not be that, hearing
of my footing with my parishioners generally, she
was prepared to resent any assumption of clerical
familiarity with her; and so, in my behaviour, any
poor innocent "bush was supposed a bear." For I
need not tell my reader that nothing was farther
from my intention, even with the lowliest of my
flock, than to presume upon my position as clergyman. I think they all *gave* me the relation I oc-
cupied towards them personally. — But I had never
seen her look so haughty as now. If I had been
watching her very thoughts she could hardly have
looked more indignant.

"I beg your pardon," I said, distressed; "I have
startled you dreadfully."

"Not in the least," she replied, but without
moving, and still with a curve in her form like the
neck of a frayed horse.

I thought it better to leave apology, which was
evidently disagreeable to her, and speak of indifferent things.

"I was on my way to call on Mr. Stoddart," I
said.

"You will find him at home, I believe."

"I fancied you and Mrs. Oldcastle in London."

"We returned yesterday."

Still she stood as before. I made a movement
in the direction of the house. She seemed as if she
would walk in the opposite direction.

"May I not walk with you to the house?"

"I am not going in just yet."

"Are you protected enough for such a night?"

"I enjoy the wind."

I bowed and walked on; for what else could
I do?

I cannot say that I enjoyed leaving her behind
me in the gathering dark, the wind blowing her
about with no more reverence than if she had been
a bush of privet. Nor was it with a light heart that
I bore her repulse as I slowly climbed the hill to
the house. However, a little personal mortification
is wholesome — though I cannot say either that I
derived much consolation from the reflection.

Sarah opened the glass door, her black, glossy,
restless eyes looking out of her white face from under
gray eyebrows. I knew at once by her look beyond
me that she had expected to find me accompanied
by her young mistress. I did not volunteer any information, as my reader may suppose.

I found, as I had feared, that, although Mr.
Stoddart seemed to listen with some interest to what
I said, I could not bring him to the point of making
any practical suggestion, or of responding to one
made by me; and I left him with the conviction
that he would do nothing to help me. Yet during
the whole of our interview he had not opposed a
single word I said. He was like clay too much

softened with water to keep the form into which it
has been modelled. He would take *some* kind of
form easily, and lose it yet more easily. I did not
show all my dissatisfaction, however, for that would
only have estranged us; and it is not required, nay,
it may be wrong, to show all you feel or think:
what is required of us is, not to show what we do
not feel or think; for that is to be false.

I left the house in a gloomy mood. I know I
ought to have looked up to God and said: "These
things do not reach to Thee, my Father. Thou art
ever the same; and I rise above my small as well as
my great troubles by remembering Thy peace, and
Thy unchangeable Godhood to me and all Thy
creatures." But I did not come to myself all at
once. The thought of God had not come, though it
was pretty sure to come before I got home. I was
brooding over the littleness of all I could do; and
feeling that sickness which sometimes will overtake
a man in the midst of the work he likes best, when
the unpleasant parts of it crowd upon him, and his
own efforts, especially those made from the will
without sustaining impulse, come back upon him
with a feeling of unreality, decay, and bitterness, as
if he had been unnatural and untrue, and putting
himself in false relations by false efforts for good.
I know this all came from selfishness — thinking
about myself instead of about God and my neighbour. But so it was. — And so I was walking
down the avenue, where it was now very dark, with
my head bent to the ground, when I in my turn
started at the sound of a woman's voice, and look-

ing up, saw by the starlight the dim form of Miss
Oldcastle standing before me.

She spoke first.

"Mr. Walton, I was very rude to you. I beg
your pardon."

"Indeed, I did not think so. I only thought
what a blundering awkward fellow I was to startle
you as I did. You have to forgive me."

"I fancy" — and here I know she smiled,
though how I know I do not know — "I fancy I
have made that even," she said pleasantly; "for you
must confess I startled you now."

"You did; but it was in a very different way. I
annoyed you with my rudeness. You only scattered
a swarm of bats that kept flapping their skinny
wings in my face."

"What do you mean? There are no bats at this
time of the year."

"Not outside. In 'winter and rough weather,'
they creep inside, you know."

"Ah! I ought to understand you. But I did
not think you were ever like that. I thought you
were too good."

"I wish I were. I hope to be some day. I am
not yet, anyhow. And I thank you for driving the
bats away in the meantime."

"You make me the more ashamed of myself to
think that perhaps my· rudeness had a share in
bringing them.—Yours is no doubt thankless labour
sometimes."

She seemed to make the last remark just to
prevent the conversation from returning to her as

its subject. And now all the bright portions of my work came up before me.

"You are quite mistaken in that, Miss Oldcastle. On the contrary, the thanks I get are far more than commensurate with the labour. Of course one meets with a disappointment sometimes, but that is only when they don't know what you mean. And how should they know what you mean till they are different themselves? — You remember what Wordsworth says on this very subject in his poem of *Simon Lee?*" —

"I do not know anything of Wordsworth."

> " 'I 've heard of hearts unkind, kind deeds
>   With coldness still returning;
>   Alas! the gratitude of men
>   Hath oftener left me mourning.' "

"I do not quite see what he means."

"May I recommend you to think about it? You will be sure to find it out for yourself, and that will be ten times more satisfactory than if I were to explain it to you. And, besides, you will never forget it, if you do."

"Will you repeat the lines again?"

I did so.

All this time the wind had been still. Now it rose with a slow gush in the trees. Was it fancy? Or, as the wind moved the shrubbery, did I see a white face? And could it be the White Wolf, as Judy called her?

I spoke aloud:

"But it is cruel to keep you standing here in

such a night. You must be a real lover of nature to walk in the dark wind."

"I like it. Good night."

So we parted. I gazed into the darkness after her, though she disappeared at the distance of a yard or two; and would have stood longer had I not still suspected the proximity of Judy's Wolf, which made me turn and go home, regardless now of Mr. Stoddart's *doughiness*.

I met Miss Oldcastle several times before the summer, but her old manner remained, or rather had returned, for there had been nothing of it in the tone of her voice in that interview, if *interview* it could be called where neither could see more than the other's outline.

CHAPTER XIII.

Young Weir.

BY slow degrees the summer bloomed. Green
came instead of white; rainbows instead of icicles.
The grounds about the Hall seemed the incarnation
of a summer which had taken years to ripen to its
perfection. The very grass seemed to have aged
into perfect youth in that "haunt of ancient peace;"
for surely nowhere else was such thick, delicate-
bladed, delicate-coloured grass to be seen. Gnarled
old trees of may stood like altars of smoking per-
fume, or each like one million-petalled flower of up-
heaved whiteness — or of tender rosiness, as if the
snow which had covered it in winter had sunk in
and gathered warmth from the life of the tree, and
now crept out again to adorn the summer. The
long loops of the laburnum hung heavy with gold
towards the sod below; and the air was full of the
fragrance of the young leaves of the limes. Down
in the valley below, the daisies shone in all the
meadows, varied with the buttercup and the celandine;
while in damp places grew large pimpernels, and
along the sides of the river the meadow-sweet stood
amongst the reeds at the very edge of the water,
breathing out the odours of dreamful sleep. The
clumsy pollards were each one mass of undivided
green. The mill-wheel had regained its knotty

look, with its moss and its dip and drip, as it yielded
to the slow water, which would have let it alone but
that there was no other way out of the land to the
sea.

I used now to wander about in the fields and
woods, with a book in my hand, at which I often
did not look the whole day, and which yet I liked
to have with me. And I seemed somehow to come
back with most upon those days in which I did not
read. In this manner I prepared almost all my
sermons that summer. But, although I prepared
them thus in the open country, I had another custom,
which perhaps may appear strange to some, before I
preached them. This was, to spend the Saturday
evening, not in my study, but in the church. This
custom of mine was known to the sexton and his
wife, and the church was always clean and ready
for me after about midday, so that I could be alone
there as soon as I pleased. It would take more
space than my limits will afford to explain thoroughly
why I liked to do this. But I will venture to attempt a partial explanation in a few words.

This fine old church in which I was honoured
to lead the prayers of my people, was not the expression of the religious feeling of my time. There
was a gloom about it — a sacred gloom, I know,
and I loved it; but such gloom as was not in my
feeling when I talked to my flock. I honoured the
place; I rejoiced in its history; I delighted to think
that even by the temples made with hands outlast-
ing these bodies of ours, we were in a sense united
to those who in them had before us lifted up holy

hands without wrath or doubting; and with many more who, like us, had lifted up at least prayerful hands, without hatred or despair. The place soothed me, tuned me to a solemn mood — one of self-denial, and gentle gladness in all sober things. But, had I been an architect, and had I had to build a church — I do not in the least know how I should have built it — I am certain it would have been very different from this. Else I should be a mere imitator, like all the church-architects I know anything about in the present day. For I always found the open air the most genial influence upon me for the production of religious feeling and thought. I had been led to try whether it might not be so with me by the fact that our Lord seemed so much to delight in the open air, and late in the day as well as early in the morning would climb the mountain to be alone with His Father. I found that it helped to give a reality to everything that I thought about, if I only contemplated it under the high untroubled blue, with the lowly green beneath my feet, and the wind blowing on me to remind me of the Spirit that once moved on the face of the waters, bringing order out of disorder and light out of darkness, and was now seeking every day a fuller entrance into my heart, that there He might work the one will of the Father in heaven.

My reader will see then that there was, as it were, not so much a discord, as a lack of harmony between the surroundings wherein my thoughts took form, or, to use a homelier phrase, my sermon was studied, and the surroundings wherein I had to put

these forms into the garments of words, or preach
that sermon.   I therefore sought to bridge over this
difference (if I understood music, I am sure I could
find an expression exactly fitted to my meaning), —
to find an easy passage between the open-air mood
and the church mood, so as to be able to bring into
the church as much of the fresh air, and the tree-
music, and the colour-harmony, and the gladness
over all, as might be possible; and, in order to this,
I thought all my sermon over again in the afternoon
sun as it shone slantingly through the stained window
over Lord Eagleye's tomb, and in the failing light
thereafter and the gathering dusk of the twilight,
pacing up and down the solemn old place, hanging
my thoughts here on a crocket, there on a corbel;
now on the gable-point over which Weir's face would
gaze next morning, and now on the aspiring peaks
of the organ.   I thus made the place a cell of
thought and prayer.   And when the next day came,
I found the forms around me so interwoven with
the forms of my thought, that I felt almost like one
of the old monks who had built the place, so little
did I find any check to my thought or utterance
from its unfitness for the expression of my individual
modernism.   But not one atom the more did I in-
cline to the evil fancy that God was more in the
past than in the present; that He is more within the
walls of the church, than in the unwalled sky and
earth; or seek to turn backwards one step from a
living Now to an entombed and consecrated Past.

One lovely Saturday, I had been out all the
morning.   I had not walked far, for I had sat in

the various places longer than I had walked, my path
lying through fields and copses, crossing a country
road only now and then. I had my Greek Testament with me, and I read when I sat, and thought
when I walked. I remember well enough that I
was going to preach about the cloud of witnesses,
and explain to my people that this did not mean
persons looking at, witnessing our behaviour — not
so could any addition be made to the awfulness of
the fact that the eye of God was upon us — but
witnesses to the truth, people who did what God
wanted them to do, come of it what might, whether
a crown or a rack, scoffs or applause; to behold
whose witnessing might well rouse all that was
human and divine in us to chose our part with them
and their Lord. — When I came home, I had an
early dinner, and then betook myself to my Saturday's resort. — I had never had a room large enough
to satisfy me before. Now my study was to my
mind.

All through the slowly-fading afternoon, the
autumn of the day, when the colours are richest
and the shadows long and lengthening, I paced my
solemn old-thoughted church. Sometimes I went up
into the pulpit and sat there, looking on the ancient
walls which had grown up under men's hands that
men might be helped to pray by the visible symbol
of unity which the walls gave, and that the voice
of the Spirit of God might be heard exhorting men
to forsake the evil and choose the good. And I
thought how many witnesses to the truth had knelt
in those ancient pews. For as the great church is

made up of numberless communities, so is the great
shining orb of witness-bearers made up of millions
of lesser orbs. All men and women of true heart
bear individual testimony to the truth of God, saying, "I have trusted and found Him faithful."
And the feeble light of the glowworm is yet light,
pure, and good, and with a loveliness of its own.
"So, O Lord," I said, "let my light shine before
men." And I felt no fear of vanity in such a
prayer, for I knew that the glory to come of it is
to God only — "that men may glorify their Father
in heaven." And I knew that when we seek glory
for ourselves, the light goes out, and the Horror
that dwells in darkness breathes cold upon our
spirits. And I remember that just as I thought thus,
my eye was caught first by a yellow light that
gilded the apex of the font-cover, which had been
wrought like a flame or a bursting blossom: it was
so old and worn, I never could tell which; and then
by a red light all over a white marble tablet in the
wall — the red of life on the cold hue of the grave.
And this red light did not come from any work of
man's device, but from the great window of the
west, which little Gerard Weir wanted to help God
to paint. I must have been in a happy mood that
Saturday afternoon, for everything pleased me and
made me happier; and all the church-forms about
me blended and harmonized graciously with the
throne and footstool of God which I saw through
the windows. And I lingered on till the night had
come; till the church only gloomed about me, and
had no shine; and then I found my spirit burning

up the clearer, as a lamp which has been flaming all the day with light unseen becomes a glory in the room when the sun is gone down.

At length I felt tired, and would go home. Yet I lingered for a few moments in the vestry, thinking what hymns would harmonize best with the things I wanted to make my people think about. It was now almost quite dark out of doors — at least as dark as it would be.

Suddenly through the gloom I thought I heard a moan and a sob. I sat upright in my chair and listened. But I heard nothing more, and concluded I had deceived myself. After a few moments, I rose to go home and have some tea, and turn my mind rather away from than towards the subject of witness-bearing any more for that night, lest I should burn the fuel of it out before I came to warm the people with it, and should have to blow its embers instead of flashing its light and heat upon them in gladness. So I left the church by my vestry-door, which I closed behind me, and took my way along the path through the clustering group of graves.

Again I heard a sob. This time I was sure of it. And there lay something dark upon one of the grassy mounds. I approached it, but it did not move. I spoke.

"Can I be of any use to you?" I said.

"No," returned an almost inaudible voice.

Though I did not know whose was the grave, I knew that no one had been buried there very lately, and if the grief were for the loss of the dead, it

was more than probably aroused to fresh vigour by
recent misfortune.

I stooped, and taking the figure by the arm,
said,

"Come with me, and let us see what can be
done for you."

I then saw that it was a youth — perhaps scarcely
more than a boy. And as soon as I saw that, I
knew that his grief could hardly be incurable. He
returned no answer, but rose at once to his feet,
and submitted to be led away. I took him the
shortest road to my house through the shrubbery,
brought him into the study, made him sit down in
my easy-chair, and rang for lights and wine; for the
dew had been falling heavily, and his clothes were
quite dank. But when the wine came, he refused
to take any.

"But you want it," I said.

"No, sir, I don't, indeed."

"Take some for my sake, then."

"I would rather not, sir."

"Why?"

"I promised my father a year ago, when I left
home, that I would not drink anything stronger
than water. And I can't break my promise now."

"Where is your home?"

"In the village, sir."

"That wasn't your father's grave I found you
upon, was it?"

"No, sir. It was my mother's."

"Then your father is still alive?"

"Yes, sir. You know him very well — Thomas Weir."

"Ah! He told me he had a son in London. Are you that son?"

"Yes, sir," answered the youth, swallowing a rising sob.

"Then what is the matter? Your father is a good friend of mine, and would tell you you might trust me."

"I don't doubt it, sir. But you won't believe me any more than my father."

By this time I had perused his person, his dress, and his countenance. He was of middle size, but evidently not full grown. His dress was very decent. His face was pale and thin, and revealed a likeness to his father. He had blue eyes that looked full at me, and, as far as I could judge, betokened, along with the whole of his expression, an honest and sensitive nature. I found him very attractive, and was therefore the more emboldened to press for the knowledge of his story.

"I cannot promise to believe whatever you say; but almost I could. And if you tell me the truth, I like you too much already to be in great danger of doubting you; for you know the truth has a force of its own."

"I thought so till to-night," he answered. "But if my father would not believe me, how can I expect you to do so, sir?"

"Your father may have been too much troubled by your story to be able to do it justice. It is not a bit like your father to be unfair."

17*

"No, sir. And so much the less chance of your believing me."

Somehow this talk prepossessed me still more in his favour. There was a certain refinement in it, a quality of dialogue which indicated thought, as I judged; and I became more and more certain that, whatever I might have to think of it when told, he would yet tell me the truth.

"Come, try me," I said.

"I will, sir. But I must begin at the beginning."

"Begin where you like. I have nothing more to do to-night, and you may take what time you please. But I will ring for tea first; for I dare say you have not made any promise about that."

A faint smile flickered on his face. He was evidently beginning to feel a little more comfortable.

"When did you arrive from London?" I asked.

"About two hours ago, I suppose."

"Bring tea, Mrs. Pearson, and that cold chicken and ham, and plenty of toast. We are both hungry."

Mrs. Pearson gave a questioning look at the lad, and departed to do her duty.

When she returned with the tray, I saw by the unconsciously eager way in which he looked at the eatables, that he had had nothing for some time; and so, even after we were left alone, I would not let him say a word till he had made a good meal. It was delightful to see how he ate. Few troubles will destroy a growing lad's hunger; and indeed it has always been to me a marvel how the feelings and

the appetites affect each other. I have known grief
actually make people, and not sensual people at all,
quite hungry. At last I thought I had better not
offer him any more.

After the tea-things had been taken away, I put
the candles out; and the moon, which had risen,
nearly full, while we were at tea, shone into the
room. I had thought that he might possibly find
it easier to tell his story in the moonlight, which,
if there were any shame in the recital, would not,
by too much revelation, reduce him to the despair
of Macbeth, when, feeling that he could contemplate
his deed, but not his deed and himself together, he
exclaimed,

"To know my deed, 'twere best not know myself."

So, sitting by the window in the moonlight, he
told his tale. The moon lighted up his pale face as
he told it, and gave rather a wild expression to his
eyes, eager to find faith in me. — I have not much
of the dramatic in me, I know; and I am rather a
flat teller of stories on that account. I shall not,
therefore, seeing there is no necessity for it, attempt
to give the tale in his own words. But, indeed,
when I think of it, they did not differ so much from
the form of my own, for he had, I presume, lost
his provincialisms, and being, as I found afterwards, a reader of the best books that came in his
way, had not caught up many cockneyisms instead.

He had filled a place in the employment of
Messrs. —— & Co., large silk mercers, linen drapers,
&c., &c., in London; for all the trades are mingled

now. His work at first was to accompany one of
the carts which delivered the purchases of the day;
but, I presume because he showed himself to be a
smart lad, they took him at length into the shop to
wait behind the counter. This he did not like so
much, but, as it was considered a rise in life, made
no objection to the change.

He seemed to himself to get on pretty well. He
soon learned all the marks on the goods intended to
be understood by the shopmen, and within a few
months believed that he was found generally useful.
He had as yet had no distinct department allotted
to him, but was moved from place to place, according as the local pressure of business might de-
mand.

"I confess," he said, "that I was not always
satisfied with what was going on about me. I mean
I could not help doubting if everything was done
on the square, as they say. But nothing came
plainly in my way, and so I could honestly say it
did not concern me. I took care to be straight-
forward for my part, and, knowing only the prices
marked for the sale of the goods, I had nothing to
do with anything else. But one day, while I was
showing a lady some handkerchiefs which were
marked as *mouchoirs de Paris* — I don't know if I
pronounce it right, sir — she said she did not believe they were French cambric; and I, knowing
nothing about it, said nothing. But, happening to
look up while we both stood silent, the lady ex-
amining the handkerchiefs, and I doing nothing till
she should have made up her mind, I caught sight

of the eyes of the shop-walker, as they call the man
who shows customers where to go for what they want,
and sees that they are attended to. He is a fat
man, dressed in black, with a great gold chain,
which they say in the shop is only copper gilt. But
that doesn't matter, only it would be the liker himself. He was standing staring at me. I could not
tell what to make of it; but from that day I often
caught him watching me, as if I had been a cus-
tomer suspected of shoplifting. Still I only thought
he was very disagreeable, and tried to forget him.

"One day — the day before yesterday — two
ladies, an old lady and a young one, came into the
shop, and wanted to look at some shawls. It was
dinner-time, and most of the men were in the house
at their dinner. The shop-walker sent me to them,
and then, I do believe, though I did not see him,
stood behind a pillar to watch me, as he had been
in the way of doing more openly. I thought I had
seen the ladies before, and though I could not then
tell where, I am now almost sure they were Mrs.
and Miss Oldcastle, of the Hall. They wanted to
buy a cashmere for the young lady. I showed them
some. They wanted better. I brought the best we
had, inquiring, that I might make no mistake. They
asked the price. I told them. They said they were not
good enough, and wanted to see some more. I told them
they were the best we had. They looked at them
again; said they were sorry, but the shawls were not good
enough, and left the shop without buying anything. I
proceeded to take the shawls up-stairs again, and, as
I went, passed the shop-walker, whom I had not ob-

served while I was attending to the ladies. ' *You*'re
for no good, young man!' he said with a nasty
sneer. 'What do you mean by that, Mr. B.?' I
asked, for his sneer made me angry. 'You'll know
before to-morrow,' he answered, and walked away.
That same evening, as we were shutting up shop,
I was sent for to the principal's room. The moment I entered, he said, 'You won't suit us, young
man, I find. You had better pack up your box to-
night, and be off to-morrow. There's your quarter's
salary.' 'What have I done?' I asked in astonishment, and yet with a vague suspicion of the matter.
'It's not what you've done, but what you don't do,'
he answered. 'Do you think we can afford to keep
you here and pay you wages to send people away
from the shop without buying? If you do, you're
mistaken, that's all. You may go.' 'But what
could I do?' I said. 'I suppose that spy, B ——,'
— I believe I said so, sir. 'Now, now, young man,
none of your sauce!' said Mr. ——. 'Honest
people don't think about spies.' 'I thought it was
for honesty you were getting rid of me,' I said.
Mr. —— rose to his feet, his lips white, and pointed
to the door. 'Take your money and be off. And
mind you don't refer to me for a character. After
such impudence I couldn't in conscience give you
one.' Then, calming down a little when he saw I
turned to go, 'You had better take to your hands
again, for your head will never keep you. There,
be off!' he said, pushing the money towards me,
and turning his back to me. I could not touch it.
'Keep the money, Mr. ——,' I said. 'It'll make up

for what you've lost by me.' And I left the room at once without waiting for an answer.

"While I was packing my box, one of my chums came in, and I told him all about it. He is rather a good fellow, that, sir; but he laughed, and said, 'What a fool you are, Weir! *You*'ll never make your daily bread, and you needn't think it. If you knew what I know, you'd have known better. And it's very odd it was about shawls, too. I'll tell you. As you're going away, you won't let it out. Mr.———' (that was the same who had just turned me away) 'was serving some ladies himself, for he wasn't above being in the shop, like his partner. They wanted the best Indian shawl they could get. None of those he showed them were good enough, for the ladies really didn't know one from another. They always go by the price you ask, and Mr.——— knew that well enough. He had sent me up-stairs for the shawls, and as I brought them he said, "These are the best imported, madam." There were three ladies; and one shook her head, and another shook her head, and they all shook their heads. And then Mr. ——— was sorry, I believe you, that he had said they were the best. But you won't catch him in a trap! He's too old a fox for that.' I'm telling you, sir, what Johnson told me. 'He looked close down at the shawls, as if he were short-sighted, though he could see as far as any man. "I beg your pardon, ladies," said he, "you're right. I am quite wrong. What a stupid blunder to make! And yet they did deceive me. Here, Johnson, take these shawls away. How could you be so stupid? I will fetch the thing

you want myself, ladies." So I went with him. He
chose out three or four shawls, of the nicest patterns,
from the very same lot, marked in the very same
way, folded them differently, and gave them to me
to carry down. "Now, ladies, here they are!" he
said. "These are quite a different thing, as you
will see; and, indeed, they cost half as much again."
In five minutes they had bought two of them, and
paid just half as much more than he had asked for
them the first time. That's Mr. ——! and that's
what you should have done if you had wanted to
keep your place.' — But I assure you, sir, I could
not help being glad to be out of it."

"But there is nothing in all this to be miserable
about," I said. "You did your duty."

"It would be all right, sir, if father believed me.
I don't want to be idle, I'm sure."

"Does your father think you do?"

"I don't know what he thinks. He won't speak
to me. I told my story — as much of it as he
would let me, at least — but he wouldn't listen to
me. He only said he knew better than that. I
couldn't bear it. He always was rather hard upon
us. I'm sure if you hadn't been so kind to me, sir,
I don't know what I should have done by this time.
I haven't another friend in the world."

"Yes, you have. Your Father in heaven is your
friend."

"I don't know that, sir. I'm not good enough."

"That's quite true. But you would never have
done your duty if He had not been with you."

"*Do* you think so, sir?" he returned, eagerly.

"Indeed, I do. Everything good comes from the Father of lights. Every one that walks in any glimmering of light walks so far in *His* light. For there is no light — only darkness — comes from below. And man apart from God can generate no light. He's not meant to be separated from God, you see. And only think then what light He can give you if you will turn to Him and ask for it. What He has given you should make you long for more; for what you have is not enough — ah! far from it."

"I think I understand. But I didn't feel good at all in the matter. I didn't see any other way of doing."

"So much the better. We ought never to feel good. We are but unprofitable servants at best. There is no merit in doing your duty; only you would have been a poor wretched creature not to do as you did. And now, instead of making yourself miserable over the consequences of it, you ought to bear them like a man, with courage and hope, thanking God that He has made you suffer for righteousness' sake, and denied you the success and the praise of cheating. I will go to your father at once, and find out what he is thinking about it. For no doubt Mr. —— has written to him with his version of the story. Perhaps he will be more inclined to believe you when he finds that I believe you."

"Oh, thank you, sir!" cried the lad, and jumped up from his seat to go with me.

"No," I said; "you had better stay where you

are. I shall be able to speak more freely if you are not present. Here is a book to amuse yourself with. I do not think I shall be long gone."

But I was longer gone than I thought I should be.

When I reached the carpenter's house, I found, to my surprise, that he was still at work. By the light of a single tallow candle placed beside him on the bench, he was ploughing away at a groove. His pale face, of which the lines were unusually sharp, as I might have expected after what had occurred, was the sole object that reflected the light of the candle to my eyes as I entered the gloomy place. He looked up, but without even greeting me, dropped his face again and went on with his work.

"What!" I said, cheerily, — for I believed that, like Gideon's pitcher, I held dark within me the light that would discomfit his Midianites, which consciousness may well make the pitcher cheery inside, even while the light as yet is all its own — worthless, till it break out upon the world, and cease to illuminate only glazed pitcher-sides — "What!" I said, "working so late?"

"Yes, sir."

"It is not usual with you, I know."

"It's all a humbug!" he said fiercely, but coldly notwithstanding, as he stood erect from his work, and turned his white face full on me — of which, however, the eyes drooped — "It's all a humbug; and I don't mean to be humbugged any more."

"Am I a humbug?" I returned, not quite taken by surprise.

"I don't say that. Don't make a personal thing of it, sir. You're taken in, I believe, like the rest of us. Tell me that a God governs the world! What have I done, to be used like this?"

I thought with myself how I could retort for his young son: "What has he done to be used like this?" But that was not my way, though it might work well enough in some hands. Some men are called to be prophets. I could only "stand and wait."

"It would be wrong in me to pretend ignorance," I said, "of what you mean. I know all about it."

"Do you? He has been to you, has he? But you don't know all about it, sir. The impudence of the young rascal!"

He paused for a moment.

"A man like me!" he resumed, becoming eloquent in his indignation, and, as I thought afterwards, entirely justifying what Wordsworth says about the language of the so-called uneducated, — "A man like me, who was as proud of his honour as any aristocrat in the country — prouder than any of them would grant me the right to be!"

"Too proud of it, I think — not too careful of it," I said. But I was thankful he did not heed me, for the speech would only have irritated him. He went on.

"Me to be treated like this! One child a . . . ."

Here came a terrible break in his speech. But he tried again.

"And the other a . . ."

Instead of finishing the sentence, however, he drove his plough fiercely through the groove, splitting off some inches of the wall of it at the end.

"If any one has treated you so," I said, "it must be the devil, not God."

"But if there was a God, he could have prevented it all."

"Mind what I said to you once before: He hasn't done yet. And there is another enemy in his way as bad as the devil — I mean our *selves*. When people want to walk their own way without God, God lets them try it. And then the devil gets a hold of them. But God won't let him keep them. As soon as they are 'wearied in the greatness of their way,' they begin to look about for a Saviour. And then they find God ready to pardon, ready to help, not breaking the bruised reed — leading them to his own self manifest — with whom no man can fear any longer, Jesus Christ, the righteous lover of men — their elder brother — what we call *big brother*, you know — one to help them and take their part against the devil, the world, and the flesh, and all the rest of the wicked powers. So you see God is tender — just like the prodigal son's father — only with this difference, that God has millions of prodigals, and never gets tired of going out to meet them and welcome them back, every one as if he were the only prodigal son He had ever had. There's a father indeed! Have you been such a father to your son?"

"The prodigal didn't come with a pack of lies. He told his father the truth, bad as it was."

"How do you know that your son didn't tell you the truth? All the young men that go from home don't do as the prodigal did. Why should you not believe what he tells you?"

"I'm not one to reckon without my host. Here's my bill."

And so saying, he handed me a letter. I took it and read: —

"SIR, — It has become our painful duty to inform you that your son has this day been discharged from the employment of Messrs. — — and Co., his conduct not being such as to justify the confidence hitherto reposed in him. It would have been contrary to the interests of the establishment to continue him longer behind the counter, although we are not prepared to urge anything against him beyond the fact that he has shown himself absolutely indifferent to the interests of his employers. We trust that the chief blame will be found to lie with certain connexions of a kind easy to be formed in large cities, and that the loss of his situation may be punishment sufficient, if not for justice, yet to make him consider his ways and be wise. We enclose his quarter's salary, which the young man rejected with insult, and,

"We remain, &c.,
"—— and Co."

"And," I exclaimed, "this is what you found your judgment of your own son upon! You reject him unheard, and take the word of a stranger! I

don't wonder you cannot believe in your Father
when you behave so to your son. I don't say your
conclusion is false, though I don't believe it. But I
do say the grounds you go upon are anything but
sufficient."

"You don't mean to tell me that a man of
Mr. ——'s standing, who has one of the largest
shops in London, and whose brother is Mayor of
Addicehead, would slander a poor lad like that!"

"Oh you mammon-worshipper!" I cried. "Because a man has one of the largest shops in London
and his brother is Mayor of Addicehead, you take
his testimony and refuse your son's! I did not know
the boy till this evening; but I call upon you to
bring back to your memory all that you have known
of him from his childhood, and then ask yourself
whether there is not at least as much probability of
his having remained honest as of the master of a
great London shop being infallible in his conclusions
— at which conclusions, whatever they be, I confess
no man can wonder, after seeing how readily his
father listens to his defamation."

I spoke with warmth. Before I had done, the
pale face of the carpenter was red as fire; for he
had been acting contrary to all his own theories of
human equality, and that in a shameful manner.
Still, whether convinced or not, he would not give
in. He only drove away at his work, which he was
utterly destroying. His mouth was closed so tight,
he looked as if he had his jaw locked; and his eyes
gleamed over the ruined board with a light which

seemed to me to have more of obstinacy in it than contrition.

"Ah, Thomas!" I said, taking up the speech once more, "if God had behaved to us as you have behaved to your boy — be he innocent, be he guilty — there's not a man or woman of all our lost race would have returned to Him from the time of Adam till now. I don't wonder that you find it difficult to believe in Him."

And with those words I left the shop, determined to overwhelm the unbeliever with proof, and put him to shame before his own soul, whence, I thought, would come even more good to him than to his son. For there was a great deal of self-satisfaction mixed up with the man's honesty, and the sooner that had a blow the better — it might prove a death-blow in the long run. It was pride that lay at the root of his hardness. He visited the daughter's fault upon the son. His daughter had disgraced him; and he was ready to flash into wrath with his son upon any imputation which recalled to him the torture he had undergone when his daughter's dishonour came first to the light. Her he had never forgiven, and now his pride flung his son out after her upon the first suspicion. His imagination had filled up all the blanks in the wicked insinuations of Mr. ——. He concluded that he had taken money to spend in the worst company, and had so disgraced him beyond forgiveness. His pride paralysed his love. He thought more about himself than about his children. His own shame outweighed in his estimation the sadness of their guilt. It was a less matter that they should be guilty, than that he, their father, should be disgraced.

Thinking over all this, and forgetting how late it was, I found myself half-way up the avenue of the Hall. I wanted to find out whether young Weir's fancy that the ladies he had failed in serving, or rather whom he had really served with honesty, were Mrs. and Miss Oldcastle, was correct. What a point it would be if it was! I should not then be satisfied except I could prevail on Miss Oldcastle to accompany me to Thomas Weir, and shame the faithlessness out of him. So eager was I after certainty, that it was not till I stood before the house that I saw clearly the impropriety of attempting anything further that night. One light only was burning in the whole front, and that was on the first floor.

Glancing up at it, I knew not why, as I turned to go down the hill again, I saw a corner of the blind drawn aside and a face peeping out — whose, I could not tell. This was uncomfortable — for what could be taking me there at such a time? But I walked steadily away, certain I could not escape recognition, and determining to refer to this ill-considered visit when I called the next day. I would not put it off till Monday, I was resolved.

I lingered on the bridge as I went home. Not a light was to be seen in the village, except one over Catherine Weir's shop. There were not many restless souls in my parish — not so many as there ought to be. Yet gladly would I see the troubled in peace — not a moment, though, before their troubles should have brought them where the weary and heavy-laden can alone find rest to their souls — finding the Father's peace in the Son — the Father himself reconciling them to Himself.

How still the night was! My soul hung, as it were, suspended in stillness; for the whole sphere of heaven seemed to be about me, the stars above shining as clear below in the mirror of the all but motionless water. It was a pure type of the "rest that remaineth" — rest, the one immovable centre wherein lie all the stores of might, whence issue all forces, all influences of making and moulding. "And, indeed," I said to myself, "after all the noise, uproar, and strife that there is on the earth, after all the tempests, earthquakes, and volcanic outbursts, there is yet more of peace than of tumult in the world. How many nights like this glide away in loveliness, when deep sleep hath fallen upon men, and they know neither how still their own repose, nor how beautiful the sleep of nature! Ah, what must the stillness of the kingdom be? When the heavenly day's work is done, with what a gentle wing will the night come down! But I bethink me, the rest there, as here, will be the presence of God; and if we have Him with us, the battle-field itself will be — if not quiet, yet as full of peace as this night of stars." So I spoke to myself, and went home.

I had little immediate comfort to give my young guest, but I had plenty of hope. I told him he must stay in the house to-morrow; for it would be better to have the reconciliation with his father over before he appeared in public. So the next day neither Weir was at church.

18*

As soon as the afternoon service was over, I
went once more to the Hall, and was shown into
the drawing-room — a great faded room, in which
the prevailing colour was a dingy gold, hence called
the yellow drawing-room when the house had more
than one. It looked down upon the lawn, which,
although little expense was now laid out on any of
the ornamental adjuncts of the Hall, was still kept
very nice. There sat Mrs. Oldcastle reading, with
her face to the house. A little way farther off, Miss
Oldcastle sat, with a book on her knee, but her
gaze fixed on the wide-spread landscape before her,
of which, however, she seemed to be as inobservant
as of her book. I caught glimpses of Judy flitting
hither and thither among the trees, never a moment
in one place.

Fearful of having an interview with the old lady
alone, which was not likely to lead to what I wanted,
I stepped from a window which was open, out upon
the terrace, and thence down the steps to the lawn
below. The servant had just informed Mrs. Oldcastle
of my visit when I came near. She drew herself up
in her chair, and evidently chose to regard my approach as an intrusion.

"I did not expect a visit from you to-day, Mr.
Walton, you will allow me to say."

"I am doing Sunday work," I answered. "Will
you kindly tell me whether you were in London on
Thursday last? But stay, allow me to ask Miss Oldcastle to join us."

Without waiting for answer, I went to Miss Oldcastle, and begged her to come and listen to some-

thing in which I wanted her help. She rose courte-
ously though without cordiality, and accompanied
me to her mother, who sat with perfect rigidity,
watching us.

"Again let me ask," I said, "if you were in
London on Thursday."

Though I addressed the old lady, the answer
came from her daughter.

"Yes, we were."

"Were you in — & Co.'s, in — Street?"

But now before Miss Oldcastle could reply, her
mother interposed.

"Are we charged with shoplifting, Mr. Walton?
Really, one is not accustomed to such cross-question-
ing — except from a lawyer."

"Have patience with me for a moment," I returned. "I am not going to be mysterious for more
than two or three questions. Please tell me whether
you were in that shop or not."

"I believe we were," said the mother.

"Yes, certainly," said the daughter.

"Did you buy anything?"

"No. We —" Miss Oldcastle began.

"Not a word more," I exclaimed eagerly.
"Come with me at once."

"What *do* you mean, Mr. Walton?" said the
mother, with a sort of cold indignation, while the
daughter looked surprised, but said nothing.

"I beg your pardon for my impetuosity; but
much is in your power at this moment. The son of
one of my parishioners has come home in trouble.
His father, Thomas Weir —"

"Ah!" said Mrs. Oldcastle, in a tone considerably at strife with refinement. But I took no notice.

"His father will not believe his story. The lad thinks you were the ladies in serving whom he got into trouble. I am so confident he tells the truth, that I want Miss Oldcastle to be so kind as to accompany me to Weir's house —"

"Really, Mr. Walton, I am astonished at your making such a request!" exclaimed Mrs. Oldcastle, with suitable emphasis on every salient syllable, while her white face flushed with anger. "To ask Miss Oldcastle to accompany you to the dwelling of the ringleader of all the *canaille* of the neighbourhood!"

"It is for the sake of justice," I interposed.

"That is no concern of ours. Let them fight it out between them. I am sure any trouble that comes of it is no more than they all deserve. A low family — men and women of them!"

"I assure you, I think very differently."

"I daresay you do."

"But neither your opinion nor mine has anything to do with the matter."

Here I turned to Miss Oldcastle and went on —

"It is a chance which seldom occurs in one's life, Miss Oldcastle — a chance of setting wrong right by a word; and as a minister of the gospel of truth and love, I beg you to assist me with your presence to that end."

I would have spoken more strongly, but I knew

that her word given to me would be enough without her presence. At the same time, I felt not only that there would be a propriety in her taking a personal interest in the matter, but that it would do her good, and tend to create a favour towards each other in some of my flock between whom at present there seemed to be nothing in common.

But at my last words, Mrs. Oldcastle rose to her feet, no longer red — now whiter than her usual whiteness with passion.

"You dare to persist! You take advantage of your profession to persist in dragging my daughter into a vile dispute between mechanics of the lowest class! — against the positive command of her only parent! Have you no respect for her position in society? — for her sex? *Mister Walton*, you act in a manner unworthy of your cloth."

I had stood looking in her eyes with as much self-possession as I could muster. And I believe I should have borne it all quietly, but for that last word.

If there is one epithet I hate more than another, it is that execrable word *cloth* — used for the office of a clergyman. I have no time to set forth its offence now. If my reader cannot feel it, I do not care to make him feel it. Only I am sorry to say it overcame my temper.

"Madam," I said, "I owe nothing to my tailor. But I owe God my whole being, and my neighbour all I can do for him. 'He that loveth not his brother is a murderer,' or murderess, as the case may be."

At that word *murderess*, her face became livid,
and she turned away without reply. By this time
her daughter was half way to the house. She followed her. And here was I left to go home, with
the full knowledge that, partly from trying to gain
too much, and partly from losing my temper, I had
at best but a mangled and unsatisfactory testimony
to carry back to Thomas Weir. Of course I walked
away — round the end of the house and down the
avenue; and the further I went the more mortified I
grew. It was not merely the shame of losing my
temper, though that was a shame — and with a
woman too, merely because she used a common
epithet! — but I saw that it must appear very
strange to the carpenter that I was not able to give
a more explicit account of some sort, what I had
learned not being in the least decisive in the matter.
It only amounted to this, that Mrs. and Miss Oldcastle were in the shop on the very day on which
Weir was dismissed. It proved that so much of what
he had told me was correct — nothing more. And
if I tried to better the matter by explaining how I
had offended them, would it not deepen the very
hatred I had hoped to overcome? In fact, I stood
convicted before the tribunal of my own conscience
of having lost all the certain good of my attempt, in
part at least from the foolish desire to produce a
conviction *of* Weir rather than *in* Weir, which should
be triumphant after a melo-dramatic fashion, and —
must I confess it? — should *punish* him for not believing in his son when *I* did; forgetting in my
miserable selfishness that not to believe in his son

was an unspeakably worse punishment in itself than any conviction or consequent shame brought about by the most overwhelming of stage-effects. I assure my reader, I felt humiliated.

Now I think humiliation is a very different con dition of mind from humility. Humiliation no man can desire: it is shame and torture. Humility is the true, right condition of humanity — peaceful, divine. And yet a man may gladly welcome humilia tion when it comes, if he finds that with fierce shock and rude revulsion it has turned him right round, with his face away from pride, whither he was travelling, and towards humility, however far away upon the horizon's verge she may sit waiting for him. To me, however, there came a gentle and not therefore less effective dissolution of the bonds both of pride and humiliation; and before Weir and I met, I was nearly as anxious to heal his wounded spirit, as I was to work justice for his son.

I was walking slowly, with burning cheek and downcast eyes, the one of conflict, the other of shame and defeat, away from the great house, which seemed to be staring after me down the avenue with all its window-eyes, when suddenly my deliverance came. At a somewhat sharp turn, where the avenue changed into a winding road, Miss Oldcastle stood waiting for me, the glow of haste upon her cheek, and the firmness of resolution upon her lips. Once more I was startled by her sudden presence, but she did not smile.

"Mr. Walton, what do you want me to do? I

would not willingly refuse, if it is, as you say, really my duty to go with you."

"I cannot be positive about that," I answered. "I think I put it too strongly. But it would be a considerable advantage, I think, if you *would* go with me and let me ask you a few questions in the presence of Thomas Weir. It will have more effect if I am able to tell him that I have only learned as yet that you were in the shop on that day, and refer him to you for the rest."

"I will go."

"A thousand thanks. But how did you manage to —?"

Here I stopped, not knowing how to finish the question.

"You are surprised that I came, notwithstanding mamma's objection to my going?"

"I confess I am. I should not have been surprised at Judy's doing so, now."

She was silent for a moment.

"Do you think obedience to parents is to last for ever? The honour is, of course. But I am surely old enough to be right in following my conscience at least."

"You mistake me. That is not the difficulty at all. Of course you ought to do what is right against the highest authority on earth, which I take to be just the parental. What I am surprised at is your courage."

"Not because of its degree, only that it is mine!"

And she sighed. — She was quite right, and I did not know what to answer. But she resumed.

"I know I am cowardly. But if I cannot dare, I can bear. Is it not strange? — With my mother looking at me, I dare not say a word, dare hardly move against her will. And it is not always a good will. I cannot honour my mother as I would. But the moment her eyes are off me, I can do anything, knowing the consequences perfectly, and just as regardless of them; for, as I tell you, Mr. Walton, I can endure; and you do not know what that might *come* to mean with my mother. Once she kept me shut up in my room, and sent me only bread and water, for a whole week to the very hour. Not that I minded that much, but it will let you know a little of my position in my own home. That is why I walked away before her. I saw what was coming."

And Miss Oldcastle drew herself up with more expression of pride than I had yet seen in her, revealing to me that perhaps I had hitherto quite misunderstood the source of her apparent haughtiness. I could not reply for indignation. My silence must have been the cause of what she said next.

"Ah! you think I have no right to speak so about my own mother! Well! well! But indeed I would not have done so a month ago."

"If I am silent, Miss Oldcastle, it is that my sympathy is too strong for me. There are mothers and mothers. And for a mother not to be a mother is too dreadful."

She made no reply. I resumed.

"It will seem cruel, perhaps; — certainly in saying it, I lay myself open to the rejoinder that talk is *so* easy; — still I shall feel more honest when I have said it: the only thing I feel should be altered in your conduct — forgive me — is that you should *dare* your mother. Do not think, for it is an unfortunate phrase, that my meaning is a vulgar one. If it were, I should at least know better than to utter it to you. What I mean is, that you ought to be able to be and do the same before your mother's eyes, that you are and do when she is out of sight. I mean that you should look in your mother's eyes, and do what is *right*."

"I *know* that — know it *well*." (She emphasized the words as I do.) "But you do not know what a spell she casts upon me; how impossible it is to do as you say."

"Difficult, I allow. Impossible, not. You will never be free till you do so."

"You are too hard upon me. Besides, though you will scarcely be able to believe it now, I *do* honour her, and cannot help feeling that by doing as I do, I avoid irreverence, impertinence, rudeness — whichever is the right word for what I mean."

"I understand you perfectly. But the truth is more than propriety of behaviour, even to a parent; and indeed has in it a deeper reverence, or the germ of it at least, than any adherence to the mere code of respect. If you once did as I want you to do, you would find that in reality you both revered and loved your mother more than you do now."

"You may be right. But I am certain you speak without any real idea of the difficulty."

"That may be. And yet what I say remains just as true."

"How could I meet *violence*, for instance?"

"Impossible!"

She returned no reply. We walked in silence for some minutes. At length she said,

"My mother's self-will amounts to madness, I do believe. I have yet to learn where she would stop of herself."

"All self-will is madness," I returned — stupidly enough. For what is the use of making general remarks when you have a terrible concrete before you? "To want one's own way just and only because it is one's own way is the height of madness."

"Perhaps. But when madness has to be encountered as if it were sense, it makes it no easier to know that it is madness."

"Does your uncle give you no help?"

"He! Poor man! He is as frightened at her as I am. He dares not even go away. He did not know what he was coming to when he came to Oldcastle Hall. Dear uncle! I owe him a great deal. But for any help of that sort, he is of no more use than a child. I believe mamma looks upon him as half an idiot. He can do anything or everything but help one to live, to *be* anything. Oh me! I *am* so tired!"

And the *proud* lady, as I had thought her, perhaps not incorrectly, burst out crying.

What was I to do? I did not know in the least. What I said, I do not even now know. But by this time we were at the gate, and as soon as we had

passed the guardian monstrosities, we found the open
road an effectual antidote to tears. When we came
within sight of the old house where Weir lived, Miss
Oldcastle became again a little curious as to what I
required of her.

"Trust me," I said. "There is nothing mysterious about it. Only I prefer the truth to come out
fresh in the ears of the man most concerned."

"I do trust you," she answered. And we knocked
at the house-door.

Thomas Weir himself opened the door, with a
candle in his hand. He looked very much astonished
to see his lady-visitor. He asked us, politely enough,
to walk up stairs, and ushered us into the large room
I have already described. There sat the old man, as
I had first seen him, by the side of the fire. He received us with more than politeness — with courtesy;
and I could not help glancing at Miss Oldcastle to
see what impression this family of "low, free-thinking
republicans" made upon her. It was easy to discover
that the impression was of favourable surprise. But
I was as much surprised at her behaviour as she was
at theirs. Not a haughty tone was to be heard in
her voice; not a haughty movement to be seen in
her form. She accepted the chair offered her, and
sat down, perfectly at home, by the fire-side, only
that she turned towards me, waiting for what explanation I might think proper to give.

Before I had time to speak, however, old Mr.
Weir broke the silence.

"I've been telling Tom, sir, as I've told him

many a time afore, as how he's a deal too hard with
his children."

"Father!" interrupted Thomas angrily.

"Have patience a bit, my boy," persisted the old
man, turning again towards me. — "Now, sir, he
won't even hear young Tom's side of the story; and
I say that boy won't tell him no lie if he's the same
boy he went away."

"I tell you, father," again began Thomas; but
this time I interposed, to prevent useless talk beforehand.

"Thomas," I said, "listen to me. I have heard
your son's side of the story. Because of something
he said, I went to Miss Oldcastle, and asked her
whether she was in his late master's shop last Thursday. That is all I have asked her, and all she has
told me is that she was. I know no more than you
what she is going to reply to my questions now, but
I have no doubt her answers will correspond to your
son's story."

I then put my questions to Miss Oldcastle, whose
answers amounted to this: — That they had wanted
to buy a shawl; that they had seen none good enough;
that they had left the shop without buying anything;
and that they had been waited upon by a young
man, who, while perfectly polite and attentive to
their wants, did not seem to have the ways or man-
ners of a London shop-lad.

I then told them the story as young Tom had
related it to me, and asked if his sister was not in
the house and might not go to fetch him. But she
was with her sister Catherine.

"I think, Mr. Walton, if you have done with me, I ought to go home now," said Miss Oldcastle.

"Certainly," I answered. "I will take you home at once. I am greatly obliged to you for coming."

"Indeed, sir," said the old man, rising with difficulty, "we're obliged both to you and the lady more than we can tell. To take such a deal of trouble for us! But you see, sir, you're one of them as thinks a man's got his duty to do one way or another, whether he be clergyman or carpenter. God bless you, Miss. You're of the right sort, which you'll excuse an old man, Miss, as'll never see ye again till ye've got the wings as ye ought to have."

Miss Oldcastle smiled very sweetly, and answered nothing, but shook hands with them both, and bade them good-night. Weir could not speak a word; he could hardly even lift his eyes. But a red spot glowed on each of his pale cheeks, making him look very like his daughter Catherine, and I could see Miss Oldcastle wince and grow red too with the gripe he gave her hand. But she smiled again none the less sweetly.

"I will see Miss Oldcastle home, and then go back to my house and bring the boy with me," I said, as we left.

It was some time before either of us spoke. The sun was setting, the sky the earth and the air lovely with rosy light, and the world full of that peculiar calm which belongs to the evening of the day of rest. Surely the world ought to wake better on the morrow.

"Not very dangerous people, those, Miss Old-castle?" I said, at last.

"I thank you very much for taking me to see them," she returned, cordially.

"You won't believe all you may happen to hear against the working people now?"

"I never did."

"There are ill-conditioned, cross-grained, low-minded, selfish, unbelieving people amongst them. God knows it. But there are ladies and gentlemen amongst them too."

"That old man is a gentleman."

"He is. And the only way to teach them all to be such, is to be such to them. The man who does not show himself a gentleman to the working people — why should I call them the poor? some of them are better off than many of the rich, for they can pay their debts, and do it —"

I had forgot the beginning of my sentence.

"You were saying that the man who does not show himself a gentleman to the poor —"

"Is no gentleman at all — only a gentle without the man; and if you consult my namesake old Izaak, you will find what that is."

"I will look. I know your way now. You won't tell me anything I can find out for myself."

"Is it not the best way?"

"Yes. Because, for one thing, you find out so much more than you look for."

"Certainly that has been my own experience."

"Are you a descendant of Izaak Walton?"

"No. I believe there are none. But I hope I have so much of his spirit that I can do two things like him."

"Tell me."

"Live in the country, though I was not brought up in it; and know a good man when I see him."

"I am very glad you asked me to go to-night."

"If people only knew their own brothers and sisters, the kingdom of heaven would not be far off."

I do not think Miss Oldcastle quite liked this, for she was silent thereafter; though I allow that her silence was not conclusive. And we had now come close to the house.

"I wish I could help you," I said.

"In what?"

"To bear what I fear is waiting you."

"I told you I was equal to that. It is where we are unequal that we want help. You may have to give it me some day — who knows?"

I left her most unwillingly in the porch, just as Sarah (the white wolf) had her hand on the door, rejoicing in my heart, however, over her last words.

My reader will not be surprised, after all this, if, before I get very much further with my story, I have to confess that I loved Miss Oldcastle.

When young Tom and I entered the room, his grandfather rose and tottered to meet him. His father made one step towards him and then hesitated. Of all conditions of the human mind that of being ashamed of himself must have been the strangest to Thomas Weir. The man had never in his life, I believe, done anything mean or dishonest, and therefore he had had less frequent opportunities than most people of being ashamed of himself. Hence his fall had been from another pinnacle — that of pride. When a man thinks it such a fine thing to have done right, he might almost as well have done wrong, for it shows he considers right something *extra*, not absolutely essential to human existence, not the life of a man. I call it Thomas Weir's fall; for surely to behave in an unfatherly manner to both daughter and son — the one sinful, and therefore needing the more tenderness — the other innocent, and therefore claiming justification — and to do so from pride, and hurt pride, was fall enough in one history, worse a great deal than many sins that go by harder names; for the world's judgment of wrong does not exactly correspond with the reality. And now if he was humbled in the one instance, there would be room to hope he might become humble in the other. But I had soon to see that, for a time, his pride, driven from its entrenchment against his son, only retreated, with all its forces, into the other against his daughter.

Before a moment had passed, justice overcame so far that he held out his hand and said:

19*

"Come, Tom, let by-gones be by-gones."

But I stepped between.

"Thomas Weir," I said, "I have too great a regard for you, — and you know I dare not flatter you — to let you off this way, or rather leave you to think you have done your duty when you have not done the half of it. You have done your son a wrong, a great wrong. How can you claim to be a gentleman — I say nothing of being a Christian, for therein you make no claim — how, I say, can you claim to act like a gentleman, if, having done a man wrong — his being your own son has nothing to do with the matter one way or other, except that it ought to make you see your duty more easily — having done him wrong, why don't you beg his pardon, I say, like a man?"

He did not move a step. But young Tom stepped hurriedly forward, and catching his father's hand in both of his, cried out:

"My father shan't beg my pardon. I beg yours, father, for everything I ever did to displease you, but I *wasn't* to blame in this. I wasn't, indeed."

"Tom, I beg your pardon," said the hard man, overcome at last. "And now, sir," he added, turning to me, "will you let by-gones be by-gones between my boy and me?"

There was just a touch of bitterness in his tone.

"With all my heart," I replied. "But I want just a word with you in the shop before I go."

"Certainly," he answered, stiffly; and I bade the old and the young man good night, and followed him down stairs.

"Thomas, my friend," I said, when we got into the shop, laying my hand on his shoulder, "will you after this say that God has dealt hardly with you? There's a son for any man God ever made to give thanks for on his knees! Thomas, you have a strong sense of fair play in your heart, and you *give* fair play neither to your own son nor yet to God himself. You close your doors and brood over your own miseries, and the wrongs people have done you; whereas, if you would but open those doors, you might come out into the light of God's truth, and see that His heart is as clear as sunlight towards you. You won't believe this, and therefore naturally you can't quite believe that there is a God at all; for, indeed, a being that was not all light would be no God at all. If you would but let Him teach you, you would find your perplexities melt away like the snow in spring, till you could hardly believe you had ever felt them. No arguing will convince you of a God; but let Him once come in, and all argument will be tenfold useless to convince you that there is no God. Give God justice. Try Him as I have said. — Good night."

He did not return my farewell with a single word. But the grasp of his strong rough hand was more earnest and loving even than usual. I could not see his face, for it was almost dark; but, indeed, I felt that it was better I could not see it.

I went home as peaceful in my heart as the
night whose curtains God had drawn about the earth
that it might sleep till the morrow.

CHAPTER XIV.

My Pupil.

ALTHOUGH I do happen to know how Miss Oldcastle fared that night after I left her, the painful
record is not essential to my story. Besides, I have
hitherto recorded only those things "quorum pars
magna" — or *minima*, as the case may be — "fui."
There is one exception, old Weir's story, for the in-
troduction of which my reader cannot yet see the
artistic reason. For whether a story be real in fact,
or only real in meaning, there must always be an
idea, or artistic model in the brain, after which it is
fashioned: in the latter case one of invention, in the
former case one of choice.

In the middle of the following week I was returning from a visit I had paid to Tomkins and his
wife, when I met, in the only street of the village,
my good and honoured friend Dr. Duncan. Of
course I saw him often — and I beg my reader to
remember that this is no diary, but only a gathering
together of some of the more remarkable facts of
my history, admitting of being ideally grouped —
but this time I recall distinctly because the interview
bore upon many things.

"Well, Doctor Duncan," I said, "busy as usual
fighting the devil?"

"Ah, my dear Mr. Walton," returned the doctor

— and a kind word from him went a long way into my heart — "I know what you mean. You fight the devil from the inside, and I fight him from the outside. My chance is a poor one."

"It would be, perhaps, if you were confined to outside remedies. But what an opportunity your profession gives you of attacking the enemy from the inside as well! And you have this advantage over us, that no man can say it belongs to your profession to say such things, and *therefore* disregard them."

"Ah, Mr. Walton, I have too great a respect for your profession to dare to interfere with it. The doctor in 'Macbeth,' you know, could

'not minister to a mind diseased,
Pluck from the memory a rooted sorrow,
Raze out the written troubles of the brain,
And with some sweet oblivious antidote
Cleanse the stuff'd bosom of that perilous stuff
Which weighs upon the heart.' "

"What a memory you have! But you don't think I can do that any more than you?"

"You know the best medicine to give, anyhow. I wish I always did. But you see we have no *theriaca* now."

"Well, we have. For the Lord says, 'Come unto me, and I will give you rest.' "

"There! I told you! That will meet all diseases."

"Strangely now, there comes into my mind a line of Chaucer, with which I will make a small return for your quotation from Shakespeare. You have

mentioned *theriaca;* and I, without thinking of this
line, quoted our Lord's words. Chaucer brings the
two together, for the word *triacle* is merely a cor-
ruption of *theriaca*, the unfailing cure for every
thing.

'Crist, which that is to every barm triacle.' "

"That is delightful: I thank you. And that is
in Chaucer?"

"Yes. In the Man-of-Law's Tale."

"Shall I tell you how I was able to quote so
correctly from Shakespeare? I have just come from
referring to the passage. And I mention that because I want to tell you what made me think of the
passage. I had been to see poor Catherine Weir. I
think she is not long for this world. She has a bad
cough, and I fear her lungs are going."

"I am concerned to hear that. I considered her
very delicate, and am not surprised. But I wish, I
do wish, I had got a little hold of her before, that I
might be of some use to her now. Is she in immediate danger, do you think?"

"No, I do not think so. But I have no expectation of her recovery. Very likely she will just live
through the winter and die in the spring. Those
patients so often go as the flowers come! All her
coughing, poor woman, will not cleanse her stuffed
bosom. The perilous stuff weighs on her heart, as
Shakespeare says, as well as on her lungs."

"Ah, dear! What is it, doctor, that weighs upon
her heart? Is it shame, or what is it? for she is so
uncommunicative that I hardly know anything at
all about her yet."

"I cannot tell. She has the faculty of silence."

"But do not think I complain that she has not made me her confessor. I only mean that if she would talk at all, one would have a chance of knowing something of the state of her mind, and so might give her some help."

"Perhaps she will break down all at once, and open her mind to you. I have not told her she is dying. I think a medical man ought at least to be quite sure before he dares to say such a thing. I have known a long life injured, to human view at least, by the medical verdict in youth of ever imminent death."

"Certainly one has no right to say what God is going to do with any one till he knows it beyond a doubt. Illness has its own peculiar mission, independent of any association with coming death, and may often work better when mingled with the hope of life. I mean, we must take care of presumption when we measure God's plans by our theories. But could you not suggest something, Doctor Duncan, to guide me in trying to do my duty by her?"

"I cannot. You see you don't know what she is *thinking;* and till you know that, I presume you will agree with me that all is an aim in the dark. How can I prescribe, without *some* diagnosis? It is just one of those few cases in which one would like to have the authority of the Catholic priests to urge confession with. I do not think anything will save her life, as we say, but you have taught some of us to think of the life that belongs to the spirit as *the* life; and I do believe confession would do every-thing for that."

"Yes, if made to God. But I will grant that communication of one's sorrows or even sins to a wise brother of mankind may help to a deeper con-fession to the Father in heaven. But I have no wish for *authority* in the matter. Let us see whether the Spirit of God working in her may not be quite as powerful for a final illumination of her being as the *fiat confessio* of a priest. I have no confidence in *forcing* in the moral or spiritual garden. A hothouse development must necessarily be a sickly one, ren-dering the plant unfit for the normal life of the open air. Wait. We must not hurry things. She will perhaps come to me of herself before long. But I will call and inquire after her."

We parted; and I went at once to Catherine Weir's shop. She received me much as usual, which was hardly to be called receiving at all. Perhaps there was a doubtful shadow, not of more cordiality, but of less repulsion in it. Her eyes were full of a stony brilliance, and the flame of the fire that was consuming her glowed upon her cheeks more brightly, I thought, than ever; but that might be fancy, oc-casioned by what the doctor had said about her. Her hand trembled, but her demeanour was perfectly calm.

"I am sorry to hear you are complaining, Miss Weir," I said.

"I suppose Dr. Duncan told you so, sir. But I am quite well. I did not send for him. He

called of himself, and wanted to persuade me I
was ill."

I understood that she felt injured by his interference.

"You should attend to his advice, though. He
is a prudent man, and not in the least given to
alarming people without cause."

She returned no answer. So I tried another
subject.

"What a fine fellow your brother is!"

"Yes; he grows very much."

"Has your father found another place for him
yet?"

"I don't know. My father never tells me about
any of his doings."

"But don't you go and talk to him, sometimes?"

"No. He does not care to see me."

"I am going there now: will you come with
me?"

"Thank you. I never go where I am not
wanted."

"But it is not right that father and daughter
should live as you do. Suppose he may not have
been so kind to you as he ought, you should not
cherish resentment against him for it. That only
makes matters worse, you know."

"I never said to human being that he had been
unkind to me."

"And yet you let every person in the village
know it."

"How?"

Her eye had no longer the stony glitter. It flashed now.

"You are never seen together. You scarcely speak when you meet. Neither of you crosses the other's threshold."

"It is not my fault."

"It is not *all* your fault, I know. But do you think you can go to a heaven at last where you will be able to keep apart from each other, he in his house and you in your house, without any sign that it was through this father on earth that you were born into the world which the Father in heaven redeemed by the gift of His own Son?"

She was silent; and, after a pause, I went on.

"I believe, in my heart, that you love your father. I could not believe otherwise of you. And you will never be happy till you have made it up with him. Have you done him no wrong?"

At these words, her face turned white — with anger, I could see — all but those spots on her cheek-bones, which shone out in dreadful contrast to the deathly paleness of the rest of her face. Then the returning blood surged violently from her heart, and the red spots were lost in one crimson glow. She opened her lips to speak, but apparently changing her mind, turned and walked haughtily out of the shop and closed the door behind her.

I waited, hoping she would recover herself and return; but, after ten minutes had passed, I thought it better to go away.

As I had told her, I was going to her father's shop. There I was received very differently. There

was a certain softness in the manner of the carpenter
which I had not observed before, with the same
heartiness in the shake of his hand which had accompanied my last leave-taking. I had purposely
allowed ten days to elapse before I called again, to
give time for the unpleasant feelings associated with
my interference to vanish. And now I had something in my mind about young Tom.

"Have you got anything for your boy yet,
Thomas?"

"Not yet, sir. There's time enough. I don't
want to part with him just yet. There he is, taking
his turn at what's going. Tom!"

And from the farther end of the large shop,
where I had not observed him, now approached
young Tom, in a canvas jacket, looking quite like
a workman.

"Well, Tom, I am glad to find you can turn
your hand to anything."

"I must be a stupid, sir, if I couldn't handle
my father's tools," returned the lad.

"I don't know that quite. I am not just prepared to admit it, for my own sake. My father is
a lawyer, and I never could read a chapter in one
of his books — his tools, you know."

"Perhaps you never tried, sir."

"Indeed, I did; and no doubt I could have done
it if I had made up my mind to it. But I never
felt inclined to finish the page. And that reminds
me why I called to-day. Thomas, I know that lad
of yours is fond of reading. Can you spare him

from his work for an hour or so before breakfast?"

"To-morrow, sir?"

"To-morrow, and to-morrow, and to-morrow,"
I answered; "and there's Shakespeare for you."

"Of course, sir, whatever you wish," said
Thomas, with a perplexed look in which pleasure
seemed to long for confirmation, and to be, till
that came, afraid to put its "native semblance on."

"I want to give him some direction in his reading. When a man is fond of any tools, and can
use them, it is worth while showing him how to use
them better."

"Oh, thank you, sir!" exclaimed Tom, his face
beaming with delight.

"That *is* kind of you, sir! Tom, you're a made
man!" cried the father.

"So," I went on, "if you will let him come to
me for an hour every morning, till he gets another
place, say from eight to nine, I will see what I can
do for him."

Tom's face was as red with delight as his sister's
had been with anger. And I left the shop somewhat consoled for the pain I had given Catherine,
which grieved me without making me sorry that I
had occasioned it.

I had intended to try to do something from the
father's side towards a reconciliation with his daughter.
But no sooner had I made my proposal for Tom
than I saw I had blocked up my own way towards
my more important end. For I could not bear to
seem to offer to bribe him even to allow me to do

him good. Nor would he see that it was for his good and his daughter's — not at first. The first impression would be that I had a *professional* end to gain; that the reconciling of father and daughter was a sort of parish business of mine, and that I had smoothed the way to it by offering a gift — an intellectual one, true, but not, therefore, the less a gift in the eyes of Thomas, who had a great respect for books. This was just what would irritate such a man, and I resolved to say nothing about it, but bide my time.

When Tom came, I asked him if he had read any of Wordsworth. For I always give people what I like myself, because that must be wherein I can best help them. I was anxious, too, to find out what he was capable of. And for this, anything that has more than a surface meaning will do. I had no doubt about the lad's intellect, and now I wanted to see what there was deeper than the intellect in him.

He said he had not.

I therefore chose one of Wordsworth's sonnets, not one of his best by any means, but suitable for my purpose — the one entitled, "Composed during a Storm." This I gave him to read, telling him to let me know when he considered that he had mastered the meaning of it, and sat down to my own studies. I remember I was then reading the Anglo-Saxon Gospels. I think it was fully half-an-hour before Tom rose and gently approached my place. I had not been uneasy about the experiment after ten minutes had passed, and after that time was doubled, I felt certain of some measure of success. This may possibly puzzle my reader; but I will explain. It was clear that Tom did not understand the sonnet at first; and I was not in the least certain that he would come to understand it by any exertion of his intellect, without further experience. But what I was delighted to be made sure of was that Tom at least knew that he did not know. For that is the very next step to knowing. Indeed, it may be said to be a more valuable gift than the other, being of general application; for some quick people will understand many things very easily, but when they come to a thing that is beyond their present reach, will fancy they see a meaning in it, or invent one, or even — which is far worse — pronounce it nonsense; and indeed show themselves capable of any device for getting out of the difficulty, except seeing and confessing to themselves that they are not able to understand it. Possibly this sonnet might be beyond Tom now, but at least there was great hope that he saw, or believed, that there must be something beyond him in it. I only hoped that he would not fall upon some wrong interpretation, seeing he was brooding over it so long.

"Well, Tom," I said, "have you made it out?"

"I can't say I have, sir. I'm afraid I'm very stupid, for I've tried hard. I must just ask you to tell me what it means. But I must tell you one thing, sir: every time I read it over — twenty times, I daresay — I thought I was lying on my mother's grave, as I lay that terrible night; and then at the end there you were standing over me and saying, 'Can I do anything to help you?'"

I was struck with astonishment. For here, in a wonderful manner, I saw the imagination outrunning the intellect, and manifesting to the heart what the brain could not yet understand. It indicated undeveloped gifts of a far higher nature than those belonging to the mere power of understanding alone. For there was a hidden sympathy of the deepest kind between the life experience of the lad, and the embodiment of such life experience on the part of the poet. But he went on:

"I am sure, sir, I ought to have been at my prayers, then, but I wasn't; so I didn't deserve you to come. But don't you think God is sometimes better to us than we deserve?"

. "He is just everything to us, Tom; and we don't and can't deserve anything. Now I will try to explain the sonnet to you."

I had always had an impulse to teach; not for the teaching's sake, for that, regarded as the attempt to fill skulls with knowledge, had always been to me a desolate dreariness; but the moment I saw a sign of hunger, an indication of readiness to receive, I was invariably seized with a kind of passion for giving. I now proceeded to explain the sonnet. Having done so, nearly as well as I could, Tom said:

"It is very strange, sir; but now that I have heard you say what the poem means, I feel as if I had known it all the time, though I could not say it."

Here at least was no common mind. The reader
will not be surprised to hear that the hour before
breakfast extended into two hours after breakfast as
well. Nor did this take up too much of my time,
for the lad was capable of doing a great deal for
himself under the sense of help at hand. His father,
so far from making any objection to the arrangement, was delighted with it. Nor do I believe that
the lad did less work in the shop for it: I learned
that he worked regularly till eight o'clock every
night.

Now the good of the arrangement was this: I
had the lad fresh in the morning, clear-headed, with
no mists from the valley of labour to cloud the
heights of understanding. From the exercise of the
mind it was a pleasant and relieving change to turn
to bodily exertion. I am certain that he both thought
and worked better, because he both thought and
worked. Every literary man ought to be *mechanical*
(to use a Shakespearean word) as well. But it would
have been quite a different matter, if he had come
to me after the labour of the day. He would not
then have been able to think nearly so well. But
labour, sleep, thought, labour again, seems to me to
be the right order with those who, earning their
bread by the sweat of the brow, would yet remember
that man shall not live by bread alone. Were it
possible that our mechanics could attend the institu-
tions called by their name in the morning instead of
the evening, perhaps we should not find them so
ready to degenerate into places of mere amusement.
I am not objecting to the amusement; only to cease

20*

to educate in order to amuse is to degenerate.
Amusement is a good and sacred thing; but it is not
on a par with education; and, indeed, if it does not
in any way further the growth of the higher nature,
it cannot be called good at all.

Having exercised him in the analysis of some of
the best portions of our home literature, — I mean
helped him to take them to pieces, that, putting them
together again, he might see what kind of things
they were — for who could understand a new
machine or find out what it was meant for without
either actually or in his mind taking it to pieces?
(which pieces, however, let me remind my reader,
are utterly useless, except in their relation to the
whole) — I resolved to try something fresh with
him.

At this point I had intended to give my readers
a theory of mine about the teaching and learning of
a language; and tell them how I had found the trial
of it succeed in the case of Tom Weir. But I think
this would be too much of a digression from the
course of my narrative, and would, besides, be interesting to those only who had given a good deal
of thought to subjects belonging to education.   I
will only say, therefore, that, by the end of three
months, my pupil, without knowing any other Latin
author, was able to read any part of the first book
of the Æneid — to read it tolerably in measure,
and to enjoy the poetry of it — and this not without a knowledge of the declensions and conjugations.
As to the syntax, I made the sentences themselves
teach him that. Now I know that, as an end, all

this was of no great value; but as a beginning, it was invaluable, for it made and *kept* him hungry for more; whereas, in most modes of teaching, the beginnings are such that without the pressure of circumstances, no boy, especially after an interval of cessation, will return to them. Such is not Nature's mode, for the beginnings with her are as pleasant as the fruition, and that without being less thorough than they can be. The knowledge a child gains of the external world is the foundation upon which all his future philosophy is built. Every discovery he makes is fraught with pleasure — that is the secret of his progress, and the essence of my theory: that learning should, in each individual case, as in the first case, be *discovery* — bringing its own pleasure with it. Nor is this to be confounded with turning study into play. It is upon the moon itself that the infant speculates, after the moon itself that he stretches out his eager hands — to find in after years that he still wants her, but that in science and poetry he has her a thousand-fold more than if she had been handed him down to suck.

"So, after all, I have bored my reader with a shadow of my theory, instead of a description. After all, again, the description would have plagued him more, and that must be both his and my comfort.

So through the whole of that summer and the following winter, I went on teaching Tom Weir. He was a lad of uncommon ability, else he could not have effected what I say he had within his first three months of Latin, let my theory be not only perfect in itself, but true as well — true to human nature, I mean.   And his father, though his own book-learning was but small, had enough of insight to perceive that his son was something out of the common, and that any possible advantage he might lose by remaining in Marshmallows was considerably more than counter-balanced by the instruction he got from the vicar.   Hence, I believe, it was that not a word was said about another situation for Tom.   And I was glad of it; for it seemed to me that the lad had abilities equal to any profession whatever.

END OF VOL. I.

Printed in the USA
CPSIA information can be obtained
at www.ICGtesting.com
CBHW051014121224
18876CB00026B/192